Bless Your Heart, Rae Sutton

OTHER BOOKS BY SUSANNAH B. LEWIS

NONFICTION

How May I Offend You Today?

Can't Make This Stuff Up!

Bless Your Heart, Rae Sutton

SUSANNAH B. LEWIS

THOMAS NELSON
Since 1798

Bless Your Heart, Rae Sutton

Published in Nashville, Tennessee, by Thomas Nelson. Thomas Nelson is a registered trademark of HarperCollins Christian Publishing, Inc.

Published in association with the literary agency of WTA Media, LLC in Franklin, TN.

Thomas Nelson titles may be purchased in bulk for educational, business, fundraising, or sales promotional use. For information, please email SpecialMarkets@ ThomasNelson.com.

Scripture quotations are taken from the Holy Bible, New International Version®, NIV®. Copyright © 1973, 1978, 1984, 2011 by Biblica, Inc.™ Used by permission of Zondervan. All rights reserved worldwide. www.zondervan.com. The "NIV" and "New International Version" are trademarks registered in the United States Patent and Trademark Office by Biblica, Inc.™

Publisher's Note: This novel is a work of fiction. Names, characters, places, and incidents are either products of the author's imagination or used fictitiously. All characters are fictional, and any similarity to people living or dead is purely coincidental.

Library of Congress Cataloging-in-Publication Data

Names: Lewis, Susannah B., 1981- author.
Title: Bless your heart, Rae Sutton / Susannah B. Lewis.
Description: Nashville, Tennessee : Thomas Nelson, [2022] | Summary: "Known for her humor and genuine Southern voice, Susannah B. Lewis brings readers the heartwarming story of a thirty-five-year-old woman mourning the recent losses of her marriage and her mother, who finds comfort in her mother's outspoken, charming, blue-haired group of friends"-- Provided by publisher.
Identifiers: LCCN 2021050562 (print) | LCCN 2021050563 (ebook) | ISBN 9780785248200 (paperback) | ISBN 9780785248217 (epub) | ISBN 9780785248279 (downloadable audio)
Subjects: LCGFT: Novels.
Classification: LCC PS3612.E9867 B57 2022 (print) | LCC PS3612.E9867 (ebook) | DDC 813/.6--dc23/eng/20211015
LC record available at https://lccn.loc.gov/2021050562
LC ebook record available at https://lccn.loc.gov/2021050563

Printed in the United States of America

22 23 24 25 26 LSC 10 9 8 7 6 5 4 3 2 1

To the motherless.
May the Lord send you someone to help fill the void.

CHAPTER 1

There was nothing to see but bottomland on the thirty-minute drive from Huntsville to Whitten. Heavy rain had caused the overflow from the Flint River to rise around the fluted trunks of the gum and cypress trees and even puddle onto the shoulder of the highway. After the sharp curve and past the neglected silo overgrown with kudzu on the left, the bottomland was in the rearview and the sleepy little town of Whitten, Alabama, appeared on the two-lane.

Brown's Store was the first cinder-block building on the right with a metal Dr Pepper sign nailed above a rusted ice machine by the front door. A marquee in the shape of an arrow sat in the gravel parking lot advertising low prices on milk and Marlboros, and, as always, "Go Warriors Go" was at the bottom in black plastic letters.

T. J.'s Auto Sales was next with a few old clunkers in the lot, and then there was Beck's Beauty Spot—a single-wide trailer with a large pair of pink shears and purple curlers painted on the white vinyl. Every blue-haired lady in Whitten went to Mrs. Beck for their cuts, colors, and permanents, and the parking lot was often filled with Buicks and Oldsmobiles purchased back in the '90s from T. J.'s competition.

Over a small, shady hill, the hub of town was visible. The railroad tracks ran parallel with Main Street and a row of the town's oldest buildings. Some had been remodeled and turned into Cookie's Bakery, Taylor Faye's Boutique, The Burger Basket, and city hall. A couple of structures still remained derelict, though, with chipped paint and yellow newspaper taped to the insides of the windows. Those buildings hadn't seen their heyday since the '50s, when my mama was a little girl and sipped a milkshake at the counter of the corner drugstore while she waited to pick up her mama's prescriptions.

Across from the railroad tracks were the newer businesses. McDonald's and Pizza Hut sat side by side, both with marquees advertising specials and supporting the Whitten Warriors. The Shell station was on the corner of Main and McLemore, and then there was the Super D Pharmacy and Tucker's Dry Cleaners.

The Baptist, Methodist, and Presbyterian churches were all in a row, separated only by massive oak and magnolia trees. Right past First Presbyterian, nestled in a grove of trees hundreds of years old, was the historic white house with columns known my entire life as Harper's Funeral Home. I waited on the traffic to slowly pass as my fourteen-year-old daughter, Molly, sniffled from the passenger seat. Without looking at her, I reached for her hand. We rested our wrists on the console of my SUV as I turned into the parking lot.

My older brother, Jamie, his wife, and their two teen-aged sons were getting out of Jamie's black truck when I pulled in to the parking spot covered in wet catkins. Jamie walked to the passenger side of my SUV in his dark suit, damp with rain, and Molly rolled down her window.

"Sweet Molly." He reached through the window and touched her arm as his wife, Dawn, stood behind him and wiped her red, puffy face.

"Jamie," I said, "would you mind taking Molly inside? Give me a minute?"

"Of course." My brother opened the passenger door. When Molly stepped out of the Tahoe in her black sundress and gray Converse shoes, her aunt Dawn scooped her into her arms.

"I'll just be a minute," I said again as they all slowly walked toward the front door of the home built in the early nineteenth century.

I stared over my steering wheel at sleepy Main Street. The rain was merely a drizzle now, and summer steam rose from the asphalt and into the humid June air. My tears fell. I looked at this little town—the place where I'd spent most of my life—and it didn't seem right. Nothing had changed in this place, and yet everything suddenly had.

I'd pulled in front of my mother's red brick home on Hazel Tree Cove only three Fridays before. Boxes and bags and Rubbermaid totes of her belongings lined her driveway shaded by overgrown crepe myrtles. She was in her carport bending next to her sedan and rummaging through a box. Bobby pins held her stylish silver bangs out of her eyes.

Molly got out of the car with earbuds draped around her

neck and walked to Mama while I searched for my purse in the back seat.

"Molly Margaret," I heard Mama say. "I bought you a Dr Pepper and a box of Fudge Rounds."

"You know the way to my heart, Nana." I watched Molly kiss Mama on the cheek and walk inside the front door as the wrought iron storm door slammed behind her.

"What's all this, Mama?" I asked when I approached her and the piles of her belongings.

"There's no need in you and Jamie going through all this when I'm gone."

"Mama, don't." I couldn't bear to think about it.

"Rae, when your grandmother died, I was left to go through fifty years of junk. There were sentimental things I kept, of course—her apron and photos and recipes and old letters, but I'm not going to put you through the painstaking process of wondering whether or not you should hold on to my old Richard Simmons VHS tapes or placemats I bought in the '80s or my ThighMaster."

"Mama." I chuckled.

"I'm doing you a great service here, Rae." She looked up from a tattered box and put her hands on her slender hips. "Your uncle Wilson already took two truckloads of stuff down to the Mustard Seed. Bless his heart. He almost broke a hip picking up that heavy box of *Dynasty* power suits with shoulder pads."

"You are going to be fine, and then what? You'll be missing those shoulder pads and that ThighMaster," I replied.

"What about all these canning jars, Rae?" She looked inside another box. "Are you ever going to can anything? Should I leave a few for you? And my pepper relish recipe? I don't know why in the world you buy chowchow from the grocery store. You were born and raised in Alabama, for heaven's sake. It's blasphemy that you don't grow peppers and can your own."

"Leave the canning jars," I said. "I'll use them."

"Have you thought anymore about what I said?" She held up a dusty Mason jar and examined it.

"About moving back home?"

She put the glass back into the box and looked to me. "The house has long been paid for. I know it's just a little brick house built in 1963, but it would be so perfect for you and Molly Margaret. I give you my blessing to nail up some shiplap and paint everything gray like that girl you love so much on the TV."

I smiled.

"You know there's hardwood under the carpet in the living room. And a big dog like Patsy needs a yard to run in. Molly Margaret can shoot basketball right here in this driveway. It would be so much better than the cramped apartment in Huntsville, yeah?"

"You're going to be fine, Mama." I shook my head. "I don't know why we keep talking about this. I don't know why you're—"

"Rae." She walked to me and tucked my long brown hair behind my ears. "Look at me, honey."

I fixed my eyes on her beautiful blue ones and sighed.

"I'm eaten up with it, Rae. You know that. It's going to win."

"But Dr. Pennington said with extensive chemo you would have more time. You . . . ," I began as my eyes glassed over.

"Don't you do that. Don't you do that crying mess, Raeley Ann." She wiped the corner of my eye with her thumb. "I'm not going through another round of chemo. I can't do it, Rae. My body just can't take it. Besides, you ought to rejoice because I'll be reunited with your daddy. I'll be with my parents and my baby sister. It's been too long since I've seen my best friend, Linda. I won't be sick anymore, honey. I won't have to worry about ThighMasters or Mason jars or anything else. Your mama is ready to go."

"I can't think about it." I stubbornly shook my head.

"I know, honey." She turned back to a cardboard box on top of her deep freezer. "My mama has been dead over twenty years now, and I still miss her every day. I'm so ready to see her again. And one day, Rae, you'll see me again, but until then, you'll get through it." She looked back at me. "Some days will be harder than others, but you *will* get through it."

I nodded.

"I sure would love to know you're back here in your childhood home and you're taken care of. I know the idea of moving back to this one-horse town isn't appealing to you, but you had a great childhood here, and Molly Margaret would too. You wouldn't have a house payment, and you'll be set with plenty of money for a while. Your sweet, hardworking daddy made sure of that," she said as she folded up a box and moved on to another. "Jamie will put in a swimming pool at his house with his share. With your portion, you can buy Molly Margaret Converse in every color and plenty of Dr Pepper and Fudge Rounds. You can splurge on some of that overpriced makeup you like so much. You can sit on the back deck and relax for a while, all right? It would do you good to get out of Huntsville and start over. And then you can go back to cleaning houses if you want. You can find plenty of houses to clean here, Rae. Jean Watkins would keep you in business for weeks on end with her hoarding piles. She's still got shampoo bottles from 1992."

I rummaged through a dusty box of Tupperware and wiped my damp eyes. I didn't want to talk about this. I didn't want to imagine a life without my mother in it.

"Better yet"—she looked back at me with enthusiasm covering her face—"use the inheritance to open a store, Rae! You can fill it with junk furniture you find on the side of the road and paint gray and wrap in chicken wire. You can call it vintage and sell each piece for three hundred dollars or more. You love doing that kind of thing. Do something you really enjoy with that money."

"Okay, Mama." I pacified her, but I wasn't sure I would do any of that. When she was gone from this world, would it be too painful for me to even step inside the house? To cook in her kitchen filled with countless memories of her dancing barefoot to bluegrass while she fried pork chops in her cast-iron skillet? To look out the living room window and see her empty rocking chair on the front porch? To walk past her bathtub and remember the nights she'd soak in it with a glass of red wine and a Danielle Steel novel?

"Now, you want to keep this, don't you?" Mama pulled one of her many violins from a box.

"You know I do."

She ran the bow across the dusty strings, and there, in her carport in a worn white T-shirt, pink seersucker capris, and flip-flops, she carefully began an elegant classical piece in F minor. I turned away and looked through a box of old *Southern Living* magazines so she wouldn't see the tears pouring from my eyes.

I was startled from my memories by a knock on my car window. I quickly wiped my face and looked to see Aunt Maxine beneath an oversize polka-dot umbrella, although the rain had completely ceased. I grabbed my black clutch from the back seat and opened the door. I stepped out and straightened my linen dress.

"Beck just did my hair, Raeley Ann. One drop of water and it'll frizz to high heaven," She patted her short silver curls.

"Hey, Aunt Maxine." I draped my arms around her petite frame and inhaled the scent of her perfumed powder.

"How are you holding up, dear?" She pulled away and placed her wrinkled hands on my damp cheeks.

"I'm okay."

"Bless your heart." She removed her hands. "Well, I knew it was coming. I thought I was prepared, but I wasn't. I'm the only one left, Raeley Ann. First Melba and now Margie. I'm the only sister left." Her voice cracked.

"I know." I nodded and patted her slightly hunched back. Her posture had stooped with the early stages of osteoporosis.

"Margie probably sent this rain!" She grabbed my arm as we both walked beneath the umbrella toward the front door of the funeral home. "She had to get the last word, you know? She loved to poke fun at me when my hair frizzed. She called me Albert Einstein."

I became light-headed when I entered the funeral home. I hadn't set foot on the squeaky heart-pine floors since my father had passed away twelve years before, but I vividly remembered the smell of the place—peppermints and flowers and musty, damp tissues. Three scents that, when combined, filled me with the darkest grief and sorrow.

Old Mr. Harper had passed away since my father's funeral, but his son, Alex, greeted me and Aunt Maxine at the door.

"I'll take your umbrella, Mrs. Maxine," he said quietly.

"Thank you, son."

"Rae." He placed the umbrella in the bronze stand and lightly touched my elbow. "I'm so sorry about Mrs. Margie. She was such a wonderful lady and music teacher. She taught me 'O Holy Night' on the piano for the Christmas pageant. I sure loved her."

"Thanks, Alex."

"We'll have the private viewing for the family first. Take as much time as you need." He ushered us toward the parlor where I saw Molly, my brother, and his family standing around the white casket topped with a spray of magnolia blossoms and pale pink hydrangeas. "It Is Well with My Soul" played softly throughout the room.

"I don't know if I can do this," I whispered to my aunt.

"You can, Raeley Ann. Come, dear." She held on to my arm, and we slowly walked down the aisle toward my mother.

Seeing Mama in a casket was surreal. My vibrant, healthy, outgoing mother with the quick wit and contagious laughter had always seemed invincible. In my mind, death was a promise for everyone but her. I was convinced she would outlive us all. I even prayed for that after my daddy died. "God, let me go before Mama. I can't bear to lose another parent."

Molly grabbed onto my other arm as tears flowed from her eyes, and we approached the casket. I placed my hand on top of my mother's. The coldness of it took me by surprise. I wrapped my fingers around hers—her nails were freshly painted pale pink—and remembered the beautiful melodies they made on the violin. The feel of them in my hair when I rested my head in her lap on the couch. Those hands held mine when I was too little to cross the street alone. They put medicine on my cuts and scrapes. They buttoned the back of my dresses before church on Sunday. They held me close on the nights we mourned my father. As Molly rested her head on my shoulder and wiped her wet eyes with a tissue, I stared at my mother's hands. I never wanted to forget them.

She was so cold and lifeless, and yet she looked so beautiful and rested there in her favorite light pink dress and pearls. She wasn't in pain. And I remembered the words she spoke in her driveway only weeks before about how she was ready to go, and a great sense of peace and comfort overcame me. Even as my brother took both me and Molly into his arms and salty tears dripped off the tip of my nose, I knew my mother was more alive now than she ever was on this earth.

———◆———

It wasn't long before the funeral home was crowded with people. Jamie, Dawn, and their boys, Logan and Liam, greeted the visitors first. Molly and I stood together at the head of Mama's casket with red noses, puffy eyes, and tissue balled in our fists. Aunt Maxine and Uncle Wilson sat on the first wooden pew in the parlor, along with several of Mama's best friends, and welcomed people after they'd all hugged my neck and said the same thing. "You're in our prayers. Let us know if we can do anything."

What could they do? Bring a casserole? Send a bouquet? Generous gestures, of course, but no one could say or do anything to heal the hurt I felt as my mother lay motionless and cold only a foot away from me.

Mrs. Nancy Babcock held both of my hands in her fragile, trembling ones as streams of tears left white streaks in her bright rouge. In her feeble voice she went on about Mama and how her visiting the nursing home to play the violin for the residents was her favorite time of the week.

"Thank you so much, Mrs. Nancy," I said. "She loved visiting everyone at Creekview. It was the bright spot in her week too."

And then Mrs. Nancy told another story about Mama. And another. And three more until the line was backed up and people looked impatient, and although I loved hearing her fond reminisces about my mother, I was ready for her to move along.

"Lord have mercy, here comes Nancy Babcock," Mama would say. *"Pull up a chair. We're going to be here awhile."*

Dawn knew Mrs. Nancy had the gift of gab and came to my rescue.

"Mrs. Nancy, would you like to sit down and visit with Aunt Maxine for a few minutes?" Dawn gently took Mrs. Nancy by her frail arm.

"Oh, where is Maxine? Did I ever tell you about the time she changed a tire for me on the two-lane, Dawn? In the snow? At night?"

"Girl, Carter just walked in," Dawn whispered to me as she led Mrs. Nancy toward my unsuspecting Aunt Maxine, who would greet Mrs. Nancy kindly but would also consider faking a heart attack to get out of the conversation.

I looked at the long line of people waiting to pay their

respects and saw my ex-husband standing tall above the congregation of stooped elderly men and women. His face was tan. His dark hair was freshly cut. He was wearing the pale yellow tie Molly had given him for Father's Day several years before.

And there, on the arm of the love of my life, was the new love of his life. Thirteen years his junior. Named Autumn . . . though she was born in July.

"He brought her?" I mumbled aloud. "He brought her here?"

"Rae." Jamie leaned into my ear. "Stay calm."

"This is our mother's funeral," I whispered through gritted teeth and squeezed the tissue so hard in my hand that it began to disintegrate.

"I know. Don't do anything rash in front of Molly. Just stay calm," he coolly whispered back before we were interrupted by another visitor.

I smiled and shed several tears with old friends from high school, but I often looked back to Carter as he stood in the slow-moving line. Our eyes locked several times, but he always looked away first. Finally, he and his twenty-three-year-old girlfriend in a sea-green dress with spaghetti straps reached my brother. He shook Jamie's hand and spoke softly while my sixteen-year-old nephew eyed Autumn from head to toe and then smiled at his football buddies sitting on the back pew.

And then he was there, standing right before me in a cloud of his familiar aftershave. Carter Sutton. The man who stole my heart decades ago and then suddenly decided one day that he didn't want my heart anymore.

"Rae, I'm so sorry," he said softly. "You know how much I loved Mrs. Margie."

"Who wears green to a funeral?" I shifted my eyes from his to the child at his side.

"Mama." Molly nudged me.

"I'm sorry about your mother," Autumn squeaked and tossed her long blond hair over her bare shoulder. She refused to look me in the eye.

"Thank you, sweetie. I'm just sorry you're with this old man when half the Whitten High School football team is here ripe for the picking," I said snidely.

"Rae." Carter sighed in disapproval before hugging Molly. "I'm so sorry about Nana, baby. She loved you so much."

"I know, Daddy," Molly answered.

"Are you still up for staying with me later this week?" he asked. "The fair will be in town if you want to go. They've already set up the concession stands in town. The funnel cake place is—"

"Is she tall enough to ride anything at the fair?" I tipped my head toward the short girl standing closely to the man I'd loved since I was eighteen years old.

Carter ignored me. "I'll call you later, Molly. Rae, again, I'm sorry about Mrs. Margie. You're in our prayers. Let us know if we can do anything."

"We?" I sneered. "As in, you and her?" I pointed to

Autumn. "I'll tell you what you both can do. You can both kiss—"

"Mama!" Molly growled at me and uncomfortably twirled a strand of her dark hair.

Carter took Autumn by the hand and they walked away, making sure to avoid Aunt Maxine (still trapped in a conversation with Nancy Babcock) because Carter was well aware of how she felt about him since our divorce.

"I'll be back," I said to Jamie as he conversed with Brother Lonnie from First Baptist.

"Mama," Molly quietly called for me. "Mama! Where are you going?"

I motioned for her to stay there before following Carter and Autumn. I didn't care who saw me in pursuit of them. I didn't care that this would be the talk of this small Southern town. I didn't care that some little old lady at Beck's Beauty Spot would say in the morning, "Did you see Rae chase her ex-husband and his young friend out of Margie's funeral? Oh, me. She looked so angry. Smoke was rolling out of her ears like Yosemite Sam. I was sure she'd shoot Carter right there in Harper's and then drag his body into one of the caskets in the showroom. Bless her heart."

A friend from high school, Kathryn, and I exchanged glances as I followed the couple out of the crowded parlor. Kathryn seemed to enthusiastically say to me with her eyes, *Get him, Rae. Get him.*

"Carter!" I called when we reached the empty foyer.

"Rae." He dropped Autumn's hand. "Are you going to make a scene at your mama's funeral?"

"I don't know." I shrugged. "Am I?"

"Look, I know—"

"I'm not talking to you with her standing here. Go get in your booster seat. Daddy will be out in a minute," I said to Autumn.

"You can't tell me what—" she began.

"Autumn, go wait in the truck, please. I'll only be a minute." He handed her his keys.

She reluctantly took them and walked out the front door.

I grabbed Carter by the arm of his crisp black suit and pulled him down a wide hallway to a small sitting room filled with antique chairs and settees. I shut the heavy old door behind us.

"Carter Sutton, I cannot believe you brought her to my mother's funeral. You had to have known how devastated I am today," I hissed as tears welled in my blue eyes. "And then I have to see you here with her? What in the world were you thinking?"

"Rae, I'm upset about your mother too," he said. "I loved her. She was the only real mother I ever had. But Autumn is my girlfriend now. She came for my comfort."

His words made me nauseated.

"She what?" I fumed and tightly folded my hands together under my chin. "She came for *your* comfort? That's why you brought your new girlfriend to your ex-mother-in-law's funeral?"

"Rae." He sighed. "I'm sorry if I upset you today."

I quickly wiped my damp face with my palms. I hated that I was crying in front of him. I hated that the heartbreak he had caused was still so evident. I didn't want him to see the power he still had over my emotions. "I know you don't love me anymore, but I would think you'd take my feelings into consideration, if only for today."

He looked down to his shiny black shoes and mumbled, "You're right. I'm sorry."

"I never kept secrets from Mama. You know that. But I didn't tell her about this. I didn't tell her about Autumn. I didn't want my mother to die resenting you, Carter. I didn't think you'd want that. I thought about your feelings. The least you can do is think of mine." I opened the heavy door and went back to my mother's casket.

CHAPTER 2

*F*ive doves disappeared into the gray sky over Cypress Creek Cemetery after my mother's graveside service, and Aunt Maxine leaned over to me and whispered, "Margie hated birds."

"Feathered demons," I answered. "That's what she called them."

"Whose idea was that?" she asked, still holding the umbrella over her head although it hadn't rained in nearly an hour.

"Alex Harper talked Jamie into it."

"Didn't he make enough money on the funeral? He had to sell us birds too?"

"I guess so," I said and twisted the damp, soggy tissue between my fingers.

"Those Harpers. Nice folks, but every one of them is greedy as a pig."

I looked over to the pearl casket beneath the navy-blue tent and then to my father's headstone next to it. It was then that I realized for the first time I was an orphan. I was a thirty-six-year-old orphan, but I might as well have been a helpless baby left on a doorstep in a basket. I'd heard when you lose one parent, it's like a comma. It slows things down. But when both parents are gone, it's a period. Done. Finished.

Mama said I would get through this, but I didn't know how it was possible.

"You're coming to the house to eat?" Aunt Maxine latched onto Uncle Wilson's arm as he pulled his handkerchief from his coat pocket and wiped his red nose.

"We'll be there."

"Dora is bringing chicken. Lena will bring a dessert. She'll pass it off in her own Tupperware, but it will be store-bought. The woman can't boil water. Bless her heart."

I stifled a laugh. "Molly and I will be by soon."

———◆———

After countless people hugged my neck and offered words of encouragement, they disappeared to their cars and their lives. Jamie, Dawn, their boys, Molly, and I were left alone in the country cemetery overlooking a field of cattails. The summer air was muggy, the sky gray. I slipped my arm around my older brother's slender waist as he rested his cheek on top of my head.

"Mama," he said. "Our sweet mama is gone."

"What will we do without them both?" I glanced to our daddy's headstone and then back to the pearl casket ready to be lowered into the ground.

"I don't know, Raeley Ann. I just don't know."

Aunt Maxine's small farmhouse was at capacity after the service. The buffet line started in the kitchen and winded through the living room and into the hallway. I couldn't eat a bite, so I sat on the couch in the den and made small talk with Dawn and family friends holding paper plates topped with fried chicken and casseroles and red Solo cups of sweet tea.

I was relieved when people began to leave and the house fell silent, except for Uncle Wilson snoring in his oversize brown recliner and Molly, Logan, and Liam huddled on the blue plaid loveseat watching Alex Trebek on the old console television. I saw my brother sneak out the front door with a pack of cigarettes in his hand, but I would save my "our mother just died of cancer so why are you smoking again?" lecture for another time.

"Girl, your mama just died of cancer and he's smoking again," Dawn said from the corduroy couch cushion next to me.

I looked to her. "How do you always know what I'm thinking?"

She shrugged her hefty shoulders and took another bite of chocolate pie from the paper plate in her hands.

"Raeley Ann," Aunt Maxine called from the kitchen. "Come in here, dear."

I stood from the couch and walked to Aunt Maxine and

my mother's best friends sitting at the round wooden table in the middle of the small kitchen with light oak cabinets and cream linoleum flooring.

"Pull up a chair, honey." Mrs. Dora motioned to the ladderback chair next to the pantry door.

"Do you call this pee-can or puh-khan, Rae?" Mrs. Fannie asked as she motioned toward the piece of pie on her plate.

"Lord have mercy, do we have to have this conversation every time we eat this pie? It's puh-khan, of course!" Aunt Maxine took a swig of her tea and then patted her hair to make sure it hadn't frizzed.

"It's puh-khan," I answered.

"Foolery, Rae." Mrs. Dora sneered in her deep Southern drawl. "It's pee-can as the day is long."

"Margie would agree with us, wouldn't she, Raeley Ann?" Aunt Maxine asked me. "It's puh-khan. Pee-can sounds crude."

"Oh, sweet Margie." Mrs. Fannie set her fork on her plate and pushed it away. "Lord, I'm going to miss her. I already do."

I reached over and touched Mrs. Fannie's ring-covered fingers. "She sure loved you, Mrs. Fannie."

At eighty, Mrs. Fannie Culpepper was the oldest of the group. She'd been Mama's Sunday school teacher at First Baptist when Jamie and I were babies, and they'd had a special bond ever since. Mrs. Fannie's late husband, Mr. Pratt Culpepper, had owned the lumber mill and was one of the wealthiest men in Whitten. Mrs. Fannie still lived in their white brick mansion on McLemore Street with rocking chairs and ferns lining the front porch. I always loved the way Mrs. Fannie dressed in diamonds and pearls and silk pantsuits and matching scarves just to run down to Beck's for a wash and dry in her oversize Cadillac. Even at her age, she was still beautiful. I imagined she'd been a real knockout in her younger years.

"I don't guess we will meet tomorrow, then?" Mrs. Dora asked before taking a sip of coffee from the antique blue toile saucer.

"No, I don't think it would be right," Aunt Maxine said. "It's too soon."

"What's tomorrow?" I asked.

"The third Thursday," Mrs. Dora answered.

For twenty years or so, Mama, Aunt Maxine, Mrs. Dora Kinney, and Mrs. Fannie met on the third Thursday of each month. Mama called it their "ministry." They alternated homes each meeting and drank coffee and ate dessert and discussed whom to send flowers to in the hospital or to whom they would deliver a meal. They read books and argued over their meanings. They prayed for their family and friends. They wrote out "Get Well Soon" cards or "Congratulations on Your Grandbaby" cards. For an hour each month, they laughed, gossiped, reminisced about days gone by, and solved all the problems in Whitten, Alabama. I went to a couple of the meetings with Mama when I was a teenager and always enjoyed their chitchat.

Several months ago, when my mother was exhausted and bedridden from chemotherapy, the ladies brought the meeting to Mama. They huddled right there in her bedroom with cups of tea and plates of pie. They spent the entire afternoon reminiscing of better days and fervently praying over my mother. I had always been so thankful that she had these ladies in her life.

"We'll resume in July, then?" Mrs. Dora asked.

Mrs. Dora was Mama's age, seventy-five, and still dyed her hair in Nice'n Easy Golden Blonde. She always wore several strands of costume jewelry bracelets on both wrists, and Mama joked you could hear her coming a mile away. Mrs. Dora's husband, Harold, was alive and well, and he still woke up at 4:00 A.M. every morning to put on overalls and feed chickens and milk cows and tend to their fifty acres on Cottonwood Road. Dora was as in love with him today as she was when they met at a honky-tonk in Huntsville fifty years ago. Those pale blue eyes still lit up when she mentioned him.

"That will be fine with me, Lord willing I'm still here," Mrs. Fannie answered.

"Fannie Culpepper, you're too classy to be talking about morbid things like death and being put six feet in the dirt. Besides, you'll probably outlive us all." Aunt Maxine laughed.

"When I do go, bury me in my finest pearls. I'd rather them be with me six feet in the dirt than to have that worthless son-in-law of mine pawn them," Mrs. Fannie retorted.

"We just buried our best friend, you old hags. Is this the best time to joke about death?" Mrs. Dora admonished.

"Oh, Dora, Margie would've laughed at that," Aunt Maxine remarked.

Mrs. Dora shrugged her shoulders in annoyance.

"Dora, don't you need to get home to Harold?" Mrs. Fannie smiled and glanced at her gold watch. "Have you ever been apart this long?"

"Where was Mr. Harold today?" I asked.

"He wanted to come, Rae." Mrs. Dora's wrists jangled loudly as she picked up her coffee cup. "He always takes a nap in the afternoon. He works so hard on the farm and has to nap at noon. Margie knew that. She knew how he loved his nap. She would understand."

"Rae, I don't mean to pry," Mrs. Fannie said, changing the subject, "but I'm curious. Have you decided what you'll to do with the house? Is Dawn going to list it?"

"It's too soon to ask her that, Fannie!" Mrs. Dora exclaimed. "As the *classy* one, you should know that."

"No," I said. "It's all right, Mrs. Dora. I'm not sure what I'll do with the house."

"Margie wanted her to move into it and fix it up," Aunt Maxine said. "She told her she could rip up the carpet and paint everything gray like that renovation woman on the TV. Jenny Gaines or something or other."

"Is that an option, dear? Moving back to Whitten?" Mrs. Fannie adjusted the sapphire on her bony ring finger.

"I'm not sure yet." I shrugged.

"Well, for what it's worth, I think it's a grand idea. I would love to have you right down the road from me. But you're thirty-six years old, Raeley Ann. You're capable of making the best decision for you and Molly," Aunt Maxine added.

"I can't believe I'm saying this, but I do actually love the idea of moving back home. When I was a kid, I couldn't wait to get out of here." I picked at the silver polish on my nails.

"One-horse town, she always called it." Aunt Maxine looked to Mrs. Fannie. "Even though there's a string of horses all over town."

"Now that I am divorced, though, the thought of coming home is comforting. I only stayed in Huntsville after college for Carter, for his job. Now that he's out of my life, there's nothing really left for me there. But it's Molly's hometown. She's already been through so much. I hate to move her here. I just don't know yet."

I watched the women exchange glances.

"Well, dear," Mrs. Fannie said, "speaking of the divorce, who was that child on Carter's arm today?"

I sighed as all of the little old ladies watched me with wide eyes and pressed teacups to their thin lips.

"Go ahead and tell them, Raeley Ann. Tell Dora and Fannie the real reason Carter left you. The cat is out of the bag now." Aunt Maxine huffed angrily and sat back in her chair. "Bless her heart."

"Well—" I began.

"Margie didn't know either," Aunt Maxine interrupted

and angrily folded her hands on the table. "She didn't know the reason Carter left was because he had a little filly on the side. She went to her grave thinking Carter Sutton had some kind of midlife crisis and just wanted a little freedom. She thought he'd clear his head and come back to Raeley Ann in no time. Oh, how she loved that boy. She would have been so upset to know he'd treated her Raeley Ann this way."

"Aunt Maxine, that's why I didn't tell her. I knew Mama wasn't going to be here much longer. I didn't want to worry her with that. She loved Carter for so long, and I didn't want her to think differently of him."

"I think that was noble of you, Rae," Mrs. Dora said.

Aunt Maxine rolled her eyes and patted her curls once again.

"How did this come about, Rae? Carter and the young girl?" Mrs. Fannie asked.

"Carter often goes out to dinner for work. They met at a restaurant. She was his server."

"Probably a server at one of those establishments where everything God gave them is hanging out for the world to see," Aunt Maxine sneered.

I shook my head at my outspoken aunt. She never failed to let everyone in the room know precisely what she was thinking, even if it included a cringe or a bruised ego. Thanksgiving with her was always a fun time. Lord forbid someone bring a dry cake or a runny casserole.

Mrs. Fannie said, "Oh, honey, I had no idea there was another woman. Maxine, how did you know?"

"Rae told me the day after Margie died. It just came tumbling out. Bless her heart."

"I couldn't keep it in any longer. I told Aunt Maxine and Dawn on the same day, but that's it. Mama never knew. Molly still doesn't. She thinks Autumn and Carter met after the divorce. I don't want her to be angry with him."

Mrs. Fannie sighed. "I'm sorry Carter betrayed you that way. You're so young, though, Rae, with plenty of life to live and men to meet."

"Shoot, Dora's sister, Ruthie, had been widowed, what, three or four times at your age." Aunt Maxine giggled.

Mrs. Dora crossed her arms. "My sister couldn't help it if they dropped like flies around her, Maxine."

"It was probably her cooking that killed them, Dora. I had her meatloaf once, and I'm surprised I lived to tell the tale." Aunt Maxine grinned.

"Ha ha," Dora said sarcastically.

Mrs. Fannie sighed again. "We sure do love you, Rae. You're going to miss your mama. Lord, there's no pain like losing your mama. My mama died in 1957, but I still remember it like it was yesterday. Mercy, I didn't know quite how to get on without her, but I made it through by the grace of God. And you can rest easy knowing you've got some old ladies who will help you through this as best we can."

They nodded in unison, and each placed their wrinkled hands atop mine on the table.

CHAPTER 3

The ride to our apartment in Huntsville that night was quiet as Molly and I both thought about the day's events and how different our lives would be now without my mother. She was everything to us. She was a friend and counselor not only to me but to my little girl. Molly Margaret and my mother shared a precious bond. Mama was always on the top bleacher cheering enthusiastically as Molly stormed down the basketball court. She taught her how to sew on a button and make homemade biscuits. They shared countless bowls of popcorn while watching Alfred Hitchcock movies. Molly was her only granddaughter, and she was spoiled well. I knew my sweet daughter riding in the passenger seat mourned her death as much as I did.

A storm rolled through that night and the booming thunder rattled the windows of the apartment. Molly slept between me and Patsy, our obese golden retriever, in my king-size bed that took up most of my small bedroom. I stroked Molly's long dark hair the same way Mama used to stroke mine and watched drops of rain stream down the window.

I wanted to call my mother. I wanted to hear her laugh. I

wanted her to tell me every mundane detail of her day. How she ran into Sue Hornsby at the Piggly Wiggly, and the automatic car wash bent her radio antenna, and Mr. Parker had finally set up his strawberry stand on the two-lane. I wanted her to tell me how in the world I would ever get used to her not being a phone call away.

Only a week before, I was lying in the same spot watching the ten o'clock news when my phone vibrated on the nightstand. Jamie told me Mama had been admitted to the hospital in Whitten. I said I was on my way and then called Carter to come get Molly because she had to be at school the next morning for final exams.

Fifteen minutes later I opened my front door to see my ex-husband in plaid pajama pants and a gray T-shirt. I wanted so badly for him to take me into his arms the way he did when my father passed away. I wanted to cry on his shoulder and tell him I was scared my mother was going to die. I wanted him to kiss the top of my head and cry with me. Instead, he kept his distance and took Molly's overnight bag from my hand.

"You'll let me know how she's doing?" he asked with concern.

"I will." I hugged our daughter, who favored him so much. "Molly, try to get some sleep tonight, okay? Get plenty of rest for your tests."

"Tell Nana I love her," Molly said as they disappeared down the stairwell of the apartment complex and headed to the home we all once shared on Sullivan Street.

When I made it to Whitten about an hour later, I walked into the dim hospital room to see Dawn and Jamie sitting in chairs next to the bed. Mama's appearance startled me. She looked so frail. Her face was pale and her usually well-kept bob was tousled on the pillow. For the first time in her life, my mother looked old and feeble. She barely had the energy to tell me hello when I walked toward her.

"Oh, Mama," I said as Jamie stood up and motioned for me to sit in his blue plastic chair.

"Where's my sweet Molly Margaret?"

"She has exams in the morning. She's with Carter." I sat next to her and took her clammy hand. "She'll be here tomorrow after school. You'll see her, Mama," I assured her.

"I'm so tired, Rae."

"I know you are, Mama." I gave her hand a light squeeze.

"I was just telling Dawn and Jamie what I told you last time you were at the house. You know, how I'm ready to see your daddy and my parents. My baby sister, Melba. I'm so ready."

I nodded and fought back tears.

"My sweet, handsome, broad-shouldered James. I knew I loved him the moment I saw him. Remember that story?"

"At the hardware store, Mama. I remember."

"I was buying sandpaper for my daddy. He was making a dining table for Mama for Christmas. There wasn't even room for Melba at our old table. He had to make a new one for all of his girls to sit together. That's all Mama wanted too. For all of her girls to sit together."

"Dad recommended the 220 grit," Jamie added.

"Two hundred and twenty grit." Mama smiled. "Do you remember your grandmother's fried green tomatoes? Lord, I miss those." She closed her eyes. "I wonder if there are fried green tomatoes in heaven."

"I'm sure there are, Mrs. Margie. I can't imagine heaven without them." Dawn sniffled and tucked her bouncy auburn hair behind her ears.

"What's that sniffling, my love?" Mama asked Dawn. "This isn't a sad occasion. This is a time of joy. I'm going home."

"You're going to be fine." The tears dripped from my chin and onto the hospital bed.

"I sure am." She smiled. "I'm going to be fine. I'm going home. I'm going to be fine."

Three days later, my mama was fine. She was finally fine. But I sure wasn't.

I spent the first two weeks after Mama died holed up in the apartment with Patsy. Molly stayed with her father the second week, and I took the opportunity to bellow and cry and lie on the floor and beat the carpet in utter despair. I crawled under the covers and shut out the world and everyone in it. I declined phone calls and ignored text messages. I refused the takeout that friends offered to bring. I watched ten years' worth of *Grey's Anatomy*. I didn't have the energy to change out of my pajamas. I lived on sandwiches and canned soup and ice cream and ordered pizza when the cabinets were bare. I just stayed there in apartment

309 and cuddled with my dog and grieved. I slept as much as I could, and when I woke up, I grieved some more.

"Rae, you have to get up," Aunt Maxine said over the telephone as I sprawled on my couch surrounded by snotty tissues and Little Debbie wrappers. "I'm with Jamie now at your mother's house. Take a shower and come over here."

"I don't know if I can come to the house, Aunt Maxine."

"Bless your heart, you can. You will. We'll see you in about an hour or so. And for heaven's sake, don't forget to take a shower!" She hung up the phone before I could argue.

I threw the dirty pajamas into the laundry basket, showered, and picked out clean pants that didn't have an elastic waist before calling Molly to let her know I was going to Whitten for the day. Then I helped fat Patsy into the Tahoe and drove to my mother's house for the first time since the funeral.

I parked behind Jamie's truck and Aunt Maxine's old Lincoln Continental and stared at my childhood home. The white rocking chair on the red brick porch sat empty, and the hanging baskets of perennials were in desperate need of watering. Several newspapers were stacked on the steps, and the mailbox by the front door was crammed with letters. My heart broke all over again.

I grabbed the stack of mail from the box and opened the wrought iron storm door to hear Aunt Maxine and Jamie talking in the kitchen. I could smell my mother before I even stepped onto the beige carpet in the living room.

"Raeley Ann? Is that you?" Aunt Maxine called.

"Yes, ma'am." Patsy followed me through the spacious den. We walked past the same cream couch where I used to watch *TRL* on MTV after school in the '90s and the coffee table covered in drink rings from Jamie's and my lack of using a coaster. Lord have mercy, Mama got so angry when we didn't use a coaster.

"Rae," Jamie said when I entered the kitchen, "are you okay? We've been worried about you."

"Yeah." I tossed the mail onto the kitchen table. "I just needed some time alone."

"I don't like when you decline my calls, Raeley Ann," Aunt Maxine said from the kitchen chair. "I'm thoroughly offended. You can decline other people's calls, but not mine."

"I'm sorry." I sat at the table where I'd eaten pounds of mashed potatoes and drunk gallons of sweet tea. "How about the both of you? Are y'all okay?"

"Yeah," Jamie answered. "I think I've taken care of everything that needs to be dealt with right now. I canceled the cable and paid some bills. I've been in touch with the attorney."

"Does he need to switch the utilities over to your name, Raeley Ann? Are you going to move in or what?" Aunt Maxine eyed me and took a drink from the Coca-Cola can in her hand covered with liver spots.

"Aunt Maxine." Jamie sighed while looking through the pile of mail I'd just thrown on the kitchen table. "Could we possibly ease into this conversation? Don't bombard her with questions as soon as she walks through the door. No wonder she's been avoiding your calls."

"What's the point of beating around the bush, Jamie? It's time to make a decision here." She snapped her fingers. "Does Dawn need to list the house? It can't sit here empty forever."

"It's only been two weeks since Mama passed. Don't rush Rae," Jamie said.

"And Huntsville is Molly's home, Aunt Maxine."

"Molly would adjust fine to Whitten, Raeley Ann."

"Still, she's been through so much change already. And honestly, I'm scared to move back here. If I do, I'll never get over Mother," I thought aloud and picked at my nails. They were nubs now. I'd bitten off every one during my two weeks of sorrow.

"Bless your heart, darling girl." Aunt Maxine leaned toward me. "You'll never get over your mother, and you don't have to."

"I know," I said, "but I don't know if it will help me to be here in her house, surrounded with memories of her day in and day out."

"You didn't quit coming here when Dad died," Jamie said. "It's painful now, Rae, and it will probably be painful for a while, but eventually coming home was comforting to you after Dad was gone, wasn't it? It was for me. It still is. This was our house. And I think it might be good for you to be here now that Mama is gone too."

"I guess." I wasn't so sure.

"As for Molly, remind her we've got the best basketball team in the state. Go Warriors!" Jamie pumped his fist.

"Fannie's nephew, Kent, is the coach at the high school. She'd be playing on a fine team. And you would have me right down the road, Raeley Ann. Your most favorite aunt in the world."

"You're my only aunt in the world."

"That too."

"We don't want to pressure you," Jamie said. "If you want to stay in Huntsville, that's fine, Rae. Dawn will list the house and we'll close this chapter in our lives."

This chapter?

This wasn't a chapter. This was my life. This house was my life. Daddy built a playhouse for me in the backyard when I was five. He installed an intercom so I could page my parents inside the house and ask them to bring me orange Kool-Aid in my favorite California Raisins cup. I watched Saturday-morning cartoons on the living room floor with a bowl of Cap'n Crunch cradled in my small hands. This was the house where my best friend, Paige, and I had countless sleepovers and prank called our teachers and talked in British accents. In my baby-blue painted bedroom, I cried over high school breakups and listened to Ace of Base and danced in front of my dresser mirror.

This was the house where Jamie would pin me down in Daddy's recliner and tickle me until I cried while Mama drowned out our noise by playing the violin in her music room. At our cherry coffee table covered in drink rings, we played Monopoly and Rook. When we finally got a computer, I screamed throughout this house for Mama to hang up the phone when I was trying to use dial-up and download music on Napster. Anytime Jamie or I won an award, we posed by the magnolia tree in the corner of the front yard. I shed buckets of tears in this house and belly-laughed more times than I could count here. No, this wasn't just a chapter. *This was the entire book.*

When I was eighteen and fresh out of high school, Paige and I could not wait to rebel and leave one-horse Whitten. We rented a crappy little apartment in Huntsville, waitressed at a steak house, and attended W.B. Hilliard College together. Paige chased a degree in social work, and I pursued journalism in hopes of becoming a bigwig reporter in New York or some city miles away from Alabama. I'll never forget Carter Sutton showing up at a party at our small loft apartment one muggy May night. He'd come with his cousin, who was a friend of a friend—or something or other. For me it was love at first sight.

This house was the place where I told my parents, while they sat at the round kitchen table shelling peas from our garden, that I'd fallen in love with a boy from not far over the Alabama state line in Tullahoma, Tennessee, who attended Vanderbilt University in Nashville.

"Vanderbilt?" Daddy's eyes had shifted over the top rim of his tortoiseshell glasses. "Wealthy, is he?"

"And smart?" Mama smiled.

"He's majoring in economics." I sat in the oak kitchen

chair next to my daddy. "He's going to be a financial advisor."

"Economics? Well, my," Mama said.

"What's this boy's name?" Daddy wiped his purple-stained fingers on the kitchen towel.

"Carter Sutton." I blushed and looked to my mother. "And he's perfect, Mama. He's just perfect."

That conversation took place at the table where I was now sitting with my brother and Aunt Maxine. It was also the same spot Carter and I sat with my parents and told them we were getting married after we'd been dating for four years. And that a baby was on the way. If it was a girl, we wanted to name her Molly Margaret. Margaret for my mother, of course.

"What's this?" Jamie interrupted my thoughts and pulled a small pink envelope from a pile of papers on the kitchen table.

"Mama's stationery," I answered.

"It has your name on it." He handed it to me.

I examined the small pink envelope in my hands and admired my mother's beautiful penmanship.

"Open it, Raeley Ann," Aunt Maxine encouraged.

I carefully unsealed the envelope, and the white-and-pink flowery paper my mother used to send notes of encouragement and thanks to others was visible.

"It's a letter. For me. From Mama." My heart palpitated. "I think I'll go back to my room and read it."

Aunt Maxine and Jamie watched me stand from the

kitchen chair and walk to the back of the house before they started quietly talking again. I entered my childhood room and waited on Patsy to follow me inside before shutting the door. My white iron bed still sat against the long wall, covered with the familiar yellow eyelet comforter. I'd refinished both my old dresser and chest of drawers for Molly's room in our house on Sullivan Street in Huntsville, and in their place were a few Rubbermaid totes, Mama's ironing board, and a pile of wrinkled shirts in a laundry basket.

I climbed onto the tall bed as Patsy turned in several circles before dropping her large, furry body onto the cream carpet. I leaned back and pulled the paper from the pink envelope.

Rae,

My darling, if you're reading this, I'm more alive than ever. I'm at peace. I'm at rest. I'm home.

I remember the first weeks after your grandmother passed away. I couldn't even pull myself out of bed. You probably remember it too. You were, what, fifteen or so, and I remember so vividly you coming into my dark room one afternoon while I was in the bed watching *Mad About You*. You were wearing one of those black band T-shirts you used to collect. Maybe it was the Pearl Jelly one. I don't know. Anyway, you sat on the edge of the bed and said, "Mama, it's time to get up." I knew right then you needed me. Jamie needed me. Your daddy needed me. I had responsibilities and a life to live. I had to get up for you all. If you're mourning like I did, it's understandable, but at some point, Rae, you've got to get up and rejoin the land of the living. Molly Margaret needs you. Patsy needs you. She has to eat every two hours or her blood sugar drops.

I feel bad for putting so much pressure on you to move into the house once I'm gone. You are a grown woman and have to make the best decision for you and Molly Margaret. It's just that I hate to think of strangers living here. I probably won't be concerned with such things once I'm in heaven, but I do have a great sense of peace, while I'm still on this earth, at the thought of Molly Margaret dancing in your old bedroom and of you shelling peas in my kitchen. You will shell peas, won't you, Rae? Please tell me you won't buy purple hulls at the store when the most fertile soil in all of Alabama is right out this back door.

You may think it will be too painful to live here once I'm gone. Maybe the house will seem empty and sad, but don't think of it like that. Think of all the happiness we had under this roof, Rae. I think you and Molly Margaret could make a lot of happiness right here at 214 Hazel Tree too.

I've always been so proud of you, my dear. I think you know that. I couldn't have asked for a more loving or caring daughter. You worry about me too much though. You always have.

On your first day of kindergarten, when all the

mommies there looked like Barbie dolls, I was forty-five years old. But I like to think I always looked good for my age. I refused to chop off my hair and wear elastic pants, and I was always on the go, wasn't I? Partly because I never wanted to seem old to you and your brother.

I've told you this story a hundred times, but you know your father and I had a world of difficulty getting pregnant with Jamie, and we sure didn't think we'd have another baby. But you came along when we were forty, and it was nothing short of a miracle! My grandmama, Mrs. Imogene Raeley, always said miracles are evidence of a loving God, and that's why I named you after her. I sure as heck wasn't going to name you Imogene (you're welcome), so you got stuck with Rae.

I've loved watching you raise Molly Margaret. You're such a good mother to her, the same way you were a good mother to all of the dogs and Cabbage Patch Kids you had when you were a little girl. Anyway, don't deprive sweet Molly Margaret of Fudge Rounds and Dr Pepper, Rae. I like to think she'll always think of me when you buy them for her.

Don't be too hard on Carter either. It broke my heart when your marriage fell apart because I've always loved him so much, from the first moment I met him. And even when you fornicated (you knew better) before you got married, I still loved him. It always brought me great joy watching him watch you when you didn't know he was looking at you. You may be divorced now, but I think there will always be a great love between the two of you.

I've rambled long enough. Just know how much I love you, dear girl. I am incredibly blessed to have you in my life. Stay close with your brother, and don't let too long go by without getting together to grill hamburgers. And for heaven's sake, don't let him start smoking again when I'm gone.

As for the house, the decision is ultimately yours. Don't do anything just because I (or Aunt Maxine) tell you to do it, okay? But (you know I always have to insert a "but"), it's been a good house to my family, and I think it would be a good house to your family.

I love you with my heart.

Until we meet again,

Mama

PS: There's another letter for you in the shed, but don't go searching for it until you've had time to rest and pray and reflect.

I paused for a few minutes while staring at my mother's words on the pale pink paper. I could picture her sitting at the kitchen table penning this letter for me for this moment. As she had gotten sicker over the last year, she insinuated time and time again how much it would please her if Molly and I moved into her home someday. Molly and I had discussed it vaguely a couple of times, but I knew a serious conversation was warranted.

I looked around my old bedroom and pictured Molly journaling in here, dreaming of some boy in here. This bedroom was certainly more spacious than her current one in the apartment. She could upgrade from a twin-size bed.

But most importantly, I felt the love in this room—in the entire little brick house. There had always been stability here. There still was. The house was bought and paid for. It was mine. Unlike so many other things, this place couldn't be taken from me. Besides, my mother seemed to think living here was a great idea. And my mother had always been right.

CHAPTER 4

As an infant, Molly slept ten hours a night and rarely cried. She didn't throw a fit when plans changed. Her twelfth birthday party at the water park was canceled because of a torrential downpour and she looked at me from the back seat of the car, in her striped swimsuit and hot-pink sunglasses, and said, "It's all good, Mama."

She'd always been an old soul, my Molly Margaret. Wise beyond her years. She listened to Fleetwood Mac and Patsy Cline. She wore Converse before it was cool for kids her age to wear Converse. She preferred taking pictures with my old Polaroid over posting on Instagram. She loved the classics like *Grapes of Wrath* and *The Old Man and the Sea*. She would rather play basketball in the driveway than watch television. People were always drawn to Molly and her cheerful, go-with-the-flow disposition. She was voted "Best Personality" her last year of middle school. For the yearbook photo she posed next to an oak tree in the schoolyard in her tattered white Converse with a confident grin on her face.

Molly had been presented with so many transitions over the last year. Not only was her body changing physically and chemically (oh, that dreaded first zit), but she was devastated to learn her father no longer loved her mother. The most upset I'd ever seen laid-back Molly was when she sat across from Carter and me at the kitchen table on Sullivan Street and heard her father tell her we were getting divorced. I let him take the lead on that conversation. Leaving me—breaking up our family—was *his* idea.

She was so angry with her dad the first few weeks. Although Carter had turned out to be an unfaithful husband, he was a devoted father. There was no doubt Molly meant the world to him. I'm not sure what he said to her later on, but he explained his decision to leave in a way that made her forgive his wrongs and fall right back in love with him. And he made sure she knew I wasn't to blame.

I respected their relationship. As hard as it was at times, I refrained from bad-mouthing her father to her. I refrained from telling her that he'd cheated on me with Autumn. I refrained from calling him every four-letter word that came to mind. I held my tongue when I wanted to verbally tear him apart. Still, I knew his leaving left a scar on her heart, and for that I resented Carter Sutton most of all.

Soon after her father and I no longer shared a home, Molly's beloved grandmother was diagnosed with cancer. She became anxious and worried. Her grades slipped a bit as she lost hours of sleep worrying Nana was going to die. The wound of abandonment, created by the divorce, resurfaced. She may have forgiven her dad, but she still felt a level of fear at the thought of losing another important person in her life.

As I explained the potential move—yet another

change—to Molly that night over an ice-cold Dr Pepper and a piece of Mississippi mud cake, she became excited at the notion of playing basketball for the best girls high school team in the state. Just the thought of scoring in a state championship made her giddy. She also realized she would still see her dad and her Huntsville friends as often as possible. My sweet girl, who had managed to adapt to change after change, not only complied with the decision to move to Whitten but sounded excited about it.

"I think I'd feel closer to Nana in that house too. Will you keep Fudge Rounds in the pantry like she did?"

I spent the next morning drinking a pot of black coffee and making phone calls from the kitchen bar in my apartment as Patsy snored on the couch. I broke my lease (much to the dismay of the apartment manager, Mr. Haskins, who said although I was an exemplary tenant, he was unable to refund my deposit) and canceled the utilities and Internet. I scheduled a U-Haul for the next day and texted friends to see if they had any moving boxes. With my savings, alimony and child support, and inheritance, I would manage fine for a few months without a paycheck, so I phoned all twelve of my clients and told them I could no longer clean their houses.

I had received my journalism degree from W.B. Hilliard College, but I never put it to use. Once I was married with a beautiful baby girl, I couldn't care less about my youthful dreams of interviewing politicians or exposing scandals in some big city in the northeast. I wanted nothing more than to be a wife and stay-at-home mother. That became my life's passion. And I honestly enjoyed every moment of it for thirteen years. It wasn't until I was divorced and could no longer depend on Carter's income that I had to get a job outside of the home. And what better occupation for a stay-at-home mother than to clean houses? I had over a decade of experience.

Once I'd made dozens of phone calls in preparation for the move, I looked around my little apartment and planned where I'd place my furniture in Mama's house. I'd eventually rip up the decades-old carpet to showcase those beautiful hardwood floors. I would probably paint every wall some shade of gray, as Mama predicted, and refinish several pieces of her furniture. I would never get rid of her massive cedar chest in the master bedroom or the kitchen table that served as the hub of the home.

When we divorced, Carter was gracious enough to allow me to take whatever I wanted from our house on Sullivan Street. Furniture was my parting gift, I suppose, but some of my favorite pieces of bulky furniture wouldn't even fit through the apartment's door. My most coveted piece, the entertainment center I bought at an estate sale and refinished in antique white, was still in my former home. I reached for my phone on the bar and called my ex-husband.

"Yeah, Rae. Hey," he answered.

"I heard Molly on the phone with you last night. How do you feel about us moving?"

"I know you've mentioned it several times, but I didn't really think you'd want to move back to Whitten.

There's nothing there, right? 'One-horse town' you always called it."

"No, it isn't hustling and bustling like good old Huntsville," I said, "but I have memories there. My mama was there. And my daddy. It's where I grew up. I really think I need to be in that house right now. I need to be around my brother and his family and Aunt Maxine. The house is paid for, and it's much bigger than this apartment. It just makes sense."

"I wish we'd talked about this more. Molly is my child, too, Rae. Huntsville High School is five minutes from my house."

"Well, Whitten High School is thirty minutes from your house. I'm not moving her to Bangkok, Carter. I'm moving her right down the road. She's really excited about playing basketball for Whitten. They are state champs. It's a great team. If she wants to play college ball, she could really stand out by playing for Whitten."

"Whatever you think is best."

"She is still free to see you whenever you want. Weekends are still fine. It's really not a huge deal at all."

"If Molly is on board with it and this is what you need to do, Rae, I understand."

"I appreciate that." I sighed in relief that the move was not going to be an issue. "Listen, your offer to take whatever I wanted out of our house last year. Does that still stand?"

"What are you wanting?"

"The entertainment center in the living room. I refinished that and I'd like to have it."

"Okay."

"Thanks," I said.

"I can deliver it if you need me to. Just let me know when. And I'll drop Molly back off at your apartment after supper tonight."

Carter was complying, and I was thankful. I guess I just wanted him to say something like, "Why don't I bring the entertainment center and all of my stuff too? I will never betray you again. I will make up my stupid mistake to you for long as we live. We'll be a family again. I still love you, Rae. I never stopped loving you."

But he didn't.

———— ◆ ————

Fourteen months ago, on a warm spring Friday night in April, Molly was at a slumber party and I was sitting on our plush L-shaped couch at my beautiful home on Sullivan Street. I had just decorated the newly painted antique white entertainment center with family photos and candles and greenery for pops of color. A stack of old books I'd placed on one of the shelves wasn't doing it for me—the feng shui was all off. I got up from the couch, moved the books to another shelf, and sat back down. I got up again, moved the books and a candle and a mini topiary, and sat back down again. Finally, it was perfect.

"What're you doing?" Carter entered the living room from the hallway. He'd just showered and his hair was damp.

He was wearing plaid pajama pants and his favorite ragged Vanderbilt T-shirt.

"I switched the old books and the candle. Looks much better," I said while rubbing Patsy's back with my bare foot. "But that magnolia leaf is too tall. It throws everything off, doesn't it?"

"Rae, forget the magnolias. I need to talk to you." He sat across from me in his leather recliner.

"Talk to me?" I grinned. "Carter Sutton, you look nervous. That makes *me* nervous."

Carter and I had been married since we were twenty-two years old. In all that time, he'd never been much for conversation. That's just who he was. He didn't enter rooms and ask if we could talk unless something horrible had happened. The last time he said these words to me was twelve years ago when my brother called to tell him my father, sick with emphysema, had taken a turn for the worse.

"I don't know how to say this even though I rehearsed it in the shower for the last fifteen minutes," he said, rubbing his palms together.

My heart was pounding in my throat. Something had happened. Had Jamie called him before he got in the shower? Was something wrong with my mother? Was my mother sick? I nearly jumped to my feet.

"I have—I just. I j-just," he stuttered.

"Spit it out."

"I don't think I can be married anymore," he blurted without looking up at me.

Dead. Silence. The ceiling fan was whirring above my head, an episode of *Dateline* was playing softly on the television, and a live band was playing at the country club only a hundred fifty yards from our back door. But I heard nothing. Dead. Silence.

"What?" That was all I could speak into the quiet.

He still wouldn't look at me. He rested his elbows on his knees and continued to rub his hands. The coward wouldn't look away from his hands.

"Carter Sutton." I stood to my wobbly bare feet, my heart pounding in my ears, no longer out of fear but anger. "What did you say?"

"I don't want to be married anymore," he said in almost a whisper. He still rubbed his hands together. Harder. Faster.

I felt my cheeks turn fire red. I felt the heat in my blood. My lips tightly pursed the way they always did when I was infuriated—the way they did when we'd argued over petty things like our budget or him missing our anniversary for a work dinner or taking a weeklong trip to Texas to hunt. I paced the living room floor as Patsy looked up at me.

"Another woman? Who is it? Tabby from your office? I've been replaced by a woman with a cat's name? Is that it?"

"There's no one else, Raeley, I swear." He finally loosed his hands and looked at me. "There's no one else. I just don't . . ."

"You don't what?"

"I just don't want to be married anymore."

My knees buckled and nausea overcame me. I leaned

against the entertainment center. It still smelled of fresh paint. I wanted to fall to the floor and weep, but I was too angry to cry. I had never been so livid, so heartbroken, so shocked—all at once.

Carter and I weren't the most romantic couple. I didn't post photos on Facebook of rose petals leading to a candlelit dinner on our dining table or bouquets he sent on random Tuesdays. We argued over small things from time to time like any normal couple. I probably lost my temper with him more times than I should have. I flew off the handle over the smallest things. Assumed the worst. Went on the defensive.

When I was a child, Mama often recited Longfellow when I was having a fit: "There was a little girl, who had a little curl, right in the middle of her forehead. When she was good, she was very, very good, but when she was bad, she was horrid." I had been horrid many times. I nagged him over dirty boxer shorts on the floor next to the hamper or him falling asleep before locking all the doors at night.

I wasn't always a kind wife, and we'd been out of the honeymoon phase for some time, but I didn't foresee ever leaving him. I didn't foresee him ever leaving me. In my visions of the future, he was sitting next to me in a rocking chair on our front porch while grandchildren played in the yard. We'd built a life together. We'd laughed and cried and prayed together for fourteen years. We'd raised a beautiful little girl. We'd watched movies together on that L-shaped couch and shared appetizers at local restaurants. We were in this for the long haul. I still loved him as much as I did on that humid May night when I saw him in my loft apartment for the first time. I had no idea he didn't love me anymore. He didn't give me any signs that I was no longer the one for him.

"I know that hurts to hear, Raeley—"

"Don't call me Raeley." I held my hand up to silence him. "You only call me Raeley when you're excited. Are you excited about this?"

"Of course not." He paused. "I do love you, Rae. You're the mother of my child. You were my first love—my only love. I just don't . . . I don't know." He sighed. "I just want out. I don't want to be married anymore. I don't know what I want."

"Is this some midlife crisis thing? You're having a midlife crisis at thirty-five, is that it? Why not just buy a convertible, Carter? How long have you been thinking about this? How long did it take you to work up the courage to tell me this?" I paced the living room, lips still pursed, face still on fire.

"A few months, I guess." He shrugged and started rubbing his hands together again. "I wanted to—"

"Stop." I shook my head and paced to the back door as tears still threatened to fall from my eyes. I looked across the dark golf course to the brightly lit country club where the live band was now playing Journey's "Small Town Girl." "To think my biggest worry was that stupid magnolia leaf only two minutes ago. Now my husband doesn't want me anymore."

"Rae, I'm sorry." He stood from the recliner. "The last thing in the world I want to do is hurt you. Or Molly."

"Oh really?" I faced him. "You're just not *in love* with me anymore? Is that it? You don't have butterflies anymore? You've grown bored with me?" I threw my hands in the air. "What are you? Sixteen? Marriage isn't about butterflies. If we're talking butterflies, I haven't felt one of those in a hot minute, but divorce has never crossed my mind." I glared at him. In that moment, I no longer saw my sweet Carter standing before me. I no longer saw my partner, my teammate, the love of my life. I saw my enemy.

"Rae—"

"Nearly fifteen years of marriage and you tell me you don't want to be married anymore! And you don't even have a good reason? No other woman? You just don't want to be married anymore? Is that what you're going to tell Molly? That you just didn't want to be married to her mother anymore?"

And then I screamed. I didn't shout. I didn't yell. I balled my fists and screamed as if I was ten years old and walking through the House of Horrors at the Whitten Elks Lodge on Halloween night. I screamed so loudly I was sure the cover band at the country club would pull the plug on the amplifiers and call the police.

"I can't even look at you anymore." I turned to stomp to our bedroom at the end of the hallway.

"I'm sorry, Rae. I don't know what else to say. I'm just sorry."

I stopped midway down the hall and looked back at him. The tears were finally streaming down my face.

"And why did you think you should put on pajamas after rehearsing this conversation? Did you think I was going to just say, 'Okay, Carter, whatever you want is fine with me. Good night, dear. Go on to bed.' I don't think so, buddy. You'd better put on your blue jeans and get out of this house."

Carter did put on his jeans. He put them on, packed an overnight bag, apologized again, and walked out the front door. Unbeknownst to me, he went straight to a young girl named Autumn . . . who was born in July. I spent the rest of the night throwing up and sobbing to my mother over the phone.

———— ◆ ————

Carter dropped Molly off at the apartment after supper. He didn't even walk her to the door. I always took that as a personal insult. He didn't long to see me anymore. He didn't want to talk to me. He no longer smiled at the sight of my face. Instead, he wanted to gaze into the eyes of a young girl named after my least favorite season.

The next morning my friend Abby, who owned a boutique in Huntsville, dropped off dozens of boxes at my apartment. We spent the day placing everything I owned inside cardboard. Abby's husband, Tim, and her teenaged son, Tyler, graciously loaded all of my furniture and boxes into the U-Haul. It didn't take long to empty the small apartment and head to Whitten.

Jamie had already taken an armoire and some of Mama's other things to his home. He hauled off Mama's massive analog big-screen television that projected a blue tint on every channel and dumped it at the local donation center.

Mama really had done me a great favor by decluttering before she passed away. I probably would've kept every knickknack and receipt and phone book from the '90s. I would've kept the power suits with shoulder pads and cardigans and tattered nightgowns. I would've kept the Tupperware containers without lids that carried the scent of her delicious chocolate cake. I would've kept anything, no matter how insignificant, if it was attached to a memory. Without her courteous act of decluttering, there would have been no room in the garage for my SUV.

But one of the most heart-wrenching events of the afternoon was removing my mother's everyday clothing from her closets to make room for mine. I couldn't bear to put anything into the donate pile. Instead, I clung to a pile of her favorite, familiar T-shirts, the seersucker capri pants she so often wore, and the terry-cloth housecoat stained with dollops of boxed hair color. I carefully folded each garment and placed them in the cedar chest that still sat in the corner of the master bedroom. As far as I was concerned, they would stay in that chest forever.

It was a long day. Boxes sat unpacked throughout the house. I finally settled my tired and aching body into the king-size bed in my mother's bedroom at around one that morning. Molly was sleeping with Patsy in the white wrought iron bed that I had slept in, had dreamed in, and had prayed in until I was eighteen years old.

I looked around the dark master bedroom. This had been my parents' bedroom since 1975. The green light from the smoke detector was right above the bed. I'd been looking at that little green light my entire life. The batteries always went dead in the middle of the night—never during the day. I'd seen my tired and incoherent daddy cuss and grumble and climb the stepladder in his flannel pajama pants and white T-shirt to change the dead 9-volt more times than I could count.

When I was a little girl and thunder clapped in the middle of the night, I'd crawl right between Mama and Daddy in this room as the wind raged through the hundreds-year-old oak tree outside the window. Mama held me close while Daddy snored so loudly even the thunder couldn't drown out the noise. After Daddy died, I stayed with Mama many weekends. Carter knew Mama and I needed each other. We put toddler Molly between us and watched *The Golden Girls*. "That Blanche is such a tramp. I'm going to get some ice cream. You want a bowl?" She'd bring back a bowl of butter pecan—it was always butter pecan—and we'd laugh and talk in her plush bed while precious Molly snuggled between us, sucking her thumb with a sippy cup cradled in her armpit.

It was strange how such a familiar place could suddenly

seem so foreign—how a place that once brought so much peace and comfort could be scary and void of my mother's presence.

I closed my eyes and felt such an incredible longing for my mother—for my father and the life I'd once known. I suddenly worried I would drift off to sleep every night in that room feeling empty inside.

CHAPTER 5

*M*ama had done a fine job cleaning out the shed too. The last time I looked in there, probably a year or so ago, it was cluttered with totes of junk and other stuff handed down to Mama throughout the years. I don't know what she did with half of the plastic bins that she'd kept, but they were gone. I thought that was a great testament of my mother's character—she always wanted to take the burden. She wanted to make things simple for those she loved.

She left two end tables in the shed. They were straight out of the '70s—octagon-shaped oak—and covered in stains and spills after sitting next to a hideous green couch in Mama and Daddy's first house by the railroad tracks. I assumed she'd left them for me to refinish.

After a week of unpacking and settling into my childhood home, I drug both tables over to a small concrete pad in a cool corner of the yard. Before Daddy built the back deck, the little slab was where he grilled hamburgers and hot dogs and his delicious medium-well New York strips that we'd eat with Mama's homemade potato salad. Jamie's and my handprints were still visible in the weathered concrete. Jamie also wrote "Mötley Crüe Rules," much to my dad's dismay. "That's garbage music, son. Those guys wear more eyeliner than your mother. Otis Redding. That's where it's at." I couldn't count how many times he played his Otis Redding record and danced with Mama, barefoot, in the kitchen.

The July sun was scorching as I dusted the end tables with a rag and prepared them for paint. They'd look beautiful in robin's-egg blue. I still had half a can of the chalk paint left from a foyer table I painted for a friend in Huntsville. I would distress the corners with sandpaper (fine grit, of course) and put the tables at either end of the L-shaped couch I was sitting on the night my husband told me he didn't love me anymore. The blue would coordinate well with the antique white entertainment center Carter had delivered a few days before.

We barely said two words to each other as he and his friend Clay brought the massive piece through the front door and put it on the long wall in the living room. I told him some more plans I had for decorating the place, and he barely nodded and went outside to talk to Molly while she sat in the swing on the back deck and read *As I Lay Dying*. He left me feeling rejected, once again.

As beads of sweat covered my temples and fell into my eyes, I opened the small, creaky drawer on one of the end tables and saw another pink note with my name written in my mother's handwriting. This was the letter Mother had said I would find in the shed. I sat on the concrete pad, right atop Jamie's dedication to Mötley Crüe.

Rae,

My darling, if you're reading this, chances are you are refinishing these tables. Your father and I bought them brand new from Felsenthal's Furniture in downtown Huntsville right after we were married. I loved the shape of them. Octagon! So funky! So groovy! So 1971! And they looked absolutely stunning next to the green corduroy couch my mother-in-law gave us as a wedding gift. Do you remember that couch? We had it until you were four or five. You fell asleep and peed on it while watching Gilligan's Island one afternoon. Looking back on it, that couch looked more like the Loch Ness Monster than a piece of furniture. Mrs. Bonnie knew it was ugly. That's probably why she gave it to me. Your grandmother wasn't my biggest fan. Never was. But that's another letter for another day.

I was so proud of the first house I shared with your father. It was on King Street right next to the railroad tracks. I know I drove you by there from time to time. It's a shame how run-down that little house is nowadays. I went by there yesterday and there was a broken recliner on the front porch and a mangy dog chained to the electric pole in the yard. Garbage and junk filled the flower beds instead of impatiens and hydrangeas. I think the man standing in the front yard wanted me to stop and buy some cocaine. It made my heart sad to see how the homeowners have let that place go.

If you're refinishing these tables, then hopefully that

means you're staying in the house. I am giddy just thinking about that possibility. I am giddy thinking of you loving this home the way I loved that little house on King Street, and the way I loved this house and raising you and your brother in it.

I remember how proud you were of your beautiful home in Huntsville. It was gorgeous sitting on that golf course with those huge river birch trees in the yard. I know you poured a lot into that place, updating all the brass lighting fixtures and ripping that awful fruit wallpaper from the kitchen walls. You made it such a lovely home, Rae. And I think you thoroughly enjoyed doing it.

I remember coming over one afternoon and you were covered in dust and Sheetrock from knocking down the kitchen wall to make the space more open. You wielded that sledgehammer like Paul Bunyan wielded his ax. I was so impressed and so proud of you for rolling up your sleeves and getting your hands dirty. You had a vision and you saw it through.

I know how painful it was for you to leave your home after the divorce, after all the work you put into it, but I want you to be excited like that again. I want you to roll up your sleeves and swing that sledgehammer. (But don't knock down the wall in the kitchen. I think it's load-bearing.)

Rae, you have a gift of making old things new. You have the gift of restoration. That gift was evident after your divorce too. You restored your life when it was so broken and made things new for yourself and for Molly Margaret. Use that gift again after I'm gone. Keep going. Restore yourself. Restore this house and make it all your own. Make it a special place for you and your daughter. Make it a home to be proud of.

These tables would be beautiful in blue, wouldn't they?

I love you with my heart.

Until we meet again,
Mama

I quietly sat on the sweaty concrete slab and held the letter in my hands. It was as if my mother knew just the words I needed, at just the right time. That was my mama. Right on cue. Even after death.

I didn't think I'd done a fine job of restoring my life after Carter left though. I was still so broken by his leaving. I constantly wondered what I'd done wrong or when the exact moment was that he looked at me and thought, *I don't love her anymore.* When my mother got sick, I didn't want to burden her with my misery. I knew she would worry about me instead of focusing on getting better, so I put on a happy face and made her believe I was healing from the heartbreak, but I was far from restored.

As I finished putting the second coat of paint on the tables, Molly busted out the back door and onto the deck in one of her father's vintage Vanderbilt T-shirts and her royal-blue basketball shorts she wore last season at Huntsville Middle.

"I'm about to outgrow my shoes, Mama. My toes are cramped up. Am I ever going to quit growing?" She bent over and tugged at the laces on her black high-tops as a panting Patsy slowly walked toward her and sniffed her shoes. "And these shorts aren't the right color for Whitten."

"You look fine, Molly. Is it already time for tryouts?" I stood to my flip-flops and dusted paint specks from my athletic shorts.

"Yes. I don't want to be late." She pulled her long brown hair into a high ponytail. "Let's roll."

———◆———

"Are you nervous?" I looked over to my daughter in the passenger seat. I'd been taking her to basketball practice since she was seven. Her shorts used to hang down nearly to her ankles, and the basketball looked more like an oversize yoga ball as her little hands attempted to dribble it down the court. But now she looked so grown, so tall, on her way to high school tryouts. I didn't know where the time had gone. I wished her daddy could see her in that moment. I wished he was right there in the car with us as she looked at herself in the visor mirror and applied Chapstick to her lips.

"Nope. I'm not nervous." She looked down at her phone. "Did I tell you my friend Morgan's cousin is going to be a freshman at Whitten too? Morgan said she's pretty cool. She already told her about me."

"Oh really? You already know someone? See? It's all

working out." I smiled and tapped the steering wheel. "And Logan and Liam will make you feel right at home too. They'll look out for their cousin. Everything is going to be fine," I said aloud, to convince myself more than her.

"I'm really fine, Mama. I'm excited about basketball and making new friends. You don't have to worry about me."

———————————— ❖ ————————————

I was flooded with memories as Molly and I walked through the open gym doors at Whitten High School. In ninth grade, I do-si-doed with Buddy Barker during physical education in this gym. I never understood why in the world we had to square-dance in PE, but Buddy loved it. He was a professional. He always wore a cowboy hat and a belt buckle, for goodness' sake. He line-danced with his grandparents down at Rodney's Tavern on Thursday nights—of his own free will. I was stuck with the only kid in high school who actually knew how to square-dance, and instead of laughing at the absurdity of it all, he took it seriously and criticized my every move.

I could still hear him shouting at me, "Raeley, pass on the right side! The *right* side!"

I went to pep rallies and watched countless Warriors basketball games in this gymnasium with my best friends. Paige and I both had our first kisses with twins Hunter and Hayden Morrison beneath the bleachers after the homecoming game in tenth grade. I'd kissed Hunter and always teased

Paige that I'd lucked out with the cuter twin. "They are identical," she'd retorted. She was just jealous because she knew I was right. Hunter was much cuter than Hayden. I will admit I looked Hunter up on Facebook not long after Carter left, out of curiosity. He was married with four kids. And he was still much cuter than Hayden.

Kevin Howell broke up with me by the water fountain in eleventh grade. I never thought I'd forget his harsh words and watching him walk out the double doors. Kevin had a cowlick that couldn't be tamed and an eight-thirty curfew. He also had halitosis. I'm not really sure why I considered him a loss.

I never thought I'd set foot in this purple-and-white gym again, except maybe for my nephews' graduations, but here I was. I was going to sit on those same old wooden bleachers and watch my little girl storm down the court as a Whitten Lady Warrior. The notion made me excited.

At least ten girls were already shooting layups as Molly set her water bottle on the bleachers and approached them. I saw the way they all looked at her, and it made me nervous for her. Twenty eyes were on my daughter, and I could tell they were wondering who she was. I would have passed out from anxiety if that had been me. I have always been such a nervous wreck around new people. But not Molly. She grabbed a ball from the rack at half-court and approached the group.

"Hey, guys, I'm Molly. I just moved here from Huntsville." She put the basketball under her left arm and extended her right hand.

SUSANNAH B. LEWIS

Their faces immediately softened. They were already drawn to this brazen girl's personality—a girl who walked in and shook hands with strangers like she was a grown-up, like she was the CEO of Nike, like she wasn't intimidated or nervous in the slightest. They watched her perfect shooting form and her five-eight frame sprint for a jump shot. They knew she'd be an asset, and they welcomed her with smiles.

"Are you Rae?" My thoughts were interrupted by a deep voice approaching me from behind.

I turned to see a handsome man wearing a Whitten Warriors T-shirt with a whistle hanging from his neck walking toward me. "Oh, yes, yes, hi." I stumbled over my words like an idiot. "You must be Coach Richardson?"

"Kent." He extended his hand to shake mine. "Aunt Fannie told me your daughter would be trying out for the team."

"That's her." I pointed to Molly shooting a three-pointer. "Molly Sutton."

This man clearly ran twenty miles a day. He drank smoothies. He was educated in the benefits of protein and knew how to calculate micronutrients. I had envisioned a Larry Bird lookalike—someone who resembled Molly's junior high coach, Mr. Barnett. Someone who used to be an athlete but twenty-five years of Budweiser and cheeseburgers had changed his physique. But I was mistaken. *This was a coach.* This man was still an athlete. He looked like a winner. He looked like a coach who would lead this team to state and then have each girl recruited to the WNBA.

"She looks good. I got a call from Coach Barnett, actually. He said she's quite the defensive player. A great rebounder too. He spoke highly of her as a teammate as well."

"Coach Barnett pushed her the last two years. She really improved. She's a hard worker and a coachable kid."

"I'm sure she'll do fine today. We will be done around four thirty, but I'll ask the girls who make the team to stay a few minutes after."

He even smelled good. Clean. Like he'd just showered with Zest.

"Okay, great. I'll be back around four thirty, then." I was suddenly concerned that my hair was in a sweaty bun speckled with blue paint.

"It's nice to meet you." He smiled. His teeth were white. And straight. He must've still worn a retainer at night.

"Nice too," I said.

Nice too. What did that mean? I turned, rolled my eyes at my own awkwardness, and left the gym.

Three hours later, Molly walked outside with a couple of girls, laughing and chattering as if she'd known them since kindergarten. She waved goodbye to them and got in the car. Her hair was dripping with sweat, and she smelled terrible.

"Well?" I asked.

"Nailed it. He played me at point guard most of the tryout. That's my favorite spot."

"That's so great!" I reached over and playfully punched her in the arm. "The girls were all nice? You already made friends?"

"Yeah, they're cool. Morgan's cousin is on the team. One of the girls has had a crush on cousin Logan since elementary school. She kept asking me all about him. It was kind of annoying, but I didn't tell her about the time he farted at the Thanksgiving table. He owes me one." She unlaced her tight shoes, removed them from her sweaty feet, and grimaced at the smell. "Practice starts next week."

"And Coach Richardson? You like him pretty well?"

"Yeah," she said. "He's pretty cute for an old guy."

"Molly." I put the car in drive.

"Well, I'm not wrong, am I?"

"No, you're not."

CHAPTER 6

*R*ain poured and thunder rumbled as I drove to Mrs. Fannie's house on Main Street on the third Thursday morning in July. Aunt Maxine had called to invite me the night before. "It's our first meeting without your mother, Raeley Ann. We'd love if you'd come to represent her. We'll have pie. Who can say no to pie?"

I had sanding and painting to do. I'd scored a few pieces of furniture from a yard sale the weekend before and already sold a foyer table to an old acquaintance from high school. But when I woke to rain that Thursday morning and knew I wouldn't get any work done outside on the concrete pad, I had no excuse not to go to my mother's "ministry." It wasn't that I particularly wanted an excuse, but I feared there would be a cloud of grief hanging over the meeting. Mother would definitely be missed.

Mrs. Fannie's big old house was beautiful—and piping hot. I never understood why one of the wealthiest women in Whitten, Alabama, refused to turn on the air-conditioning. Instead, box fans sat in the corner of every room and window units roared. The heat was not remedied. The stagnant, summer Alabama air recirculated around the front parlor decorated with antiques. In that room it was as if time had stood still in 1955. The couch was a Victorian-style rolled-arm and uncomfortable as all get out.

Mrs. Fannie rolled in a brass serving cart topped with a toile teapot of coffee, four matching cups and saucers, and dessert plates full of pecan tarts. Real linen napkins folded into triangles rested on every plate.

"This is an awful fancy affair," I said. "Should I have dressed up a little?" I looked down at my running shorts and tank top.

"Maybe a bit, Raeley Ann." Aunt Maxine pinched her fingers together and frowned at my attire.

The ladies looked ready for Sunday services. Mrs. Dora and Aunt Maxine had on pastel blouses and freshly pressed khaki slacks and rings on nearly every finger. Mrs. Fannie's pearls, the pearls she'd rather be buried with than let her son-in-law obtain, hung over her A-line dress with a small floral pattern.

I noticed a photo of Kent in a silver frame on the secretary in the corner. He was young, in his twenties, posing with Mrs. Fannie and Mr. Pratt on the front porch of the very house we sat in, sweating. A huge Kimberly queen fern was behind them. Judging by his vintage rugby shirt and long Leonardo DiCaprio bangs, it must've been taken in the '90s.

"Oh, you see that photo of Kent, dear? He said Molly did wonderfully at tryouts." Mrs. Fannie handed me a toile teacup of dark coffee.

"Oh, yes, ma'am. She made the team. She is so excited."

"I love that boy like a son. I'm so glad he moved back here. Did you ever meet Kent when you were younger, Rae?" Mrs. Fannie slowly sat in an olive-green high-backed chair and pressed the teacup to her red lipstick.

"No, ma'am. I don't think so," I answered.

"He's my baby brother Theo's son. They moved from Whitten to Birmingham not long after Kent was born. Did you know he played basketball in Tuscaloosa? He was a stellar athlete. He moved back a few years ago when we put Theo in the nursing home here. I thought he'd leave after Theo died, but he didn't. I think he stays to keep an eye on me. Keep me out of trouble."

"Well, good thing for that." Mrs. Dora sat next to me on the antique sofa as her costume jewelry jingled on her wrists.

"Has he been married? Kent?" I asked.

"Oh, heavens no." Mrs. Fannie waved her hand at such folly. "Kent's always been a bachelor. He's broken plenty of hearts, I will tell you that. Cora England's girl latched onto him the first five minutes he was in Whitten. I talked him out of that."

"All those England girls have a reputation, you know?" Aunt Maxine winked at me from a chair identical to the one Mrs. Fannie sat in.

"Oh, I know! I have the grandest idea." Mrs. Fannie set the teacup on the coffee table coaster and clapped her small, jewelry-covered hands. "You and Kent, Rae! Oh, that's perfect. That would be just heavenly, wouldn't it, Maxine?"

"I don't see a problem with it." Aunt Maxine shrugged nonchalantly.

"No, no." I shook my head and put my saucer on the glass coffee table. "No, Mrs. Fannie."

"Well, why on earth not? I'll tell him to give you a call. That's what I'll do. That's exactly what I'll do!"

If you had told me a year and a half ago that I'd be sitting, motherless and single, at a meeting in a sweltering hot antiquated home and an eighty-year-old woman would be playing matchmaker for me, I wouldn't have believed it.

"No, Mrs. Fannie. Don't do that. I'm not ready to date anyone."

"Fannie, butt out of that girl's life. She said no," Mrs. Dora chimed in.

Mrs. Fannie pretended to hold a phone to her ear and smiled at me while I shook my head again.

"Let's move on to business now. I'll open with prayer," Aunt Maxine said. "Dear Lord, thank You for the friendships and family represented here. Thank You for the opportunity to do the work of Your hands. Let us leave this meeting better than when we arrived. Tell Margie we love her. Amen."

"Amen."

"Amen."

"Amen."

"Now, Margie always gave the hospital and nursing home report, but I got that together this month," Aunt Maxine began.

Aunt Maxine and Mrs. Fannie put on identical black readers from the Super D pharmacy and produced notepads and pencils from their purses. I felt ill-equipped. I didn't have readers or a sheet of paper.

Aunt Maxine proceeded to read off a list of names of those they knew admitted to or discharged from Whitten General over the last month. They made notes to check on those who were home and send flowers to those who were still in the hospital. They argued along the way.

"Eleanor Martin is still there after breaking her hip. That's Kitty Applebee's sister, you know?" Aunt Maxine read from her list as the glasses rested on the tip of her nose.

"No, it isn't, Maxine. Eleanor is Darcille's sister. Kitty is their first cousin," Mrs. Dora corrected her.

"I know that isn't right, Dora," Aunt Maxine huffed. She removed her glasses and shook her head.

"They were close like sisters, yes, but they are actually cousins. Don't argue with me on this."

"I think Dora's right, Maxine," Mrs. Fannie interjected. "Eleanor and Darcille were Benjamin's daughters. Kitty's dad was named William."

"Now, that's not right at all. I know that Kitty and Eleanor were—" Aunt Maxine began.

"Don't start, Maxine. Let's move on. Someone send Eleanor some flowers. I don't care whose sister she is," Dora declared.

"I'll send them. To *Kitty's* sister, Eleanor." Aunt Maxine wrote on her notepad. "Now, Robin Percy's daughter just had her fourth baby. We need to send them a gift too. I'll pick up a baby blanket from Clooney's and drop it off. They live in that white house on Maplewood."

"Which daughter?" Dora inquired.

"Rachel."

"No, Maxine. Samantha had the baby. Rachel isn't even married," Ms. Dora argued. Mrs. Fannie looked to me and gave an exasperated sigh.

"Dora! I know darn well Rachel is married. She married Martha Nell's son. The one with the big teeth and beard. Don't tell me. I went to the wedding, Dora." Aunt Maxine decisively shook her finger.

"Moving on." Fannie scribbled on her notepad and changed the subject. "Now, we all know Paul Dixon died on Tuesday. Do we want to ride together to the funeral home tomorrow?"

"Was he sick?" Dora asked.

"Only since 1957, Dora," my aunt replied.

Mrs. Dora rolled her pale blue eyes and made a note on the pad resting on her khaki slacks.

Mrs. Fannie said, "I'll just walk to the funeral home. Dr. Talbot says I need to exercise."

"Then we'll meet you there, Fannie. Dora, I'll swing by and get you at twelve thirty. Does Harold want to go?"

"You know he won't be up from his nap yet. And he never liked Paul Dixon. I didn't much either. I'm only going for his boys. I taught them in school. Sweet kids."

"Paul Dixon had girls, Dora. Two of them. You're

thinking of Edward Dixon's boys." Aunt Maxine removed her glasses, again, and glared at Mrs. Dora.

"Maxine, I know good and well who Paul Dixon *and* his sons are!"

I couldn't help but to laugh out loud and ask, "This is what y'all do? You argue for an hour over family trees?"

"We serve others, Raeley Ann. That's what we do. And speaking of, I haven't heard you volunteer to send a single card, flower, or baby blanket." Aunt Maxine frowned.

"I'm sorry, Aunt Maxine. Tell me what you want me to do."

"Find out if Paul Dixon had sons or daughters. Pull out that phone of yours and look them up on that Facebook."

"Yes, ma'am." I took my phone from my purse resting on the hardwood floor.

"Look up Tate or Marshall Dixon. I guarantee they'll mention their father, *Paul*," Dora insisted. "Paul didn't have girls. How silly. I couldn't even imagine Paul Dixon with girls."

"Dora Kinney, did you even grow up in Whitten? I can't tell that you did." Aunt Maxine chewed on the end of her glasses.

I laughed while I opened the social media app and searched for the Dixon boys. Or girls.

"While Rae is gathering evidence, I think we should have some dessert," Dora said as they all slowly gripped the arms of their chairs, stood their aching bones, and approached the shiny cart beside the coffee table. "Now, are these pee-can or puh-khan tarts, Fannie?"

"Lord, don't start that mess," Aunt Maxine said.

"I hate to inform you, Aunt Maxine, but Tate Dixon posted, 'We will miss my father terribly. Please keep us in your prayers.'"

"Ha ha! I told you Paul had sons. Tate and Marshall! I told you." Dora nearly started dancing right there on the Persian rug. "Your memory is fading, old woman."

"You can't trust anything you read on that Internet." Aunt Maxine walked back to the high-back chair with a small dessert plate.

I tossed my phone back into my purse, wiped the beads of sweat on my brow, and reached for a tart. "So, what do we do now? We've decided who needs flowers and gifts and prayers. We cracked the Dixon case."

"Well, now we just visit, dear." Mrs. Fannie slowly chewed the tart. Her ruby lipstick was smudged at the corner of her thin lips.

"Should we choose a book to discuss at next month's meeting?" Dora asked.

"I only have time to read *Guideposts*, Dora. Not everyone wants to read those Harlequin things you always recommend," Aunt Maxine scoffed. "Raeley Ann, you should see the book Dora suggested a few months ago. I'd already blushed before the second paragraph. Your mama said she was too embarrassed to read it in the waiting room at her chemotherapy appointment. The man on the cover was wearing a loin cloth."

"Filthy." Mrs. Fannie shook her head.

"Now, listen!" Mrs. Dora sat on the edge of the couch. "They are romance novels, not filth. I happen to appreciate a good love story."

"What's Harold think of you reading that rubbish?"

"He doesn't know she reads it, Maxine. She waits until he's taking one of his naps." Mrs. Fannie laughed and picked up the saucer from the coffee table.

Mrs. Dora sighed. "Do you see how they treat me, Rae? It's despicable." She tapped me on the arm. "Why don't we change the subject? Tell us how things are coming along at the house, dear. You've been there several weeks now. Maxine says the place looks lovely."

"It's so cute. She's really updated it. She's painting furniture too. Already sold some things to . . . what's her name, Raeley Ann?"

"Marcy Powell," I said.

"That's right. Now, that's Dolly Powell's daughter, isn't it?"

"That's right, Aunt Maxine."

"See, Dora, I *do* know some things." Aunt Maxine stuck her tongue out at Mrs. Dora.

"I found some old bottom kitchen cabinets at the junk store on Route 118 and refinished them. I tore off the countertops and replaced them with butcher block. Marcy is going to use them for her outdoor kitchen."

"Oh, how perfectly lovely!" Mrs. Fannie exclaimed. "And you made good money on that?"

"Yes, ma'am. I didn't charge her as much as I should

have, but I still made a decent amount of money." I finished the delicious tart.

"You're a single mother now, Rae. Every bit of income helps. Don't be afraid to know your worth and charge for it." Aunt Maxine nodded at me.

"I always loved refinishing things like that," Mrs. Fannie said. "When I was a little girl, we were so poor. And we'd get nearly everything second- or thirdhand and have to repair it in some way. Poor Theo didn't have a crib. He slept next to Mama and Daddy in a dresser drawer on the floor." She took the last gulp of her coffee. "Anyway, my daddy brought home an old armoire that Mr. Meriwether gave him. I mean, we didn't even have a closet for our clothes and there were four of us. We worked on that old armoire every night after suppertime. It was busted and broken and smelled awful. I think a possum or something had died in it. But when we were done working on that armoire, it was such a beautiful piece of furniture."

"It's right over there, Raeley Ann." Aunt Maxine slowly turned in the chair and pointed to the corner of the parlor at the massive Louis XV–style armoire with carved floral accents and parquetry inlaid doors.

"Oh, wow." I tossed the linen napkin to the coffee table, stood, and walked to the magnificent piece of furniture.

"Isn't it lovely? Oh, I wish you could have seen that thing before my daddy got a hold of it. It was kindling. That's all it was."

I ran my fingers across the shiny oak embellishments.

"You know, Rae," Mrs. Fannie said in her sweet Southern voice, "I didn't just keep that piece because it's gorgeous and it holds my departed mother-in-law's fur coats. I kept it to remind me of several things."

I sat back on the couch as she spoke.

"I kept it because it signifies hard work. It took many nights to bring that piece back to life. And it signifies restoration. Nothing is too damaged or broken for our good Lord, our Maker's hands, to restore. And it reminds me of where I came from too."

"Fannie has a beautiful rags-to-riches story." Aunt Maxine folded her hands on her lap.

"Well, it is, Maxine." Mrs. Fannie looked to my aunt. "We grew up in a clapboard house on the two-lane. You could see daylight through the walls. The floors were nothing more than dirt and plywood. My daddy, God bless him, drank like a fish and couldn't hold a steady job. He was a good man. He was a good father. He loved each one of us, but he just couldn't get ahold of that drinking. I think he rebuilt every one of the shelves in that chest with liquor on his breath. But he was finally restored of that too."

"How was that, Mrs. Fannie?" I asked.

"He stumbled into a tent revival out on Route 118 one summer night. I'd already married Pratt by then. And Lord mercy!" She threw her hands into the air. "Pratt's mama sure wasn't keen on him taking a poor white-trash girl as his wife. But she grew to love me. It took some time, but our relationship was restored too. She even left me her precious fur coats and finest silver when she died." Mrs. Fannie smiled and shook her head. "But Daddy, bless his heart. He stumbled into that tent revival stone-cold drunk. That hefty preacher—"

"Brother Willard Callery," Dora interjected.

"Yes, Brother Callery, he just kept right on preaching while Daddy drug his feet toward him. The congregation was whispering and pointing at drunk old Walter Watkins making his way to the altar. And Brother Callery didn't stop preachin' for a second! He just opened his arms and took my daddy into them and kept on preachin' the gospel right there in front of all those people. And then he started praying over my sweet daddy. He held him in his arms, my daddy in his tattered clothes that reeked of whiskey, and he told everyone to quit their whispering and gossipin' and come up and lay hands on him. And my daddy, just as drunk as a skunk and crying his eyes out, gave his life to Jesus right then and there. And he was made new, Rae. Just like that old piece of furniture. He was made brand new."

"Brother Callery was a fine man," Dora said. "He sure was a fine man. Preached my mama's funeral. A fine man."

"My daddy spent the rest of his life on fire for Jesus and what He'd done for him, the way He changed him. Daddy never drank another drop of whiskey. He made amends for all the ways he'd hurt my sweet mama and his children. Restored. At sixty-seven years old."

"Never too old for restoration." Aunt Maxine lifted a hand to heaven in praise.

Mama had talked about this in the letter she left for me in the shed. She talked about restoration and making old things new. It sounded cliché, but my heart was like that old armoire or the furniture I found at the junk store or on the side of the road. Beaten and battered. Bruised and dented. Worse for the wear. I was mourning the loss of my dear mother and my husband. And some days I didn't know how I'd get out of the bed. I didn't know if my heart, my mind, would ever be restored. If what my mother's friends said was true, God would have to do it. If what Mrs. Fannie said was true, only He could dust me off, sand away the scars, and make me new. I couldn't do it. He'd have to.

But was He going to do it? I didn't know.

CHAPTER 7

Mama was an incredibly talented musician. She played both violin and piano. She never took a lesson in her life and mostly played by ear, but she taught herself how to read music and was qualified to teach the subject at Whitten Middle School, which she did for nearly thirty years. She favored calling her violin a fiddle. She called it a fiddle when she played "Blue Moon of Kentucky," and she called it a fiddle when she played "Partita in D Minor" by Johann Sebastian Bach. Her daddy, a Birmingham coal miner until 1937 and later a hay grower who supplied all the horse farmers and cow operations within a hundred miles of his small homestead, was a country boy who didn't dare play the violin. He played the fiddle, so that's what Mama always called it too.

She kept her favorite, most reliable fiddle—a satin antique Mendini 4/4—propped against the wall in the corner of the living room for easy access. But she had a collection of ten or so. They lived in her music room and were displayed on hooks along the walls.

The music room was a small add-on that Daddy built off the laundry room when Jamie and I were small. Mama painted it her favorite shade of pale pink and hung framed sheet music on the walls between the fiddles. She bought a small spinet piano from Mrs. DeBerry, the local piano teacher, and placed it on the long wall of the room next to a pink-and-green floral chaise longue. A white bookcase filled with music books and gifts she'd received from music students over the years—miniature porcelain fiddles and knickknacks—sat in another corner. I had decorated the rest of the house as my own, but I didn't dare touch my mother's music room, and I never planned to do so.

The day after the meeting at Mrs. Fannie's house, I walked into the music room with Patsy following and pulled a spruce viola from the pink wall. I sat on the floral lounge and ran the bow across the dull strings. Patsy seemed to grimace. I could only play a few chords correctly. Mama always wanted me to play a musical instrument, but I never had the patience or the rhythm. I took piano lessons from Mrs. DeBerry for a year or so but retired with only one song, "Ode to Joy," in my portfolio.

I placed the viola back on the wall and paced the small room, admiring the violin collection. On top of the spinet piano, I saw the familiar pink envelope with my name written in Mama's cursive on the front. I didn't know how I'd missed it in the handful of times I'd been in the room over the last month, but a smile covered my face as I sprawled across the lounge and peeled it open.

Rae,
　　You're in my favorite room in this house. How many

times did I escape to this room and play the fiddle while you and your brother bickered or your father watched the Crimson Tide? I came here when the bills were overdue and stress sank in. I came here when I was grief-stricken at the loss of my parents. I cried in this room. I prayed in this room. I healed in this room.

Music has always been such a comfort to me. It's been a gift. I can't begin to describe what a glorious and exhilarating feeling it is to hear your own hands make beautiful melodies. I would sit in this room for hours on end and play and cry and smile. I would always exit this room better than when I entered.

I wish you'd learned to play an instrument, but you hated every lesson with Mrs. DeBerry. You refused to practice the piano and vomited the morning of your only piano recital. But each time you played "Ode to Joy" for me, my burdens were a little lighter. I think yours were too.

Do you remember when Jamie took drum lessons? Oh, me. I was thrilled when he showed an interest in music—even when my head pounded as he banged the tom-tom for hours on end. I nearly died of liver failure from all the ibuprofen I took during his stint with the drums, but it was worth it.

Because I know the power in turning to music during hard times.

The afternoon your grandmother, Mrs. Bonnie Reeves, died, your father was at her bedside. He phoned to tell me she'd passed away, and thirty minutes later he walked through the front door of our little house on King Street. I was standing at the kitchen counter, rolling out biscuits, and he silently wrapped his arms around my waist and rested his head on my shoulder. I'd known your father for a long time and had never seen him cry until that moment. I held him there in the kitchen for a good long while until he walked to the record player in the living room and put on his favorite Otis Redding song, "These Arms of Mine."

"Dance with me," he said.

And there, on that cold linoleum floor in my bare feet, your father and I danced. His mother had only been dead an hour, and we danced in that kitchen. I don't know why your father picked that song. I don't know why his first instinct after his mother died was to dance, but that's what we did. And I think the music helped him. I know it did.

When that boy with the bad breath—oh, what was his name? Kevin Howell! When Kevin Howell broke up with you, you came home from school and ran straight to your bedroom. The door shut and soon the song from that prostitute movie with Julia Roberts was blaring from the other side. "It Must've Been Love." You played it on repeat. You finally exited with puffy eyes and joined your father and me at the dinner table. My heart hurt so terribly for you in that moment—your first heartbreak. But you were better than when you ran into your room that afternoon. You and that prostitute song worked it out.

I can still see you and your father dancing to Etta James at your wedding. I can still see you and Carter swaying to Percy Sledge at the country club. I can still see you and Jamie dancing in front of the television. I can still feel your father's arms around my waist. He always liked to dance while I was trying to cook. I burned more fried green tomatoes because your daddy put on an Otis Redding album.

If you decide to stay in this house, I hope you'll dance in it. I hope you'll take Molly Margaret's hand and spin around the living room. I hope you'll dance while putting away the laundry or drying the dishes. I hope the next love of your life will make you burn the fried green tomatoes.

Music, Rae. It's a beautiful thing.

I love you with my heart.

> Until we meet again, and
> dance on streets of gold,
> Mama

I wiped my eyes and immediately went to the kitchen to grab my phone from the counter. I pressed shuffle on my music playlist and Bonnie Raitt's "Angel from Montgomery" reverberated through the small house. I twirled alone in the kitchen. I remembered Mama doing the same in bare feet and her apron. I'd open the cupboards for a snack and she'd grab my wrist and spin me around, laughing all the while. I smiled at the memory until the song was interrupted by the ringing of my phone.

"Hello?"

"Rae? It's Coach Richardson. Well, Kent," the voice answered.

"Oh." My eyes grew wide, and I immediately began to pace the small gray rug in front of the kitchen sink. "Hey there."

Hey there? That was the best I could do? Why not *How are you?* Or *Good to hear from you?*

"Congratulations to Molly on making the team. I'm looking forward to working with her this year."

"Oh, she's very excited. We both are." I twirled my brown hair between my fingers. "Thanks for giving her the opportunity."

"Sure."

Awkward silence.

"Aunt Fannie told me to . . ." He paused. "Aunt Fannie said I should . . ."

Oh, good Lord.

"Would you be interested in having dinner tomorrow night?" he blurted.

Oh, good Lord.

"There's a band playing down at Bea's tomorrow night. Do you like bluegrass?"

"I love bluegrass," I said.

"So dinner, then? Would that be okay?"

"Sure. I love bluegrass," I repeated.

"Great. I'll meet you there tomorrow night at six?"

"That would be fine. I love bluegrass."

How many times was I going to tell him that I loved bluegrass? The man probably thought I listened to Bill Monroe on repeat.

"All righty. Looking forward to it," he answered.

"See you then." I frantically pressed End.

Bonnie's voice resumed in my speaker and I screamed.

———————◆———————

"Coach Richardson! I still can't believe it," Molly said the next night as I stood in the master bathroom and applied my eyeshadow.

"I'm as surprised as you are, Molly." I blended the brown shade on my eyelid.

"If you start dating Coach Richardson, I'll be teased by the other girls on the team. I just know it." She sighed. "And what if they think the only reason I made the team is because the two of you are dating?"

"We're not *dating*. And that's nonsense, Molly Margaret." I turned around to look at her lying on my bed. "They've seen your defense. You shoot three-pointers like Steph Curry. You're a wonderful basketball player and everyone on that team knows it."

"Yeah, maybe. But this is still weird." She rolled over to her belly and kicked her legs behind her in the air.

"I know it is," I said. "But apparently Mrs. Fannie thought we'd be a good match. I'm just going to dinner with the man. I'm not marrying him, okay?"

"I've never thought about you with someone else. I mean, Daddy and Autumn. That's weird enough. But you and another guy?"

"Molly." I stepped over fat Patsy snoring on the floor to sit by her on the tall bed. "It's just crab cakes and bluegrass at Bea's. That's it. I'm sure I'll be home by ten."

"I'm fine with it, Mama. I just . . ."

"I know this is weird for you." I looked at the eyeshadow brush in my hand. "This is weird for me. I haven't been on a date with another man since I was a teenager. Your father was all I ever wanted."

"He broke your heart, didn't he?" She gazed at me.

"Your daddy is a good man." I paused and patted her back. "But, yes, he broke my heart. I didn't think I'd ever go on another date again in my life. Your daddy was it for me."

"Go, Mama. Have a good time."

"You sure you're okay with this?"

"It's all good." Molly smiled. "Actually, this could be good for my basketball career. Ask Coach Richardson if I can be the starting point guard."

———— ◆ ————

Bea's was located in a red-painted cypress building parallel to the railroad tracks on Main Street and was Whitten's answer to Red Lobster. It had been in business since I was a kid, and my mother knew Mrs. Bea personally. She was a rough-looking woman with embedded crow's-feet surrounding her green eyes and orangish, frizzy hair. She hotboxed Pall Malls and drank whiskey on the rocks, but she never failed to appear at First Baptist's early service. Her two sons drove down to the Gulf Coast every weekend for the freshest catch of fish, and the food was delightful. Her restaurant was a staple in Whitten, and I'd had many plates of coconut shrimp and crab cakes in the dimly lit dining room adorned with lobster photos and rusted anchors.

I walked into the buzzing restaurant foyer and saw Kent standing in the dark corner in a light blue Polo and dark jeans. I won't deny that he looked handsome. His hair was thick and brown and his skin was tanned from the sun. He looked like he smelled good. Aftershave, no doubt. He reminded me of Carter. Would I ever meet a man who didn't remind me of Carter Sutton?

My heart pounded in my throat as I walked toward him. "Kent?"

"Rae!" His eyes were wide. He seemed pleased at the sight of me.

He looked at me the way Carter used to—before he was tired of being my husband. Before he met a young girl named Autumn, who'd just celebrated her birthday with him on July Fourth on Windemere Lake. They probably shared the same cabin we all shared as a family. Did she know I stepped on a rusted nail on the back deck one summer and had to get a tetanus shot? Did she know our baby girl caught a crappie at the dock with a Barbie fishing pole? I bet Carter and Autumn did more than ski and watch fireworks and roast marshmallows for her birthday. I bet they—I couldn't even think of it.

"Have you been waiting long?" I nervously tucked my dark hair behind my ear.

"Should I have picked you up?" He lightly touched my arm. "I should have picked you up, shouldn't I? Rae, I'm no good at dating. I never know the right thing to do."

I smiled. "No, meeting here was fine. You're obviously nervous. I am too. I haven't had a date with anyone in nearly twenty years. Let's just relax, okay?"

He nodded. "I think our table is ready."

We followed the hostess to the back of the crowded restaurant and sat at a rustic table overlooking sleepy Main Street. The members of the bluegrass band were still unloading their instruments near the bar, but we had a clear view of them.

We made awkward small talk and ordered our food. He had the flounder. I had the crab cakes. I'd never been a drinker, but Bea's hurricane seemed like a good choice. Maybe I wouldn't say such awkward things after a good dose of rum. Or maybe I'd say the most foolish things ever. Only time would tell.

"Aunt Fannie didn't put me up to this," he assured me as I ate my crab. "I really did want to ask you out. On my own. Without the influence of my eighty-year-old aunt."

"She had *nothing* to do with this?" I smiled.

"Well." He set his fork down and sat back in the booth. "She told me all about you, and I made the decision to give you a call."

"And what did she say about me?"

"She said you are a fine young lady. She said you are sweet and kind and caring. And when I saw you at the basketball tryout, well, I knew you were someone I wanted to know better."

I blushed. "I had paint in my hair."

"I saw the paint." He smiled.

"I'm curious. Why haven't you ever married?" I drank the last drop of my hurricane as the band tuned their guitars and fiddles.

"I came close. Twice." He leaned forward and placed his elbows on the table. "I don't know. Just didn't work out, I guess. My first fiancé cheated on me, and my second, well, she didn't like basketball." He laughed. "Do you like basketball, Rae?"

"I love basketball," I said. *And bluegrass.*

"She didn't like basketball, but she did like her married coworker. So I've been cheated on in both of my serious relationships. I haven't dated much since my last breakup. Trust issues, I guess."

I knew exactly how he felt.

"I'm so sorry about the loss of your mother, Rae. Aunt Fannie sure adored her. I met her a couple of times. Remarkable woman. Incredibly talented on the violin."

"Fiddle," I said. "She always called it the fiddle."

"Fiddle," he repeated.

At that moment, the band introduced themselves as the Osgood Brothers and began a slow melody of guitar, keyboard, and, of course, fiddle. It was a melody that would've caused my mother to sit at attention. She would've watched the fiddle player contently, watching every rosin of the bow, every finger placement. I found myself doing that very thing.

"She would've loved this," I said.

Kent and I talked over the sounds of the bluegrass band for the next hour. Because of the band's volume, he eventually moved from the opposite side of the booth to beside me. We talked basketball. We talked about our aunts. We talked about one-horse Whitten, Alabama. His hand grabbed for mine on the seat of the booth. He said he needed a new coffee table. I promised to find one for him and refinish it in dark walnut.

Carter kept intercepting my thoughts. When Kent reached for my hand, each time he looked at me with a gaze of satisfaction, I thought of the man who had possessed my heart, my mind, and my soul for so many years. I thought of the nights we shared at the Grille in Huntsville as a cover band played and we danced on the parquet floor. I thought of the nights he told me I was beautiful. And that I was the love of his life. I thought of the contentment I felt when he rested his arm behind me on the pew at church on Sunday mornings.

Was it all a lie? Was every morning, afternoon, and

romantic night we spent together all those years a lie? And did he ever think of me when he spent these same kinds of nights with Autumn?

I consciously put Carter out of my mind and enjoyed the time with Kent. When our stomachs were full and our faces were sore from laughter, Kent walked me to my SUV. The orange streetlight cast a glow on his face as he gave his spiel—he'd had a nice time and he hoped we could do it again soon. He said, again, that he looked forward to coaching Molly. My heart fluttered beneath my white tank top. Was this man going to kiss me? I hadn't kissed another man in so long. Who did I last kiss before Carter? Was it Kevin Howell? I think it was. I think it was Halitosis Howell. What year was that? Nineteen ninety-nine. I hadn't kissed a man other than Carter since 1999?

"Good night, Rae," Kent said as he turned from me and walked to his truck.

"Good night," I called after him.

I didn't have to worry about a kiss, and I was relieved.

CHAPTER 8

Grief comes in waves. You think you're fine and you've accepted your new normal, and then you're suddenly not fine. Nothing is fine. You feel as if you've been abruptly taken under by the deepest, darkest, suffocating wave. You find yourself in the fetal position on the floor next to an afghan blanket and wads of tissue, sobbing hysterically. Calm, then chaotic. Fine. Not fine. That's how grief works. At least that's how it was working on me.

On the Sunday afternoon after the date with Kent, I'd been pelted by a wave of sadness. The sound of Molly shooting basketball in the driveway, dribble after dribble, filled my ears, but salty tears filled my eyes. My face was so swollen it hurt. My cheeks were tightly stretched across their bones. My face hurt; my heart hurt. In that moment I was shattered. Broken. Everything was dark and foreboding. My life—the good life, the complete life, the comfortable life—as I'd known it was over.

I was thirty-six years old, curled on the floor next to Patsy, wanting my mother. Needing her. I needed a parent. I needed a safe place to land. I also wanted Carter there to rest on the floor with me and hold me in his arms. I wanted to bury my face on his broad shoulder and cry into his tattered Vanderbilt T-shirt. I needed to feel his kiss on top of my tangled hair and his strong hand stroking my back. I needed him, the only love of my life, to console me, to guide me. I needed his wisdom and counsel.

My security blankets were all gone.

When the ball stopped bouncing outside, I picked myself up from the living room carpet and wiped my damp, bloated red face with the sleeve of my shirt. I scooped up the worn tissues, tossed the afghan to the couch, and rushed to the kitchen and pretended to be busy when Molly entered and grabbed a bottle of water from the refrigerator.

Keeping my back to her, I asked, "Good workout?"

"Yeah, I think I'll take a shower. It's like 110 degrees out there."

"Sounds good." I stifled a sniffle and placed some coffee cups from the dish rack into the cupboard while Patsy curled next to my feet on the cool linoleum floor.

"You okay, Mama?" she asked.

"Yeah." I nodded, still refusing to let her to see my swollen face and red eyes.

"Okay." She left me alone in the kitchen.

I continued to put the dry dishes resting on the rack into the cabinet and remembered the afternoon when Mother called to tell me her doctor found a spot on her lung. I was sitting on the couch on Sullivan Street. She was probably standing right where I was standing now—in front of the kitchen sink, looking out the window to the large, shady backyard and the cotton field beyond it. This was the spot where she always talked on the phone. I could still see her, in the days of my youth, waving a blue-and-white dish towel in one hand with the cordless phone pressed to her ear with the other, gabbing with Aunt Maxine about something or other.

The spot on her lung was probably nothing, she'd said. She told me not to worry, and although we'd only been apart for a week and I detested him for leaving me, my first instinct when I hung up with my mother was to call Carter. He was staying at the Holiday Inn Express while we worked out the details of our separation, but I called and poured my anxiety onto him anyway. And he was wonderful in every way. I hated and resented his decision to live his life without me by his side, but I accepted his comforting words about my mother and my burden was lifted in the moment.

Carter could always ease my fears. That's what he did. And I needed him to lift the burden I was bearing right now. I thought maybe I should call him. But I envisioned Autumn beside him as they watched television or golfed or fished on that Sunday afternoon, and I refrained. I definitely didn't want to confide in him with a twentysomething blonde on his arm.

I didn't know much about Autumn. I will admit, though, she was a beautiful young lady. Her hair was poker straight and didn't frizz in humidity. I assumed her stomach was like a washboard, yet to be riddled in stretch marks. Molly reported that she was kind to her when she visited her father. Autumn never stayed the night at our home on Sullivan

Street when Molly was there. She even bought Molly a Dr Pepper T-shirt when she visited family in Texas. But I wasn't ready to get to know Autumn. I wasn't ready to co-parent with her or attempt to be her friend. To me, she was just the girl who stole my husband, and I wasn't ready to accept that. Or forgive it.

My thoughts were interrupted by the sound of my phone ringing on the kitchen table. Dawn said she was on her way over with lunch. I didn't feel much like company, but my sister-in-law never took no for an answer. Twenty minutes later, she bounded into my kitchen with sacks of food and two foam cups in her hands. I was still standing by the kitchen sink, wiping my nose and staring out the window.

"Girl, I brought two choices from Sally's Sandwiches." She threw the bags onto the table. "You want bacon, lettuce, and tomato with Duke's mayo, or chicken salad? The chicken salad does not have grapes, which is blasphemy, but I thought you might eat it anyway. You pick. I'll have either."

"The BLT is fine, Dawn. Thank you." I pulled out a kitchen chair and sat down. Patsy looked up at me from the floor, her brown eyes begging for a slice of bacon.

"Does Molly want some of my chicken salad sandwich? The thing is huge." She rustled through the plastic sack.

"No," I said. "She's in the shower and she already ate lunch."

She pulled the bistro chair from the table and sat down. "Here's a bag of Sally's chips. A little greasy for my taste, but they'll do. There should be a pickle in the bag with your sandwich."

"What made you decide to do this?" I unwrapped my food and immediately tossed a crumble of bacon to my dog.

"Do what, girl? I just got out of church. It's lunchtime. Jamie and the boys went to the Chinese place, but I was hungry for a sandwich. I thought you may be hungry too." She shrugged her shoulders covered in a flowy leopard print blouse.

"Yeah, right. You know I went out with Kent Richardson last night, don't you?" I took a bite of the wheat bread.

"Maybe." She winked at me.

"Who told you?" I asked.

"The better question is why didn't *you* tell me?" She pushed the cup of iced tea toward me and then took a sip of her own.

"I'm sorry, Dawn," I said. "I didn't know if it would be worth mentioning."

"Well, now that the date is over, you know if it is worth mentioning. Is it?" She chomped into her chicken salad and tucked her thick auburn hair behind her ear.

"Who told you? Has word spread that fast? I had forgotten what it's like to live in Whitten. I'd forgotten everyone around here can tell a thing or two about a thing or two."

"So," she said between bites, "Marla Halbrook was at Bea's last night. She texted me when she saw you and Kent sharing a booth. You can imagine my embarrassment when I didn't know what in the world she was talking about. Rae,

I'm your sister-in-law. I need to be prepared to answer texts like that."

"Marla Halbrook has always been a nosy heifer." I wiped mayo from the corner of my mouth with my napkin.

"So? The date? How'd it go?"

"It was okay, Dawn. It was just okay. I like him. He's handsome and kind and all of that. Kent is nice."

"But he isn't Carter?" she asked, and I shook my head.

"He isn't Carter. And Mama is dead. And nothing seems right. And this isn't the life I envisioned having at thirty-six." I refrained from crying onto the dill pickle in my hand.

"Oh, sweet sister." She sighed. "You think my life is how I imagined it would be? The doctor says my blood pressure is through the roof and my bad cholesterol is up and my good cholesterol is nonexistent. I'll probably have a stroke before I'm forty-five."

"Dawn Abigail Reeves, you just compared my dead mother and crumbled marriage to your cholesterol."

"Girl, bad cholesterol is a big deal!" she screeched. "My point is nothing goes as planned. Do you think I ever thought I'd weigh two hundred seventy pounds? You do remember me in high school, don't you, Raeley? Size four. Cheerleader, doing all my little backflips on the basketball court. Rah-rah-rah!" She waved her hands above her head. "I wore miniskirts. And tube tops. I was a toothpick. But things have changed. That's what life does—it changes. Sometimes it's scary and not what we at all expect. But it goes on, right? Life goes on, Rae. You've got to keep on living. Keep on going. I've got to take up Jazzercise. And buy a treadmill. And swear off pasta. From the looks of fat Patsy lying there on the floor, she needs to do those things too. But we keep on going."

"I know, but what if Jamie left you, Dawn? What if he left you for a young girl with a twenty-nine-inch waistline? Just fell out of love with you without warning? What would you do? I don't know what to do. Tell me what to do."

"Girl, I'd probably eat half the pantry. And I'd cry. And I'd hate him for a long while and plot his and his floozy's death because I watch too much *Dateline*. And I'd grieve for my boys. And then one day, I imagine, I'd wake up and realize it's time to get over it. I'd keep going, like I just said. I did that when my daddy died. You remember what a wreck I was when Big Bob died? But I picked myself up and kept going."

"I remember." I took a swig of tea.

"Rae, you keep forgetting this is all new to you. Mrs. Margie has only been gone a few weeks. You haven't been divorced that long either. Time heals wounds. You haven't had enough time yet. It's okay to feel this way and ask the questions that you're asking. It's okay to grieve all your losses. Remember when Mr. James died? You were devastated, and so was your brother and your mama, but you all healed with time. You'll do it again."

"I had Mama and Carter when Daddy died. They helped me heal."

"Girl, stop this pity party. You don't give yourself enough credit, Raeley!" She shook her head and took another bite of the chicken salad. "You're a tough broad. You don't see that yet?"

"I just miss Mama so much." I tossed the half-eaten sandwich to the napkin and buried my face in my hands. "And Carter. I'm so heartbroken, Dawn." The stupid tears began to pour again.

"Hey." She stood from her chair, bent over, and draped her arms around me. She smelled like her favorite lotion, Sweet Pea. Always Sweet Pea. Sweat Pea when she was a size four, tumbling across the Whitten High School gymnasium, and Sweet Pea now. "Hey, girl, listen to me."

"I know I'll get through this with time, but the time isn't now, Dawn. I've got such a long way to go. What am I going to do?" I muttered between sobs.

"Hey, you're going to do what we just said. You're going to keep on living. You're going to do what Mrs. Margie and Mr. James would want you to do. You're going to be strong for that sweet niece of mine. And you're going to find true love again, Rae. You really will. You've still got so much life to live and so many wonderful things to do."

She pulled away as I sniffled and wiped my face with the palm of my hand.

"But right now, you're going to finish this BLT. And then we're going to sit on the front porch in your mama's rocking chairs. We're going to talk about the hydrangeas and how to properly trim those unruly crepe myrtles by the driveway. And we're going to talk about Kent Richardson, and I'm going to tell you that if you like him even the tiniest bit, then you're going to go out with him again. And then we're going to talk about Marla Halbrook and her horrendous haircut and her terrible taste in shoes. And then I'll probably come inside and get a Fudge Round because my sugar is dropping and my stomach is rumbling. And then we're going to talk about the exercise equipment I'm going to buy and whatever else we want to talk about. We're going to keep on talking. And keep on living, girl. You understand?"

I nodded and grinned. She wrapped her arms around me again as I buried my face into her soft shoulder.

Dawn and I did all the things she said we'd do. We talked about Mama's flowers and she made me promise to trim the crepe myrtles next spring. "But not crepe murder, girl! Don't butcher the poor things."

Molly joined us on the porch as we discussed my date with Kent. She'd already asked me a million questions when I'd returned home from Bea's the night before, but she asked them all again, much to the delight of my nosy sister-in-law. Dawn rooted for me to go on another date with him. She suggested I call and invite him to go out. I adamantly refused but Molly agreed with her aunt and added, "I really don't mind, Mama. Did you ask him about point guard?"

After our conversation about Marla Halbrook's horrendous mullet and white woven sandals that she wore in the winter with socks, Molly went inside to call her best friend, Lauren, in Huntsville, and Dawn excused herself from Mama's wooden rocker to rummage through the pantry for chocolate. When she returned with a Little Debbie in hand, she told me Dr. Talbot really was worried about her cholesterol and imminent diabetes. He'd told her at her last appointment that she had to make a change, so we talked about nutrition and I committed to work out with her several mornings a week. After all, I'd put on a few pounds while grieving Mama and Carter, and it wouldn't hurt me to do a jumping jack or two.

Dawn didn't want to go to the Beast Factory on the outskirts of town because she said the instructor was "an extremely judgmental drill sergeant with biceps the size of tree trunks who forced her students to throw tractor tires over their heads and eat grass." Besides, she had no interest in becoming a beast; she simply wanted to get healthy. We made a pact, instead, to join the 6:00 A.M. boot camp at Bodyworks. She personally knew the trainer, who had struggled with sugar addiction most of her life but dropped more than a hundred pounds with diet and exercise. She was known to be tough but was also known to be kind and encouraging.

"Rae, I want to ask you one more thing before I go home and eat lasagna. I never should have married a man who can cook . . ." Her voice trailed off as we continued to slowly rock on the porch that muggy July afternoon. The sun was slowly setting to our left and the sky was a beautiful hue of orange and pink. Mrs. Murphy's Boston terrier, Hugo, barked at us from the driveway across the street, and Mr. Delk fired up his John Deere lawnmower next door.

"Okay," I said. "Go ahead."

"How are you spiritually?"

"Spiritually?"

"Your parents were devout in their faith. Outspoken even. It was such an important part of their lives, and your brother's life, too, but you never mention God or church or anything."

"I like to sleep on Sunday mornings, Dawn." I looked away from her and sipped from the sweating water bottle in my hands.

"Well, it's not even about church or religion. I'm asking about your relationship."

"With God?" I asked.

She nodded from the chair beside me.

"I'm not really happy with Him right now."

"Girl." She turned toward me in the wooden rocker. "You must know that sad things happen. That's just par for the course in this fallen world. Not everything is rosy. You know that."

"I do know that, Dawn, and I believe in heaven and that Mama is at peace there, but all this at once?" I threw my hands in the air. "Carter and then Mama? Both of them gone. Back-to-back? I thought God never gives us more than we can handle. Isn't that true?"

"That is not true." She shook her head. "Sweet sister, when we have more on us than we can bear, we have to let *Him* bear it. There's comfort and peace in sweet surrender. There's a relief in saying, 'I am broken. Only You can help me.'"

"And what's He going to do, Dawn? Is He going to bring my mama back? Is He going to make Carter fall back in love with me? Is He going to strike Autumn Nance dead? That's what would really help me. What's He going to do if I throw my hands up and scream out that I'm broken?" I snapped. "Is He going to come down on a cloud, Dawn?"

"He's going to give you rest. That's what He gives us when we are battered and drowning in more depression and despair than we can possibly bear. That's what He gives us when we let go of the rope. He catches us and gives us rest—rest from the struggle and the hopelessness."

I shrugged nonchalantly and sipped from the water bottle again.

"Jesus went through incredible pain. He hung on a cross. Battered. Beaten. Ridiculed. Mocked. He endured pain we cannot even comprehend. Yet the purpose of His suffering was realized on Sunday when the stone was rolled away to reveal an empty tomb. Rae, there *is* purpose in all of this. There's purpose and perseverance in your pain, your grief and longing. Let Him take the burden from you and hang it on the cross. And let Him turn it into a thing of beauty. All you have to do is ask Him. And rest."

"Dawn, I just don't think my mother dying and my husband abandoning me will ever be a thing of beauty."

"Whatever brings us closer to God, no matter how painful or debilitating, is worth it. Maybe that's the silver lining in all of this. To bring you back to Him?" She reached over and placed her hand on top of mine. "Oh, how He loves you,

Rae. And I do too." She stood and walked toward her Jeep shaded by the crepe myrtles. "I'll see you at Bodyworks in the morning?"

"If I'm up in time."

"You slept in this morning, didn't you? How many mornings a week do you need to sleep in?" She slyly grinned.

"Okay, okay." I smirked. "I'll be there."

"Then I'm off to eat my last carb supper. Bye, girl."

CHAPTER 9

I was on time for the 6:00 A.M. Bodyworks boot camp. I had crust in my eyes, mismatched socks, coffee breath, and forgot to put on deodorant, but I was on time. After doing burpees, jumping jacks, and running around the building in the morning humidity, I vomited in the trash can and told Dawn I wouldn't be back. She didn't seem too disappointed because she knew half the women in the class and they already proved to be a much better support system than I would ever be. They weren't the type to let a little heat and heave deter them from their fitness goals.

Once I'd showered and somewhat recovered from the morning's workout, I sat inside my car in the high school parking lot, waiting on Molly to walk out the gym doors. She soon exited, strands of her dark hair damp from sweat and sticking to her forehead. Her cheeks were rosy red as she talked and waved her hands around and the girl beside her smiled and nodded. As she opened the passenger side door and climbed into the Tahoe with her large basketball bag and water bottle, I saw Kent coming through the gym doors in basketball shorts and a gray T-shirt that was also damp with sweat around the collar.

While Molly tried to make room in the floorboard for her bulky bag, Kent noticed me and held up his finger and mouthed, "Wait a minute." He was soon at the driver's door. I rolled down the window to let in the hot, stagnant air and his scent—musky but not disgusting, thank the Lord.

"Hey," he said as Molly continued to wrestle with the bag. "Listen, I, uh—"

"You want to have dinner tonight?" I interrupted him and he immediately grinned.

"Sure, I'd enjoy that."

"Our house? Molly, is that okay with you?" I looked to my daughter, whose cheeks became even more flushed with embarrassment.

"Yeah, that's, uh, that's fine," she said completely caught off guard.

"Do you like lasagna?" I turned back to Kent at the window. "It's my brother's recipe. Shipping supervisor by day, chef by night. Six o'clock okay?"

"Yeah, that would be great. Do I need to bring anything?"

"Just your appetite."

"Will do." He patted the car's windowsill and walked to his shiny truck on the other side of the parking lot.

"'Just your appetite'? Lame." Molly sighed. "Do you know how awkward that was for me? You just invited my basketball coach to dinner while I was sitting *right here*."

"I thought you were okay with this?" I put the car in Drive.

"I am okay with it. I just didn't expect him to be coming to our home for dinner so soon. It's still weird, Mama."

"You're right, Molly." I immediately felt guilty. "I don't know how to navigate this. I don't know what is acceptable. I don't know how much time you need. Or how much time I need. I don't know when is the right time to move on." I pulled onto the street. "I don't know what came over me. I can cancel."

Molly paused. "It'll be fine. I'll have someone to talk ball with. That would be fun, I guess."

"I know it's been a hard two years for you with the divorce and Nana passing away and moving to a new town. You'll talk to me, yeah? You'll always let me know how you feel? You are the most important thing to me, Molly," I said as she nodded.

"Do we have time to drive to Huntsville to get Lauren before dinner? Can she spend the night? That would help ease my awkwardness. She likes ball and lasagna too."

"Sure," I said. "I think that's a great idea."

———— ◆ ————

I popped the lasagna into the oven and raced toward my room to get ready. When I passed Molly's closed bedroom door, I could hear her and Lauren giggling. They'd been inseparable since Lauren's family moved into the house next door to us on Sullivan Street nearly ten years before. They missed not being neighbors and going to school and playing basketball together, so Lauren's mom and I committed to shuffling them to and from Huntsville as often as we could. When Molly stayed at Carter's, Lauren usually stayed there too.

Carter. As I ran the straightening iron down strands of my hair, there he was, right back in my memories as always . . .

"I like your hair wavy," he had said. He was sitting on the closed toilet lid and watching me in the bathroom mirror.

"I'm blessed with Aunt Maxine's hair. One drop of humidity in the air and I look like I've been electrocuted." I placed the iron on the vanity and picked up the brush.

"That's not true."

We were in the cramped bathroom of the apartment I shared with Paige during our college years. I'd only been dating Carter for a month or two, and he'd arrived early for our date that evening. He always showed up early, sometimes by an hour or more. He said he couldn't wait to see me. We'd only been together a short period of time and he'd already seen me without makeup, wavy hair, still in pajamas, with stains on my sweatshirt. He said he thought I was gorgeous anyway.

"Leave it natural, Rae. Really. It's beautiful."

"It's really not, Carter."

He stood and tucked a strand behind my ear. I remember what Paige was playing on the stereo in the living room. Mazzy Star. "Fade into You." And then Carter leaned in and kissed me gently. His arms wrapped around me in that bathroom crowded with makeup and reeking of Paige's Sunflowers perfume and whispered in my ear, "It's beautiful. You're beautiful." It was what I would affectionately refer to for years to come as a moment from our very own '90s movie. It was as if a producer were sitting on the toilet lid with a camera and the bathroom were a set in Hollywood. I was Jennifer Love Hewitt. Or Sarah Michelle Gellar. Or Rachael Leigh Cook. I was some actress with three names, Raeley Ann Reeves. I was living the moment that made every girl in overalls and Birkenstocks with Rachel's haircut from *Friends* say, "Awwwww."

"How many cheesy chick flicks have you seen to know girls eat this kind of stuff up? You don't even have sisters," I asked when he pulled away.

He shrugged and chuckled.

I had a couple of boyfriends in high school and not one ever tucked wavy strands of hair behind my ear or whispered that I was beautiful. No one, no boy, ever acted like this.

Not to mention, he was a handsome boy. He wasn't a boy with chronically bad breath or acne or coarse hair that barely fit beneath a ball cap. Carter was intelligent, handsome, with a souped-up truck and a future. He was a perfect gentleman who hadn't pressured me once to do anything I didn't feel comfortable doing. A boy who held my hand in the movies and told me I was beautiful when half of my hair was straight and the other half was wavy.

Carter Sutton. He was my sweet Carter Sutton. I didn't

know who he had become, but I didn't think I'd ever get over the old him.

Kent knocked at the front door right on time, not a minute early, bearing Chianti in a green bottle with a yellow label. He'd had a haircut since I'd seen him earlier that afternoon and smelled like a hint of aftershave. His straight teeth gleamed white against his tan, clean-shaven face. He reached down to rub Patsy's ears as she sniffed his shoes. "Hey, old girl," he said to her.

"Well, this is nice, but you didn't have to bring anything." I took the wine and motioned for him to follow me to the kitchen.

"I didn't want to come empty-handed. I hope it's okay that I brought wine. I know Molly will be joining us for dinner, but—"

"You didn't bring Jägermeister and shot glasses, Kent. The wine is perfectly fine." He chuckled as I set the bottle on the Formica counter and rummaged through a drawer for a corkscrew.

"You look lovely, and it sure does smell good in here." He nervously shoved his hands into the pockets of his blue jeans as I popped open the bottle and retrieved two glasses from the cupboard. "Where's Molly?"

"She and her friend from Huntsville, Lauren, are in her room," I said. "The lasagna should be ready in about fifteen minutes. You want to have a glass of wine and sit in the living room while we wait?"

"Sure."

We sat on opposite ends of the L-shaped couch with our glasses of red wine, and Kent looked around the living room.

"Aunt Fannie said you're updating the place?" he asked.

"Ah, I just slapped a few coats of gray paint on the walls. I still have a lot I want to do in the kitchen and bathrooms. My next project is to rip up the carpet. There's beautiful hardwood beneath it. I don't know why in the world my mama ever decided to cover it up with this shaggy mess." I rubbed my bare foot across the beige floor and sipped from my glass.

"I live in a little white ranch-style on Elkmont. I did a lot of renovations on it and pulled up the carpet and refinished the original floors. You should stop by sometime. To see the floors, I mean. If you're in the neighborhood. Or if—" He was interrupted by the sound of someone entering the kitchen door.

"Raeley Ann?" Aunt Maxine's voice called over the slamming storm door. "Whose truck is that in the driveway?"

"We're in the living room, Aunt Maxine." I grinned at Kent and shrugged my shoulders.

"Oh, Kent," she said when she entered, holding Tupperware, and saw us sitting on the couch. "Well, I'll be, Raeley Ann. I didn't know you were having company tonight. I guess I should have called. I look a mess. I'm covered in strawberry stains." She brushed at her yellow short-sleeved button-down blouse.

"Hi, Mrs. Maxine." Kent stood to greet her.

"Oh, sit down, son. It's not as if the queen of England just entered the room." She motioned for him to stay put and walked toward us. When she reached the sectional, she carefully bent down to kiss my cheek and then sat between us.

"What brings you here?" I asked her and took another sip of my wine.

"What's that you're drinking, dear?" She gave the glass a curious inspection while Patsy sniffed her pants. "Go on, Patsy. Go on, now."

"Kent brought Chianti. We're going to have lasagna as soon as it's ready."

"Wine is known to give terrible hangovers, honey," she scolded. "I was just stopping by to drop off some strawberry cake." She leaned forward and placed the Tupperware on the coffee table. "I bought five pints from Mr. Parker a few days ago and made cake and pie and muffins and shortcake. Well, your uncle Wilson said he's about had enough strawberries to last a lifetime. Said he was liable to turn red if he ate another bite, so I brought you what was left. I know Molly enjoys it."

"Oh, good, Aunt Maxine. You do make the best strawberry cake."

"Well." She patted her gray curls. "There's really nothing to it, Raeley Ann. You do have my recipe, don't you? With the Jell-O mix?"

"Yes, ma'am, I have it."

"Kent, do you like strawberries, dear?" Aunt Maxine

turned to him on the other end of the couch and the scent of her perfumed powder filled the room with her movement.

"I sure do."

"Well, tell Raeley Ann here to let you have a piece before you go this evening."

"Yes, ma'am."

"So, how did this dinner come about?" She folded her tiny manicured hands on the lap of her khaki pants and looked us both over.

"I ran into Kent after Molly's basketball practice today and invited him to dinner."

"Well, that's nice. It's nice that you are spending some time together. Fannie told me you went to Bea's a few nights ago. I was glad to hear that. You should have told me, Rae."

We sat in awkward silence for a few moments.

"Where's Molly? Is she at Carter's tonight?"

"No, ma'am. She and Lauren are in her room. Do you want me to get her?" I began to stand from the couch.

"Oh, no. Let them be." Aunt Maxine shook her head. "Sit back down, honey. You're on a date. No need to call the young'uns in."

"Well, it's not exactly a date," I said.

"It's not?" She looked to Kent and smiled. "Two single adults with lasagna and wine sounds like a date to me. Your uncle Wilson and I used to go on plenty of dates. Never with wine though. We've never been the type to partake in spirits. Our dates usually consisted of sweet tea. Maybe a Coke."

The buzzer on the oven chimed and I felt an incredible

sense of relief, as if I'd been saved by the bell. I prepared to stand to my bare feet, step over Patsy, and rapidly exit the room.

"Raeley Ann, you let me get that lasagna." Aunt Maxine slowly stood in her white Skechers tennis shoes with air-cooled memory foam. "You and Kent keep visiting. I'll get that lasagna out and let it cool. Do I need to pop some bread in the oven? Toss the salad?"

"Aunt—"

"Don't fret for a minute. I'll get it all ready. Just keep sipping that Chi-ann-tay. And try not to get a headache."

"Chianti," I said.

"Well, that's what I said. Chi-ann-tay," she said as she disappeared into the kitchen.

"Kent, I'm so sorry," I said quietly when she was gone.

He smiled and stifled a laugh. "Don't apologize for a thing. I've got an aunt just like her."

"She'll probably stay for dinner. She knows no boundaries, you know?" I gulped the rest of the wine.

"I don't mind a bit, Rae. Really." He smiled. "However, I am a little disappointed that you said this wasn't a date. I was under the impression that it was."

Aunt Maxine said she hadn't eaten a thing all day but strawberries. That she had been so busy baking that she hadn't had time to cook Uncle Wilson a proper supper either. He'd eaten a fried bologna sandwich and potato chips and homemade pickles for supper before retiring to his recliner with a bag of popcorn to watch one of his many John Wayne tapes. When I asked her to join us for supper, she acted like it would be a huge inconvenience for everyone, but complied anyway.

I glanced across the basket of garlic bread to Kent sitting opposite of me at the kitchen table and shrugged. He gave me a wink as if everything was perfectly fine while Aunt Maxine told Molly to hold her shoulders back and instructed Lauren to put her napkin in her lap like a "good Southern girl." Lauren had made enough trips with us to Whitten over the years to see my family, so she was familiar with Aunt Maxine's quirks and happily placed the napkin in her lap.

"That Dora sure is ornery," Aunt Maxine said as she dabbed marinara sauce from the corner of her lips. "I swear, Raeley Ann, she could make a preacher cuss. I've known the woman the better part of my life, but she's getting crabbier with age. The nerve to tell me who Paul Dixon's children are!"

"But she was right, Aunt Maxine." Kent and I exchanged a smile while I drizzled Italian dressing on my salad. "Paul Dixon did have sons, not daughters."

"Don't tell me what for, Raeley Ann. She was wrong. And that Facebook was wrong. Paul Dixon's daughter is—"

"Please, Aunt Maxine, you've got to let it go. I can't go through the Dixon family tree again."

"Well, you're about as ornery as Dora, Raeley Ann," she huffed while Molly and Lauren giggled softly.

"Molly, your shot looks great. Are you excited for the season?" Kent interjected.

"Yes, sir."

"I'm sure glad to have you on the team this year. I think you'll be a great asset. We almost went to state last year. We were so close. Maybe we can do it this year."

"I sure hope so," Molly said.

"I hope you don't," said Lauren.

"Oh, Lauren, what if we have to play each other? I would just die if I had to break your ankles."

"You won't get past me, Sutton. I've got two inches of height on you," Lauren playfully teased through a mouth full of lasagna.

"I'm sure it's tough not playing with your friends this year. Have you girls been together a long time?" Kent asked Molly.

She shrugged and poked at her food with her fork. "I've played basketball with them since I was in elementary school, but it's okay. I think Whitten has a much better chance at state than Huntsville does."

"Hey!" Lauren interjected. "I'm the best freshman post in the state of Alabama."

"You talk a big game, Lauren Landry."

"We need a good post. Maybe we can recruit you, Lauren." Kent smiled. "Are you interested in wearing the purple and white?"

"No, sir," Lauren replied. "I'm a Huntsville High Tomcat through and through."

"What position do you play, Molly Margaret?" Aunt Maxine took a swig of tea from an amber glass.

"I was point guard in middle school." Molly finished her last bite and placed the fork on her empty plate.

"What's that? Uncle Wilson only watches Alabama football. I don't know a point guard from a running back."

"A point guard directs the entire offense. Kind of like the quarterback in football."

"And are you a good quarterback?" Aunt Maxine glanced at Kent.

"Yes, ma'am. She's the best I've had in quite a few seasons," he replied as Molly's face flushed red with delight at his compliment. She looked at me and I gave her a proud smile.

"I'm looking forward to coming to some games. I'll have to bring a cushion. Those bleachers will wreak havoc on my back. I don't think I've watched you play since I rode with Margie down to Huntsville a couple of years ago, Molly Margaret. I think you were still in elementary school. The ball was bigger than you were."

"She's come a long way since then, Aunt Maxine. She's put in a lot of hard work," I said. "I'd love for you to come sit with me at the games. I'll buy you a padded bleacher seat."

"Your uncle Wilson gets pretty rowdy at sporting events. Do you remember when he got thrown out of one of Jamie's Little League games? He kept heckling the umpire for being blind as a bat and was yelling out the number of his optometrist, Dr. Keegan. That parks and recreation director . . . oh, what's his name? The one with the crossed eyes? He told him he needed to leave, and Wilson gave him Dr. Keegan's number too."

"Maybe Uncle Wilson should stay home," Molly said.

Once our plates were empty and only crumbs were left in the bread basket, the girls retired to Molly's room and Aunt Maxine helped me clean the kitchen. Kent offered to load the dishwasher, but Aunt Maxine insisted he sit on the couch and watch something manly, like baseball. I expected her to make a pot of coffee and serve us strawberry cake before sitting between us on the couch until Kent went home. To my surprise, though, she fixed a to-go plate for Uncle Wilson and bid us good night.

"You want to sit on the deck with another glass of wine? It's a nice night. Storm will be rolling in later, so it's cooled off quite a bit." I motioned toward the back door.

"Sure, I'd like that."

I poured us both another glass of Chi-ann-tay, and he and Patsy followed me out the back door. We were greeted by the sounds of bullfrogs and cicadas and a warm wind rustling through the overgrown magnolia and oak trees in the backyard. We sat beside each other at the wrought iron patio table my parents purchased from Sears when I was in high school. It had held up nicely over the years and didn't have one speck of rust. I lit the citronella candle in the middle of the table to keep the pesky mosquitos at bay and leaned back in the cushioned chair. The lamps in the living room shone through the windows and cast a soft glow across the deck.

"I'm sure sorry Aunt Maxine—"

"Don't you apologize for a thing," he said as Patsy rested her head on his leg and he rubbed her golden ears. "Our aunts are one and the same. That's probably why they are such good friends. Aunt Fannie has overstayed her welcome and overstepped her boundaries plenty of times. Who can get mad at them though?"

"I sure can't," I said.

"When I moved to Whitten before my father died, Elise England and I went on a few dates. Do you know Elise?"

"Oh, yes," I answered. "She's a beautiful woman, but she doesn't have the best reputation. I've always felt a little sorry for her. She's been run through the Whitten rumor mill."

"Well, apparently Aunt Fannie had heard about her too. She barged in on us one evening when I invited Elise over for dinner. She wasn't nearly as sweet as Maxine though. Elise and I were just about to sit down at the dining table, and Aunt Fannie flat-out told her she was too experienced for her precious, albeit thirty-five-year-old, nephew and that she should leave."

"No!" I gasped. "She said that? She called her *experienced*?"

"She sure did. Elise grabbed her purse and stormed out. Aunt Fannie didn't bat an eye. She just said, 'Well, dear, that steak looks delicious' and sat down in Elise's chair."

"Oh, Mrs. Fannie!" I covered my mouth. "She chased her off and then ate her steak? That's awfully harsh."

"So please don't apologize for Aunt Maxine joining us this evening. At least she let me stay and finish my meal."

"Oh, me." I took a sip of wine.

"Thank you for inviting me tonight, Rae," he said. "I've really had a good time."

"I have too," I replied. "This evening has been a much-needed de-stressor. I've had a rough couple of days missing my mother. I'm still struggling with my divorce too. This is nice. Sitting here with you is nice."

"You—"

"I guess I shouldn't have said that, should I?" I interrupted him. "I shouldn't have mentioned my divorce. That's probably not the best topic during a date, is it?"

"Ah, so this *is* a date?" he simpered.

"Wine. Lasagna. My aunt sitting between us on the couch. My daughter and her best friend talking about basketball. If that isn't a date, I don't know what is."

"I've had a great time, and I know a good date from a bad date. I've had so many bad dates. I've had bad relationships. I have often contemplated giving up. I watched a documentary the other night about this man in his midsixties. He never married. And he lived in Saskatchewan or somewhere ridiculously cold and raced sled dogs. Those dogs were his life. He said they treated him better than any woman ever had. And I was on board with that for a minute. I thought, *I'll be okay if I never marry or have kids. I'll just retire somewhere remote and buy a bunch of dogs and live off the land.* But the documentary got more depressing as it went on. The poor guy lived in a one-room shack on a frozen lake and ice fished, and he commented he didn't even like fish. He peed in a coffee can. He kissed the dogs on the mouth. Repeatedly. He looked miserable in that heavy snowsuit. And then I thought, *No, Kent. Don't give up on finding love. Not yet.*"

I laughed. "I can't picture you wearing a snowsuit or kissing a dog on the mouth."

"Pucker up, Patsy." He looked down at her lying at his feet.

I grinned. "Tell me about basketball. You played for Tuscaloosa? That's pretty incredible."

"Oh, the good old basketball days." He leaned back in his chair and sighed. "The best time of my life, Rae. What's Springsteen sing about? Glory days?"

"Did you want to be a high school basketball coach after college?"

"I wanted to be an NBA coach. Golden State Warriors. That's been my team since I was a kid. Chamberlain. Barry. Hardaway. But Steve Kerr got to them first."

"You ought to be proud though. You've been in Whitten for what, three years, and you've taken both the boys and girls to state twice? That's quite the accomplishment. You're pretty respected around here. You know how Whitten feels about their Warriors. Football, basketball. It's a big deal in a Southern town."

"I can't complain. I love coaching those kids. It's the next best thing to the NBA. I truly am content coaching the Whitten Warriors instead of the Golden State Warriors. And I don't have to deal with the egos and the drug abuse you find in professional ball. I don't foresee doing anything else. What about your ex-husband? He a sports guy?"

"He's a golfer," I said. "And not a good one. He golfs with clients. He couldn't care less about sports. He loves to watch Molly play, but he's not a jock by any means. We went to an Auburn game with some friends—"

"Not Auburn!"

I laughed. "And he pretended to care about the game, but he didn't have a clue what was happening. He called Uncle Wilson during halftime for a quick lesson on sacks and safeties. Carter's dad wasn't a sports buff either. Mr. Sutton was a CEO, not an athlete, so Carter got it honest."

"But you . . . you like sports? Would you go with me to an NBA game? Crimson Tide football?"

"I like sports. I wasn't great, but I played a little basketball in high school. I watch the NBA with Molly."

"Who's your favorite team? Don't say the Lakers."

"You won't believe it." I shook my head and grinned.

"Don't say the Lakers," he repeated, "or I'll have to leave right now."

"Golden State," I answered. "Curry. Durant. Thompson."

"This is too good to be true. Is it too soon for a marriage proposal?" He dropped from the patio chair to the deck on one knee as we both laughed. And then we stopped laughing. And the only sounds to be heard were the sounds of summer—frogs and crickets and heavy green leaves blowing in the wind. Kent leaned in and my heart pounded. My eyes closed. And for the first time since I met

Carter Sutton seventeen years ago, my lips touched another man's lips.

And it was heavenly.

CHAPTER 10

When Kent kissed me goodbye after our lasagna date as we stood on the front porch and a slight drizzle fell from the dark summer sky, my heart fluttered. It literally fluttered as if I had chased an entire pot of dark coffee with a Monster energy drink.

I hummed as I got ready for bed. I nearly twirled a time or two. I was floating on air. I couldn't sleep (and not because Patsy was pinning me beneath the comforter or because Molly and Lauren were laughing loudly in her bedroom). I couldn't sleep because my thoughts were consumed with Kent Richardson and the smell of his aftershave and gorgeous hazel eyes and gleaming white teeth.

And then my thoughts went in another direction and I couldn't sleep because I worried why such an attractive, athletic, humorous man had never been married or found the right woman. I worried he was mentally unstable or a knife-wielding psycho with skeleton upon skeleton stacked in his closet. I worried he was the unidentified murderer in the show I'd seen on the ID channel the night before. But my thoughts veered back to his eyes and the way he'd kissed me twice that evening and I eventually fell asleep, smiling and content, because I was giddy over a man who wasn't Carter.

———————◆———————

The Golden Age Senior Center was a small beige cinder-block building on a dead-end side street behind First Presbyterian Church. Aunt Maxine was the director of the nonprofit that hosted activities for the senior citizens in Whitten. A column ran in the hometown newspaper every week announcing events like "Gospel quartet to perform at Golden Age this weekend. Refreshments provided." Or "Rook tournament at Golden Age this weekend. Refreshments provided." Or "They're going SEW CRAZY at Golden Age this weekend. Refreshments provided."

A frantic Aunt Maxine called me the morning after my attempted date with Kent because the decoration bin in the closet at the center was completely void of crepe paper streamers and they were going to be hosting Lilith Powell's hundredth birthday celebration at noon. She pleaded over the line, "The woman has lived through wars, the Great Depression, and four husbands, Raeley Ann. She deserves crepe paper streamers! Please buy some and bring them by."

I pulled up to the little square building a few minutes after I dropped off Molly at the school for basketball practice. I parked between Aunt Maxine's Lincoln and Mrs. Dora's sedan with a dented bumper because "some jackleg with a cellular phone glued to his ear" backed into her at Clooney's Pharmacy a few days before.

"Raeley Ann! Praise the Lord. Did you get the streamers?" Aunt Maxine's humped frame emerged through the front door and onto the weathered stoop.

"I got them." I held up a roll of yellow and a roll of red.

"Mustard and ketchup colors? Oh, good heavens. You couldn't find anything more feminine? Ms. Lilith was a florist for eighty years. She created beautiful bouquets. She doesn't serve hot dogs."

"This was all they had, Aunt Maxine," I responded. "What did Mama used to say? 'You get what you get and you don't pitch a fit'?"

"I always hated that saying. Okay, okay, come on in."

I stepped inside and was met with the scent of menthol. I was certain no octogenarians had been puffing cigarettes in the building; therefore the smell had to be attributed to pain cream.

"Rae, good to see you, honey." Mrs. Dora entered the recreation room from the small kitchen at the back of the building. "Did you get the streamers?"

"Yes, ma'am. Red and yellow."

"Oh." She grimaced. "The store didn't have pastels? Lilith loves pastels."

"Uh—"

"It's going to look like a concession stand in here, Dora. We just have to work with what we have. Bring me the stepladder from the closet. Let's get the streamers and the banner up on the wall. Guests will be here in less than an hour."

"I don't think you should be climbing a stepladder, Aunt Maxine."

"Don't be silly. I'm a seventy-seven-year-old woman with osteoporosis and a weak knee. *You're* going to climb the ladder. You tape the streamers and the birthday banner to the wall while Dora and I set the tables and finish preparing the hors d'oeuvres." Then she muttered under her breath, "Red and yellow."

I rolled my eyes at her comment about the streamers while Mrs. Dora brought me the ladder, her costume jewelry rattling.

"Maxine, Reggie knows to pick up the cake, doesn't he?"

"He knows, Dora. He said he would get it on the way."

"Well, the man doesn't have the best memory. Remember the fiasco with the pancake breakfast? Thirty men and women choking down pancakes with tap water because Reggie forgot the orange juice and coffee. I don't know why in the world you let him volunteer. He's liable to walk in here without the birthday cake. No cake. Red streamers. What a disaster!"

"Well, Lilith is half-blind anyway, Dora. Bless her heart. I don't think she can have sugar, either, so maybe she won't even notice the gaudy streamers or the lack of cake. Just go check on the quiche and quit worrying about it."

"Well, you're the director. It's your reputation on the line." Dora huffed and jingled into the kitchen.

I softly snickered while taping strands of the condiment colors to the cinder-block walls.

"Tell me about last night, Raeley Ann. Kent?" Aunt Maxine asked while situating pale blue hydrangea center-pieces on the round tables in the rec room.

"It was nice," I said. "We had a nice evening."

"He didn't stay the night, did he?"

"Aunt Maxine!" I exclaimed and looked down on her from the stepladder. "No, he didn't stay the night."

"Well." She shrugged. "You were drinking those spirits. I didn't know if—"

"That's a pretty brazen accusation, isn't it?"

"I've been called brazen my whole life, dear."

"I won't argue with that." I turned back to the wall and affixed the pink birthday banner. It looked horrible next to the bright red and yellow strands of crepe paper.

"You think there's a future there?" she asked as I climbed down.

"I don't know. I'm not thinking that far ahead."

"So you're just having a *good* time?" She smoothed the wrinkles from a tablecloth.

"Aunt Maxine, your mind is certainly in the gutter this morning, isn't it? Have you been reading one of Mrs. Dora's romance novels?"

"You know I haven't," she retorted. "I was just kind of shocked to see you sitting on the couch with him last night. I mean, I was pleased to see it. I want to see you happy, Raeley Ann. I'm just not sure inviting a man over for dinner is wise, that's all. Seems a little too inviting. Wrong idea. Mixed signals."

"Aunt Maxine, do you really think I'd let anything inappropriate happen with Molly at home with us? Is that why you played chaperone half the evening? You think I've gone buck wild since my divorce? You think I'm making bad decisions?" I folded the ladder and leaned it against the wall.

"Of course not, honey." Aunt Maxine stopped setting the tables and looked to me. "I just know he courted Elise England for a while, and that poor child is, well, bless her heart," she whispered, "*loose as a goose*. I don't know what kind of morals the man has. He's Fannie's nephew. He comes from upstanding folks. I just . . ." She paused. "Raeley Ann, I just feel a sense of duty. I feel like I need to look out for you now that Margie is gone. Your uncle Wilson and I weren't blessed with children, and I've always thought of you and Jamie as my own children, but since your mother passed, I just want to protect you, my love."

"Oh, Aunt Maxine." I walked to her. "You know I love you. Thank you for your concern, but I promise I will be all right, okay? I still have a pretty good head on my shoulders."

She patted her tight curls. "You're right. I'm sorry I intruded. I love you."

"Come here, you old biddy." I took her small frame into my arms.

"I'm still disappointed in those red and yellow streamers though. Not your best decision."

———◆———

When I picked Molly up from basketball practice, I waited on Kent to walk out too.

"Are we going to go, Mama?" Molly asked after she'd removed her basketball shoes and had been buckled into the passenger seat for a good minute and a half.

"Yes." I pretended to read an article on my phone. "I'm just trying to finish this post on painting. I'm restoring a chest of drawers for one of Aunt Maxine's friends. It's got some good tips."

"You're stalling." Molly called my bluff.

"Stalling?" I chuckled. "Molly, I'm trying to finish this article. It will only take a minute."

"You're waiting on Coach Richardson, aren't you?" She rolled her eyes. "He's going to be a minute, Mama. He's locking up."

"Molly, I am not—" I halted when Kent walked through the purple gym door and into the hot sun.

Molly followed my gaze. "Well, lookie there. Right on time. I swear, Mama, you're worse than Ella."

"Who is Ella?" I checked my lipstick in the rearview mirror.

"The girl on the team who has a crush on Logan. She already told me she is going to learn his schedule when school starts back and make me wait with her by the bathroom until he walks by. Do you know how much time I am going waste standing there with her waiting to see my cousin, who once pinned me down on the couch and farted in my face?"

Kent saw me admiring him through the windshield and enthusiastically smiled. I expected him to sprint toward me and pull a box of chocolates from the duffel bag hanging from his arm.

"I'm going to vomit," Molly muttered.

"Hey!" I rolled down the window as he approached my SUV.

"Hey, you," he said. "Molly had a great practice today. Nice job, girl."

"Thank you!" She feigned a smile.

"So, do you have anything planned this evening?" he asked.

I could feel the car rock from the weight of Molly's eye roll.

"I don't think so. Molly is going to her dad's house later. I was planning to paint some furniture."

"Maybe we could get together? If you don't want to go out to dinner, we could order in and I could help you with the furniture. Or do you want to be alone while you paint? Whatever—"

"No, as a matter of fact, you can help me. I'm restoring a chest that needs some sanding and a busted drawer needs replacing."

"I'm at your service. Do I need to bring anything? Besides food?"

"I have everything. I'll see you around five thirty or six?"

"It's a date." Kent smiled and walked toward his truck.

"Mama, I cannot even deal with this," Molly said when the window rolled up.

"What?" I looked to her.

"I don't have a problem with you dating Coach Richardson. I really don't. I think he's a nice guy. But the flirting! I swear I'm going to throw up. I'm going to vomit on you or on him and he'll cut me from the team for vomiting on him and there goes my chances of ever playing ball in college. Your flirting is ruining my future! 'I would love for you to sand my furniture. I'm at your service.' I cannot even!"

"Wait until you start dating, Molly Sutton. I just may vomit."

Carter was supposed to pick Molly up at four thirty that afternoon, but at four fifteen he texted her he was running late. He said he was still in Huntsville and didn't know when he'd be done with his last client of the day. I immediately began to panic. The thought of Carter and Kent being in my presence at the same time made me want to, in Molly's words, vomit.

"Text your dad again. Ask him what time he's picking you up. Ask him his ETA. Ask when he'll be here."

"Mama, that's the same question asked three different ways. I'm not texting him again. He's working. He'll be here when he gets here. Chill."

I contemplated telling Kent to come over much later. Before I could, though, he texted me that he had already placed the order at Rubio's and would pick up our enchiladas at five thirty and then head to my house. I broke out in a cold sweat and paced the living room. Patsy slowly followed my every step.

At 5:43 P.M., Kent's shiny truck pulled in to my driveway . . . and Molly Margaret was still in her room FaceTiming some girls from the basketball team.

I threw open the storm door as Kent walked onto the front porch with a large brown sack in his hand. "They gave us an extra cheese dip by mistake. Score, right?"

"Yeah, score," I nervously said as he walked inside. I poked my head back out the door and surveyed the street for Carter's black Ford.

"Everything okay?" Kent walked to the kitchen while Patsy quickly followed the smell of chicken and salsa.

"All right. Here's the deal." I put my hands on my hips and paced the kitchen. "Molly is still here."

"So?" He set the food on the kitchen table.

"So, Carter hasn't been by to get her yet. You're going to meet him. This is going to be so awkward," I said as I raked my hair out of my eyes.

"Hey." He smiled and turned to me. He gently placed his hands on my arms. "Just calm down. Everything is fine, Rae."

"I-I just—" I stammered. "He has no idea about us."

"There's an us now, huh? An *us*?" Kent playfully squeezed my arm.

"You know what I mean. Carter has no idea we've been on dates. This just—this is just too much for—"

"Rae, I'll be a perfect gentleman. I'm not going to challenge the man to a fight in the driveway. And he'll get to see that you're moving on, right? Isn't that a good thing?"

"Yes, that's a wonderful thing. I am moving on. I want him to know I'm moving on. I just wasn't prepared for you to meet him this soon. Or in my kitchen while we eat chips and salsa. I'm freaking out, I know. I'm overreacting. I'm sorry, Kent."

"Don't apologize. Can I at least ask him about sports? What he thinks about the Crimson Tide this fall? The quarterback they just recruited? The legacy of Bear Bryant?"

I sighed and grinned at the handsome man holding my hand. "Don't you dare."

I'd scarfed down half the enchilada I was eating when I heard Carter's loud truck pull in in front of the house. I could only imagine the expression on his face when he saw Kent's truck parked in the middle of the driveway. He probably thought it was Molly's new boyfriend—her first boyfriend. An upperclassman with his driver's license. He certainly wouldn't think poor, pitiful Rae had a new man in her life.

"He's here," I said, eyes wide.

"And?" Kent said. "Do you want me to take off my shirt and go to the door?"

"Kent, stop!" I smiled. "Be serious! Just help me through this, okay?"

He nodded. "I got you."

I heard two raps on the front door, then I exhaled and stood from the kitchen table.

When I saw Carter standing on the other side of the glass, I felt dizzy. He looked handsome as ever in a white-and-green plaid button-down, khaki shorts, and the flip-flops I'd given him summer before last. They were nice flip-flops I'd purchased from Macy's. That's what he had requested for his birthday. "Rae, I want some *nice* flip-flops I can wear to church and out to dinner. You've always said I had pretty feet, well, for a man. It's time I show these puppies off at early service and the Grille."

I pushed open the storm door and nearly fainted at his familiar scent. Polo by Ralph Lauren. A green bottle of the cologne had sat on the vanity next to his toothbrush for the last twenty years.

"Whose truck is in the driveway?" he immediately asked.

"Molly's basketball coach is here," I said quickly and backed away from the front door. I began frantically chewing my thumbnail.

"Why?" he asked as the door slammed behind him.

"He, uh, he's Mrs. Fannie's nephew. You know Mrs. Fannie, right? It's her nephew. He's here."

"Okay. Why?" He shrugged.

"He's here to, well, he's here . . ." I fanned the collar of my navy-blue T-shirt as beads of sweat broke out on my neck. I wiped my sweaty hands on my white shorts.

"Rae, what's wrong with you? Have you been drinking?"

"No," I said. "I just, well, Kent is here. He's Molly's basketball coach."

"I get that. Molly's basketball coach is here. I'm asking why he is here, Rae? Why is our daughter's basketball coach at your house on a Friday night? That's the question, Rae. Do you follow?" He was annoyed.

"He's here to see me, Carter. We're having dinner." I looked down at my bare feet on the beige carpet.

"Oh," he said, surprised. "He's here as a friend? Or you're dating Molly's basketball coach?"

"He's not just my friend," I said, somewhat sheepishly, as if I didn't want him to be disappointed in me. And then, out of nowhere, I suddenly had a flashback of Autumn standing at my mother's casket in that tacky green dress with spaghetti straps. She gripped her bright nails around my ex-husband's arm. He stood tall and proud of the young blonde at his side. That vision of them only weeks before abruptly emboldened me. It was like a shock down my spine. A jolt of lightning. A burst of caffeine. A cold shower. I came to. I shrugged off any guilt I had possessed only seconds before. I was immediately proud. And I was eager to make Carter Sutton feel a hint of jealousy or regret or one of the million other negative emotions he'd made me feel when he paraded around with another woman on his arm. "You know what, Carter? Yes, I am dating Molly's basketball coach. He's a great guy. He's in the kitchen. You want to meet him?"

"Well." He clicked his tongue and cocked his head. "Sure, I guess so."

"Kent?" I called for the attractive, athletic man who was eating cheese dip at my kitchen table.

"Yes, Raeley Ann?" he answered. He'd never called me by my full name. I knew he was just trying to get under Carter's skin, and I was okay with it.

"Kent?" I entered the kitchen with Carter at my heels. "This is my ex-husband, Carter Sutton. Carter, this is Kent Richardson."

"Hey, man." Kent stood from the table and extended his right hand.

"Hey," Carter muttered and extended his.

"Molly's a great kid. She's looking really good in basket-ball practice. I'm glad to have her on the team this year," Kent remarked as Patsy nuzzled by his side. I knew this probably infuriated Carter. Patsy had been his couch buddy for years, but she didn't even acknowledge him. She was more concerned with the scent of Spanish rice on the napkin Kent held in his left hand.

"That's good to hear," Carter said dryly. "Um." He looked to me with brows furrowed in confusion. "Is Molly ready, Rae? I was hoping to get to the movie theater in Huntsville by seven."

"Go on back to her room and get her, Carter. I'm going to finish my dinner. Kent?" I motioned for him to sit with me at the table.

Carter cleared his throat and walked down the hallway to Molly's room.

I looked at Kent and grinned.

"Great job," he said quietly.

A few minutes later, Carter reappeared in the kitchen with Molly at his side. She gave me a hug and kissed my cheek and told her coach goodbye.

"Carter!" I called from the kitchen table before they walked out the front door, "Kent played Crimson Tide basketball. Isn't that something?"

"Yeah, that's something," he said, an edge in his voice before walking out the front door.

I raised my eyebrows and Kent shrugged.

"Well, that was fun," I said.

Patsy rested her stomach against the cold concrete of the carport as the warm July breeze whipped around us and dried the first coat of paint I had applied over the freshly sanded piece. Music played softly from the speaker of Kent's phone as we stood back and eyed the chest of drawers.

"Looks nice. Can't even tell that drawer was busted. You did good." I punched him in the arm.

"I watched *This Old House* with Bob Vila a lot as a kid."

"It shows."

"Shh. Listen," he said as he held up his finger.

The intro to "Wild Horses" by the Rolling Stones echoed from his phone on the brick steps.

"Dance with me while we wait on that coat to dry?" He held out his hand as I blushed and nodded.

Kent wrapped both of his arms around my waist and I wrapped mine around his neck. We began to sway back and forth beneath the dim, bug-filled light on the carport ceiling. I rested my head on his broad shoulder and slid my flip-flops across the cement.

I closed my eyes and relished the thought of Carter mulling over the evening's encounter. I had a wonderful vision of him driving down the two-lane toward Huntsville, past Beck's Beauty Spot and the old clunkers in T. J.'s parking lot. He'd see the marquee in front of Brown's Store claiming support for the Warriors—the renowned basketball team coached by the man who was holding me close that very minute. He probably fidgeted in the leather seat of his truck as he sorrowfully realized poor, pitiful Rae had moved on.

Did he expect me to cry over him forever? He left me. This was his own doing. He made the decision to break our family apart. I would still be with him, watching some crime documentary on the L-shaped couch at our home on Sullivan Street and digesting frozen pizza, if he hadn't chosen young Autumn over me. I had nothing to feel guilty about.

So why was I thinking of him instead of relishing the moment with Kent? I squeezed my eyes tighter to erase any vision of Carter Sutton. I didn't want to dwell on the things I adored and missed about him, and I didn't want to delight in thoughts of him being saddened and jealous that I was dating again. I didn't want to think of him at all.

Kent's arms squeezed me tighter and I sighed in relaxation. This was a new movie. Not one about college kids kissing in a bathroom in the '90s while Mazzy Star played on the living room stereo. This movie was about thirtysomethings who were wise and hardened to the ups and downs of life and listened to the Rolling Stones. There were no actresses with three names in this movie. This scene was better suited for an educated thirty-six-year-old Julia Roberts.

The song ended, and before pulling away, our lips met. Neither one of us were nervous anymore, as if we had been together for years. It was exciting and new, but comfortable. It was safe to say, I was smitten with Kent Richardson.

———— ◆ ————

The first coat had dried quickly in the summer air. I knelt onto the drop cloth and began applying the second coat as Kent sat next to me in a lawn chair and sipped sweet tea from a beloved Tupperware cup that had been in our family for decades. A few cars sailed down the sleepy neighborhood street, and Mrs. Murphy's dog yipped at us from the front porch across the street while she and Mr. Murphy rocked in decades-old red metal sled-based chairs and cooled themselves with paper fans.

"How'd you get into this? Painting furniture?"

"Carter and I bought a run-down house in Huntsville right after we were married and spent years renovating it. I did most of the work and found that I really enjoyed it. I even knocked down a few walls and busted out some windows."

"It was hard to leave that house, yes?"

"Yeah, it was." I dipped the brush into the can of Dusty Olive paint. "I wanted to stay there after the divorce, but I couldn't afford it. Carter is still there. I'm glad he kept the house. That's always been Molly's home. I'm happy it still is."

"My sister in Mobile is an interior designer. She doesn't bust down walls, but she makes a pretty decent living picking out couches and curtains and whatever else it is she does. She uses the word *swatches* a lot."

I smiled. "Tell me about your family. You don't talk of them much."

"There isn't much to tell really. I have an older sister, Kara, who has never been married and will never get married because she is so devoted to couches and curtains and swatches that she doesn't have time to date. Besides, she could never find a man who dresses the way she prefers him to dress or speaks the way she prefers him to speak. He would end up another design project and finally grow so tired of her trying to change him that he leaves. At least, that's what has happened to her last dozen or so boyfriends."

"I find that sad," I said. "I'm sure she's lonely, right? Being married to swatches must be unfulfilling."

"Ah, she's got one of those hypoallergenic lap dogs and the most beautifully decorated home in Mobile, Alabama. She will be fine."

"And your mom?"

"She hasn't been the same since my father was put into the nursing home here. Aunt Fannie paid for his care because Mother and Daddy couldn't really afford it. He had Alzheimer's."

"I didn't know."

"Horrible disease." Kent frowned. "He would look at the woman he loved for forty-four years, the mother of his children, and not have a clue who she was. He changed. He turned into a cruel man who said awful things. He wasn't my father anymore, that's for sure. It broke my mother's heart to see him that way. At first Mother made the hour-and-a-half drive to visit him every day, but she cried all the way back to Birmingham. She eventually quit coming very often because he said such mean things. She wanted to remember her husband the way he was before dementia. I knew Whitten had a basketball coach opening, so I applied and moved down here to keep watch over him until he died."

"That's terrible, Kent. Your poor father. And your mama watching him fade away like that. I'm so sorry."

"She has her bridge club and book club and crochet club. She stays busy. She won't move here, as much as I plead with her to. She's content, I guess. It's just sad to watch, isn't it? To watch our parents grow old and feeble? To watch their hands wrinkle and their eyesight fade and their steps slow? They're no longer young and vibrant and energetic. No longer those young adults picking us up from elementary school with long, beautiful hair and bright eyes and stylish clothes. And then they're gone. Too soon. And it means we're pushed right to the head of the line."

I nodded and looked down to the can of paint.

"Rae, that was insensitive of me. Your mother just passed away. I shouldn't have . . ." He leaned forward in the lawn chair.

"No." I shook my head. "No, Kent. Don't apologize. You just verbalized things that have weighed on my mind ever since my mother was diagnosed with cancer."

"Still, I'm sorry. We've had a nice evening. I didn't mean to bring up a painful subject."

"You know I'm a mess, right?" I put the brush on the drop cloth and turned to him. "My mom has only been dead for six weeks, and I'm far from healed of it. I've only been divorced for a little over a year. I just moved back to my hometown after being away for almost eighteen years. I'm living in my parents' house, raising a teenager who is just as emotional as I am. I'm dealing with so many things. Maybe this isn't the right time for me to be in a relationship, Kent. Maybe I'm too vulnerable right now. I like you very much, but it isn't fair for me to subject you to all of this, to this mess of—"

"I'm not scared, Rae." He shook his head and smiled. "I'm not scared of any of that. I've got a shoulder that would be honored for you to lean on."

I quickly wiped the tear that streamed down my cheek. "You don't think you're a rebound? That maybe I'm incapable of making any kind of relationship decisions right now because of my emotional neediness or possible remaining feelings toward Carter or unresolved—"

"I know what a rebound is in every sense of the word. I

am a basketball coach, and I've had my fair share of failed relationships." He smiled. "Do you pray, Raeley?"

I shrugged. "Sometimes. I don't know. My parents taught me to pray. I just don't know what good it does."

"I prayed for this. For you."

"For an overly emotional and recently divorced woman with a teenage daughter and two parents in the ground and tacky shag carpet in her living room?"

"With an obese golden retriever." He glanced at Patsy snoring beside us.

I laughed and wiped my eyes again.

The chest was finished by midnight, and Kent went home. I crawled into bed thinking of his hazel eyes and our dance and the way he bid me farewell for the evening, with a kiss on the hand—like a prince would before riding away on his stallion. I settled into my pillow and Patsy's mane, content and joyful.

But still, the thing that gave me the most satisfaction was envisioning Carter lying alone in our bedroom on Sullivan Street, wide-eyed, not sleeping—and not because Lauren and Molly were laughing loudly down the hall. But because he faced the realization that I was no longer the depressed, distraught divorcee he thought I'd always be.

CHAPTER 11

On Sunday afternoon I stood over my mother's cast-iron skillet and poked at the green tomatoes frying in piping hot oil. I looked like she did when she was young. My long brown hair was pulled into a messy bun. My shorts were covered with her half apron, sewn by her own hands via a Simplicity pattern in the '70s—yellow and orange roses with groovy ricrac trim at the waist and hem. I was barefoot, just as she was so many times she stood over this stove. Grease had splattered from this same skillet onto her pink-painted toes.

The front door opened as I pulled the heavy skillet from the eye and placed the fried green tomatoes on a paper towel atop a plate. Some of the crispy coating fell from the tomatoes and grease soaked into the paper.

"What are you cooking?" Molly walked into the kitchen.

"Hey, sweetie." She kissed my cheek and tousled the hair on Patsy's ears. "Nana's fried green tomatoes. They smell delicious, don't they? You want one?"

"Maybe later. Dad and I ran through a drive-through on the way home. I'm full." She walked back to her room with Patsy following.

"Hey, Rae," Carter said as he slowly entered, his hands shoved into the pockets of his blue jeans.

"Oh, hey." I was startled to see him. I turned back to the stove.

"Those your mama's fried green tomatoes?"

"Yeah." I hesitated. "You want one?"

"Please. Two," he said, followed by the sound of the kitchen chair sliding away from the table.

Without looking back to him, I pulled one of Mama's daisy-covered plates from the cupboard and put two tomatoes on it. "You want remoulade?"

"You know I do. And—"

"Tabasco."

"Yes, please."

I turned to see him at the kitchen table, rubbing his hands together in anticipation. I placed the plate before him and then returned for the hot sauce, remoulade, and a fork. I also poured freshly brewed sweet tea into a glass and set it before him.

"Thanks, Rae."

I fixed my own plate and joined him at the small, round table as he chomped on the tomato. He always chewed loudly, as if his jaw was about to crack. I'd teased him about it since our first date so many years before. We'd planned to go to a nice restaurant, but we were running late to catch *Men in Black* at Regal Cinema so we stopped at Burger King. With the first bite of french fry, he sounded like a cow chewing cud. It grew annoying over the years, but as he sat next to me, I unexpectedly realized I'd missed the noise.

"Tastes just like Mrs. Margie's."

"Thanks."

We ate in awkward silence for a few minutes until I finally said, "What are you doing?"

"What do you mean?"

"Why are you sitting at my table eating fried green tomatoes? Why didn't you just drop Molly off at the door like you usually do? What's your motive, Carter?"

"Motive?" He laughed and put his fork on his empty plate. "You watch too much ID channel, Rae. I don't have a motive."

"Why are you here?" I repeated and wadded my napkin in my hands.

He pushed the plate away and shifted in the bistro chair. He wiped the corners of his mouth with his fingers and crossed his arms.

"I've been thinking a lot about Dale and Donna Jameson."

"Who?" I asked, ruffling my brown in confusion.

"My best friend back home, Adam Jameson? We went to his wedding, remember? I've talked about him a million times."

"Yeah?"

"His parents divorced when we were in elementary school. It was a shock to the whole town. No one could believe Dale and Donna Jameson weren't together anymore."

"Well, it happens, I guess." I sighed.

"They both eventually remarried. And guess who you'd see down at Catfish Cabin every Friday night? Dale and his new wife and Donna and her new husband all sharing a table, laughing. They played cards together. They sat at high school football games together. They were friends." He paused and looked to me. "I want that for us, Rae. I want us to still be friends."

"Carter." I shook my head adamantly. "I don't know if I can ever eat at Chuck E. Cheese or play Go Fish with Autumn."

He grinned. "She's not *that* young, Rae."

"Please! She probably drives a Big Wheel."

"We broke up about a week ago." He uncrossed his arms and rapped his fingers on the table.

"What? You and Autumn broke up?"

He nodded. "She, uh, she found a younger guy."

"Younger than her? Where did she meet him? Disney on Ice? Tumble Tots?"

"That's pretty good." He chuckled. "I mean, I'm fine with it. You're right—she was too young for me. We didn't have much in common, really. I didn't expect us to last forever."

"But she was worth throwing away your marriage?" I stood from the table, grabbed his plate and mine, and placed them in the sink.

"Rae," he said as I leaned my back against the sink and faced him. He looked down to his hands.

"Don't do that. Don't look down at your hands. Why do you do that? Why can't you look me in the eye?"

"I can't look at you," he said quietly. "I can't look at you because I'm ashamed. I'm ashamed of tearing our family apart because I was going through some kind of premature midlife crisis. I'm sorry for bringing a date to your mother's funeral and strutting around with her like she was a trophy. I'm just sorry, Rae."

I crossed my arms and stayed silent.

"You have no idea how sick I felt when you called to tell me your mom had cancer. I wanted to tell you, right then on the phone, that I was coming home. I thought, *My God, I've left the only woman I've ever loved at a time when she's going to need me the most.* I was disgusted with myself."

"And why didn't you tell me?" My eyes glassed over with tears.

"Pride." He looked to me. "My stupid pride. I don't know how else to apologize, but I do apologize. And I would really like for us to be friends like Mr. Dale and Mrs. Donna. I want us to take Molly places together too. She needs us to be on the same team. You think you can forgive me?"

"Carter, you left me for another woman. A beautiful, young—so, so, so young—"

"I get it, Rae." He grinned.

"—woman. You caused pain to our daughter that she certainly didn't deserve. I don't know if I can forgive that just yet."

He quietly nodded and continued to look at his hands. He picked his nails.

"I will work on it though. I'll work on the forgiveness and the friendship. For Molly."

"Thank you." He looked right at me and smiled. "So, Kent? There's something significant there?"

"Y-yeah, yeah," I stammered. "I mean, I care about him. He cares about me. We have a good time together." I couldn't help but feel awkward saying those words about another man to Carter.

"I asked Molly about him this weekend. She said he's a nice guy. A great coach. I asked her if she liked the two of you together. She said she thought he was good for you."

"Well," I began, "I'm glad she approves. I did talk with her about this, Carter. I made sure she was comfortable with the idea."

"How did you even get together?" He shifted in the chair as I looked around the kitchen, now avoiding eye contact with him.

"His aunt suggested we meet. And then, well, I don't know, I saw him at basketball and we ended up going to dinner."

"Do you love him?" His question took me by surprise.

"Well, that's an intrusive question, isn't it?" I shrugged and waved my hands. "I don't want to talk about this with you." I turned away from him and looked out the kitchen window to a squirrel scampering across the deck.

"You're humble. You're still considerate of my feelings,

aren't you? Even after the way I've treated you. You're behaving the opposite of the way I behaved with Autumn."

I turned back to him. "It was always supposed to be you. I wasn't supposed to be dating at thirty-six. I didn't ask for this. When you came to the decision to leave me, did you think of the possibility that I'd move on? Or were you only thinking about your moving on? Did you think I was just going to live the rest of my life alone?"

"I'll be honest. I didn't think about it," he answered. "I just thought about playing poker with the guys as late as I wanted or taking off to the lake to fish all week or ordering takeout at eleven at night. I just thought about being free."

"Free?" I asked. "You mean free of me, don't you? You weren't thinking about poker or fishing or Chinese food. You were thinking about Autumn. You left me for her, Carter." My face began to burn red.

"I know, Raeley." He shook his head and looked away from me. "I know leaving you was the most selfish thing I've ever done. I told you, I was—"

The living room door opened, and suddenly Aunt Maxine was poking her head inside the house. "Raeley Ann?"

Carter's eyes widened and he gave me a quick, worried glance.

"Hey, Aunt Maxine." I took a deep breath to calm down. I walked to the den and held the door open for her as she came into the house.

"I hope I'm not interrupting. I just ran by to—" She stopped short when she saw Carter stand from the kitchen table.

"Oh, that is your truck out front? I thought Kent was here." She looked to me.

"Kent has a Chevy. Carter has a Ford," I clarified.

"Chevrolet, Ford, Buick, Studebaker. I can't tell one from the other anymore." She walked into the kitchen and peered at my ex-husband.

"It's nice to see you, Aunt Maxine." He hesitantly stepped forward and began to reach his arms out to hug her.

"Don't you dare put your arms around me, boy." She pointed her finger at him. "Sit down."

"Aunt Maxine . . ." I sighed.

"This has been a long time coming, Raeley Ann. You know it has." She pulled a chair out from the table and sat across from Carter. I sighed again, knowing I couldn't stop her, and walked to the sink to rinse the dishes.

"No, ma'am, you sit down with us too," she instructed.

I tossed the dish towel to the counter and sat down, arms crossed.

"Carter Sutton," she began, "I loved you like a son. I loved you just as much as my sister, Margie, did. I thought you hung the moon. I thought you were an answered prayer to my Raeley Ann."

"Yes, ma'am." He looked down at his hands again. I guess he couldn't make eye contact with Aunt Maxine when he was ashamed either.

"What you did—walking out on your wife and your child the way you did—"

"I didn't walk out of their lives, Aunt Maxine. I still see

my daughter multiple times a week. I didn't abandon her," he argued, somewhat timidly.

"But you hurt Molly, Carter. And you certainly abandoned Raeley Ann, didn't you? Bless her heart." She pointed a wrinkled, crooked finger at me. "That woman did nothing but love you and take care of you for how many years? And you grew bored of her, was that it? You robbed a cradle quicker than an alcoholic robs a liquor store. You jumped ship for some little wild-eyed thing. Lust, that's all it was. Despicable."

"Quiet, Aunt Maxine. Molly is in her room," I said as Carter continued to stare silently at his hands folded on the table. He offered no defense.

"Wilson and I have not had a perfect marriage. I'm sure there have been plenty of times he's grown bored of me. I'm sure he's wondered if there was someone more exciting out there. I bet he eyed Shirley at physical therapy a time or two. And I bet he's wondered what it would be like to be on his own without my nagging or nit-picking or complaining about his snoring. Lord knows I've spent plenty of sleepless nights wondering if I made a mistake in marrying someone who inhales the drapes. But you know what, Carter?" She tapped his hands and he looked to her. "We'll be married fifty-three years next April."

"Yes, ma'am."

"You don't just leave. You don't act on emotion. Feelings are fickle and fleeting. Love isn't a feeling, Carter. It's an action. The Good Book says love isn't self-seeking. It says love always perseveres. And I've never known the Good Book to be wrong, son."

"What do you want me to do, Aunt Maxine?" he asked her.

"I want you to show this woman—the mother of your child—and Molly Margaret that you're sorry every day of your life. I don't mean I want you to live in guilt or to grovel, but I want you to make it up to the both of them the rest of your days in ways of love and kindness."

"I can do that." He looked to me and then back to her. "And I'm sorry, Aunt Maxine."

She sat back in her chair and sighed. "You're still a good person, Carter. I don't deny you love your daughter or that you're a good father. I don't deny you loved Raeley Ann well for all those years you were married. And if you do marry again, don't make the same mistakes. Remember what I said. It's an action. Not a feeling."

"Yes, ma'am," he repeated while I quickly wiped the corners of my eyes and stood to rinse the dishes.

———◆———

"Happy humpty day, Raeley Ann," Aunt Maxine said into the phone bright and early Wednesday morning.

"Excuse me?" I pulled my phone away from my ear to check the time: 6:50 A.M.

"Humpty day. Wednesday?" I could hear oil popping in her skillet in the background.

"It's hump day, Aunt Maxine," I said and buried my head beneath my heavy comforter. A disgruntled Patsy rolled over and huffed at the early morning chitchat. "It's the middle of the week. The hump. Hump day."

"Oh, mercy, I thought it had something to do with Humpty Dumpty. I never quite understood. I assumed he fell off the wall on a Wednesday. Bless his heart."

"Why are you calling so early?" I yawned.

"I know you enjoy sleeping in most mornings, including Sunday, but you don't go to bed early on Wednesday nights, do you?" she asked.

"I rarely go to bed early."

"Wonderful!" The grease continued to sizzle. "I would love for you and Molly Margaret to attend prayer meeting tonight. Fannie is going to sing 'My Anchor Holds.' Oh, Raeley Ann, you've not lived life to its fullest until you've heard Fannie Culpepper sing 'My Anchor Holds.'"

"I don't know, Aunt Maxine—"

"Brother Lonnie is preaching a wonderful sermon on being brokenhearted. I think it would be an encouraging word for you. And it wouldn't hurt to have Molly Margaret come as well. High school can be a tumultuous, confusing, and tempting time. The poor dear has had a rough year. Being at church would do her soul good."

"We went to church in Huntsville, Aunt Maxine. Molly was really involved with her youth group on Wednesday nights. You act like we've never stepped foot inside a church. We aren't over here sacrificing cats and drinking blood."

"Oh, Raeley Ann! What a profane thing to say." She huffed. "I'm just saying that I would love to have you visit this evening. We have quite a few girls Molly's age in the youth program. It would also be a good way for her to make some new friends. The Potter girls are around Molly's age. Six thirty?"

"As you wish, Aunt Maxine. Can I go back to sleep now so I'll be well rested for tonight?"

"As you wish, Raeley Ann."

I attended First Baptist Church on Main Street every Sunday morning and Wednesday evening until I moved out of my parents' home when I was eighteen. It didn't matter if I stayed the night with a friend on Saturday night or if I had a ton of homework to do on Wednesday, I'd better be on time to sit with Mama, Daddy, and Jamie on the right side of the sanctuary, fourth pew from the front.

Brother Jerome "Jerry" Gatlin was the pastor all those years. He was a heavyset man with a shiny bald head who was on fire with the Spirit and jumped up and down while shouting about redemption and salvation and the sweltering fires of hell. He regularly steadied himself against the sturdy oak pulpit before pulling a handkerchief from his front pocket and dabbing the perspiration dripping from his brow.

My Sunday school teacher was Mrs. Arlene Pennington, long dead and gone. She smelled of peppermint and a staunch perfume that made my eyes water. Her hair was the color of a Twinkie and piled high atop her head. Her rouge was bright, her nails were long, and her laugh was boisterous. She was a sweet soul who loved to give hugs and leave bright red kisses on the cheeks of all "her girls" before we exited her class with our colorful drawings of the garden of Eden or arks made of Popsicle sticks.

Molly and I opened the heavy white door and stepped onto the burgundy carpet, and I immediately recognized the greeter for the evening, Mr. "Mac" McElhenny. He used to be one of the middle-aged ushers who sang bass in the choir and always had cherry suckers in his pocket for the kids. Now he was an old, hunched-over man who didn't recognize me. Still, he had the same inviting smile he'd always had, and I even noticed the stick of a sucker poking out of his pocket.

I saw Aunt Maxine and Uncle Wilson sitting in a pew a few rows back from where I used to sit with my parents. They were conversing with another couple on the bench in front of them as Molly and I approached.

"Well, here they are. Raeley Ann and Molly Margaret." Aunt Maxine smiled and motioned for us to sit next to her. "Do you remember Sylvia Potter?" She pointed to the petite lady adjacent to us. "She did that needlepoint picture that hung in your mother's bathroom for a hundred years."

"'Sprinkles are for cupcakes, not toilet seats,'" I said and smiled.

"I always thought that was the cutest thing." Aunt Maxine clapped her delicate hands together.

"Rae, I haven't seen you since you were this pretty thing's age. This is your daughter?" Mrs. Sylvia nodded at my girl.

"Hi," Molly said.

"I sure loved your grandmother," Mrs. Sylvia said to Molly. "She was a dear friend to so many, including me."

"Thank you, Mrs. Sylvia."

"Now, Sylvia's granddaughters are around your age, Molly," Aunt Maxine said.

"Nadia will be a freshman and Emmie will be a junior." Mrs. Sylvia smiled warmly at Molly. "They are in youth group if you'd like to join them tonight, honey? I'd be glad to walk you back there," she offered.

"Yes, ma'am, okay."

"You're sure?" I asked Molly as she stood to her Converse.

"It's all good, Mama," she said quietly and followed the small lady with a short bob dyed the color of rubies.

"Well, isn't that just wonderful?" Aunt Maxine beamed. "Oh, Raeley Ann, do you remember Sylvia's husband, Harvey?" She reached out and tugged on the sleeve of Harvey's shirt as I nodded to the man who also nodded but looked perturbed that Aunt Maxine had interrupted his and Uncle Wilson's conversation. "Let's see here, who else do you know? Well, everyone knows you, but who do you remember? It's been such a long time." Aunt Maxine scanned the sanctuary.

"Maxine, leave the girl be," Uncle Wilson said as Harvey faced forward. He reached for my hand and gave it a quick squeeze hello.

"Calm down, Wilson. I'm just excited my baby sister's girls are back in her church. Is it a crime to show them off?"

Uncle Wilson ignored her, as he often did, pulled his glasses from the front pocket of his short-sleeve button-down, and placed them on his face.

Aunt Maxine continued to babble as I glanced around the room. I recognized some of the members and couldn't believe how much they had aged. What were youthful faces when I was a child were now sagging and wrinkled and cur-tained by short white hair. A handful of people my age and younger filed into the sanctuary as it filled with the sounds of chatter and laughter. Some I knew and some I didn't have a clue who they were. I felt a bit saddened that I once knew every person who sat on these pews beneath brass chande-liers, but now many were strangers.

A young, stylish woman sat at the red oak grand piano, and Aunt Maxine leaned over and loudly whispered to me, "That's Julie Harper, Cathy Emmitt's granddaughter."

As she began to play, the congregation stood and the words came back to me without even looking at the blue hymnal in my hands. "Jesus Saves," "Sweet By and By," "The Old Rugged Cross." Mrs. Fannie finally graced the stage in an elegant navy-blue dress and shining emerald earrings and ended the set with her beautiful rendition of "My Anchor Holds." There was no applause afterward, only *amens* echoing throughout the large sanctuary. I thought I heard a sniffle or two as well.

Brother Lonnie stood from the deacon's bench and took his place behind the pulpit.

"Mrs. Fannie Culpepper sure is a blessing, isn't she, church?" he asked as the parishioners again nodded in agreement and murmured amens. "When Brother Craig told me Mrs. Fannie would be singing that song this evening, I knew right then the Lord must have placed it on her heart. It is so appropriate for tonight's message on being brokenhearted. And so, I titled tonight's sermon, 'My Anchor Holds.'

"'My Anchor Holds' was written in 1902 by William C. Martin, and no doubt it was penned from a broken heart, but many times that's how God works, amen?

"'Troubles almost 'whelm the soul; grief like billows o'er me roll; tempters seek to lure astray; storms obscure the light of day: but in Christ I can be bold, I've an anchor that shall hold,'" Brother Lonnie said in singsong.

Brother Lonnie asked the parishioners to open their Bibles to Hebrews 6:19 and read aloud, "'We have this hope as an anchor for the soul, firm and secure.'"

I sat in that stiff cherry pew next to my aunt, who smelled of Estée Lauder powder and chewed on a cherry Life Saver and soaked in the words Brother Lonnie spoke from behind the pulpit. I allowed myself to be saturated in them, like my brushes absorbed chalk paint. Every adjective he used accurately described my heart in this season of life—lonely and longing, confused and broken.

I had often described my grief as waves that tossed me about—enormous, angry waves that would suddenly appear as I stood at the kitchen sink, as I lay in my bed, while sprawled on the living room floor, or while I sat at a stop light in my car. Those ominous, foreboding waves threatened to pull me under and fill my lungs, leaving me unable to breathe, to function. And yet I'd never envisioned an anchor to keep me steady. An anchor was never the answer. No anchor—no help—seemed attainable when I was caught in a storm. I certainly didn't think of God.

My parents were people of great faith. They raised me on God's Word and the devastating, yet glorious, story of Jesus' brutal death on the cross and magnificent resurrection three days later. I believed it. I believed hell was hot and heaven was real. I believed God was an all-knowing, all-seeing deity who healed and cured, and when He didn't, that was His will too.

Yet still, in a lifetime of being taught those things by my mother and father, Mrs. Arlene, and Brother Gatlin as I sat in that sanctuary twice a week for eighteen years, I never felt that God was mine—personally mine. His power applied to people who were once addicted to cocaine but were now missionaries. It applied to the people who survived car wrecks and cancer. His promises never applied to me—a middle-class girl who had never struggled with addiction or disease or utter heartbreak. My difficulties were never important enough for Him to intervene. I never thought of myself as the one sheep He sought out while leaving ninety-nine behind.

Even when my father died, I pushed through on my own.

I did send up a prayer for strength for my mother now and again, but I handled it. I got through without weeping and begging for God's help.

But as much as I adored my father, the grief I experienced when my mother died was more substantial. The waves were bigger, rougher, more sinister. Not only was I heartbroken at watching Mama die of cancer, but my unfaithful husband's choices left me punctured with insecurities and loneliness like nothing I had ever known. My divorce and my mother's death both left gaping wounds in my soul.

I'd been tossed to and fro, so weathered and beaten, that I knew I could no longer steer the ship alone. I had to throw the anchor overboard. I had to rely on it to keep the boat, my life, from being submerged. The storm was too great this time. The waves too rough. Drowning was imminent without an anchor that would hold. Brother Lonnie assured me through Scripture, and Mrs. Fannie assured me through song, that it would. It would hold. It would save me. It would keep my head above water. It would allow me to breathe and go on to find dry land to shake myself off and recover wholly. And I believed it. For the first time I really, truly believed it.

When Brother Lonnie was done teaching, encouraging, promising me that God would be an ever-present help in my time of trouble, we stood to sing the invitation. With the first chord of "Just As I Am," I was nudged. A still, small voice prompted me to go to the altar and fall to my knees before God and the entire congregation. I immediately denied it with all my being. What would people think? Would they whisper? Would they think I was kneeling for attention? Pity? What would Aunt Maxine do? Would she make a spectacle? Would she gather people to come pray over me and draw more attention than necessary? Would Brother Lonnie stop the service and point out this wounded soul kneeling on the burgundy carpet?

I didn't know, and I didn't want to find out. So I denied it. I pushed it away. I tried to think of other things—Kelly Wooley's coffee table in my shed that was ready to be sanded, the hardwood floors beneath the carpet in the living room. Had I forgotten to give Patsy her heartworm pill this month? I forced my mind to go elsewhere.

And then Brother Lonnie said aloud, in the most comforting and inviting tone, "Come. Give the Lord every hurt. Every burden. Every heartache. As the billows roll, rely on the anchor. Come."

Without even fully realizing what I was doing or the movements my legs were making, I stepped past Aunt Maxine and Uncle Wilson and walked directly to the front of the church just like Mrs. Fannie's daddy did, drunk, so many years before at a tent revival on Route 118. I, too, in a sense, felt drunk. I didn't quite know what I was doing, and everything seemed hazy, dizzy even. I knelt down on the bottom step of the altar and let my tears fall onto the carpet. I tuned out the notes of the song, the thought of the hundred eyes on the back of my head, and I rested, prostrate, and simply muttered, "God, help me." That was all I said.

That was all I could say. I didn't go into a lengthy prayer or requests or describe my grief in detail. Brother Lonnie had said God already knew all of that anyway. All I could muster were those three words, one time, "God, help me."

I don't know how long I knelt there. When I stood, my eyes puffy and my face warm, I kept my head down and watched my brown strappy sandals move down the aisle and back to my aunt and uncle. I took my place back on the pew, and without looking to me or saying a word, I felt Aunt Maxine's hand grab mine. She gave it a light squeeze until the song was over and we were dismissed.

CHAPTER 12

With summer vacation coming to an end, Jamie and Dawn decided to host a back-to-school cookout. Their once lovely large yard with impeccable landscaping now looked like a dirt bike track. As Mama predicted, he and Dawn were putting in a swimming pool with their share of the inheritance. The concrete had yet to be poured, so the kidney-shaped body of aqua water filling the liner was surrounded by mud and sheets of cardboard that served as a walkway.

Logan and Liam invited some friends, including a couple of girls, and Molly seemed to fit right in with them. They repeatedly walked the cardboard path and jumped into the cool water. Molly laughed and splashed around with her cousins and their friends, and I knew she would adjust to a new school just fine. She had such a big, inviting personality that people were drawn to. I envied that about her.

Aunt Maxine and I sat at the vintage wooden picnic table on the patio and shooed the flies away from the potato salad and baked beans as Jamie manned the grill. Uncle Wilson stood close to him and stared at the flames surrounding the hamburgers.

"James Jr., it's time. Flip them now," he demanded.

"No, sir. Not yet."

"They are going to burn, boy. Flip them!"

"Not yet, Uncle Wilson."

Beads of anxiety-induced perspiration formed on Uncle Wilson's wrinkled brow as he stared at the blaze. Any second he was going to grab the spatula out of Jamie's hand and flip the burgers himself. Finally, Jamie turned them over on the charcoal briquettes and Uncle Wilson heaved a sigh of relief and then took a swig of tea.

"You're going to give me a heart attack, son," he said before shuffling inside the house.

"Raeley Ann, you should have invited Kent." Aunt Maxine rested her elbows on the red-and-white checkered tablecloth. "Fannie could have come, too, and brought her peach cobbler. What I wouldn't give for a piece of her peach cobbler. I don't think she's made one all summer."

"I told her to invite Kent, Aunt Maxine," Jamie said.

"I've seen him nearly every night this week. I don't want to smother him. Besides, he's volunteering at the school tonight. He's getting classrooms ready and helping some teachers move things around. I know he's busy."

Dawn came through the back door with a jar of pickles, mustard, ketchup, and mayonnaise. Uncle Wilson followed her with a bag of buns, a tray of lettuce, Dawn's garden-grown tomatoes, and onions.

"Just set those right there, Uncle Wilson. Thank you," Dawn said before sitting next to me at the picnic table.

"You're looking great." I nudged her arm.

"Well, thank you, girl. Boot camp is kicking my butt. I'm twelve pounds down though. It's so fun to see that number drop on the scale instead of rise. I can't wait to see Dr. Talbot next week and have my labs drawn. I'm certain my cholesterol has improved. I'm having a bun-less burger tonight. And no potato salad, although I know it's delicious, Aunt Maxine."

"You're a beautiful girl with or without the extra weight," Aunt Maxine said and Dawn thanked her. "I know you've worked hard, so I won't heckle you for not eating the potato salad. Although, I used Yukon gold potatoes and added a pinch more sugar this time around. It ought to be just delectable."

"Going through life without potato salad is no way to live," Uncle Wilson muttered.

"I'm proud of my baby. She's looking all fine and svelte." Jamie winked at Dawn from the grill.

"Gross! Stop! You two and your kissy talk. It's annoyed me since I was fourteen. Remember how you used to call each other pet names like poochie and schnookums? It made me nauseated."

"Oh, hush, Rae." Dawn laughed and slapped at my hand. "It was pookie and snookie."

"Even worse." I grimaced.

"Well, I sure wish poochie and snookie had been at the service on Wednesday night. Raeley Ann came," Aunt Maxine said to Dawn.

"You did?" Dawn's face lit up. "Girl, you went to church?"

"What is with you people? You keep acting like I'm—"

"Do not reference sacrificial cats and blood again, Raeley Ann," Aunt Maxine interrupted. "It's no way for a Southern lady to talk."

"How was it?" Dawn asked.

"I really enjoyed the sermon. It was exactly what I needed to hear. It was eye-opening and gave me peace. I've been reading my Bible again. I will be back on Sunday," I said as I took a drink of ice water from the Mason jar. I wasn't ready to share my sacred experience at the altar with my family, and I was relieved, and surprised, that Aunt Maxine didn't tell them about it either.

"Wonderful!" Aunt Maxine clasped her petite hands. "Wilson, did you hear that? Raeley Ann is coming back to church on Sunday. Oh, I'm so thrilled. We can have lunch at my house afterward. The whole family. I'll make chicken and rice casserole. Wilson, did you hear that? Raeley Ann and Molly Margaret will be back at church on Sunday."

"I'm not deaf, Maxine. I heard her. But she isn't going to keep coming if you make a big fuss about it every time. Ain't nothing to chase a person out of church quicker than people making a fuss." Uncle Wilson puffed and watched the kids in the pool.

"Fellowship is a wonderful thing—belonging to a church family. Iron sharpening iron. It's so healing, Rae, to be filled with the Word and then go into the world to fill others up." Dawn gave my hand a quick, comforting squeeze.

"You going to pull those burgers, son?" Uncle Wilson glanced over at the grill.

"Not yet," Jamie answered. "Just hold your horses, Uncle Wilson."

"I'd like to hold a burger that isn't burnt," he replied.

"The kids sure look like they're having fun," Dawn said. "Molly seems to be hitting it off with Megan and Lila. They've been friends with Logan and Liam since elementary school. They are good girls."

"Molly's going to be just fine at Whitten," Aunt Maxine added. "She's a resilient kid with a big personality. I know she'll make tons of new friends."

"Okay, Uncle Wilson, are you ready to eat the best burger of your life?" Jamie walked to the table with the plate of patties and set them before us.

"I don't know about that, son. Your daddy was the grill master. I don't think anybody could out grill James Reeves. I miss his barbecued chicken as much as I miss him."

"Well, my name *is* James Reeves Jr., isn't it?"

We ate the delicious food and conversed while the kids continued to splash and squeal in the pool surrounded by mud. I couldn't help but think of my mother. She loved a good cookout. Nothing made her happier than enjoying grilled chicken or a burnt hot dog on a patio in the sweltering summer humidity. Uncle Wilson was right about my daddy being a master at the grill. He cooked for us several nights a week during the summer months, and we'd all gather on the back deck with family and friends. When the food was gone and the sun began to set, the crickets and cicadas serenaded us as we played cards at the patio table surrounded by the scent of citronella. Barbecuing was a family tradition, and I was thrilled to be back at a picnic table on an August night, even risking splinters and mosquito bites, to enjoy a good meal and a bout of laughter with my family.

There was a void, though, without Mama there to refill our Mason jars with tea and rush to take the stuffed eggs and potato salad back into the cool house before they went bad and gave us all food poisoning. I missed the sound of her boisterous laugh and the way she doused everything on her plate in Duke's mayo while Jamie and I (who both abhorred mayonnaise) referred to it as "the devil's white sauce."

I felt a wave of grief approaching as I sat at Jamie and Dawn's picnic table without her. Aunt Maxine and Uncle Wilson were bickering over something ridiculous while Jamie and Dawn laughed, but I knew the wave was coming. I sensed it. I tuned them out and focused on the anchor. I focused on the anchor that was promised to hold me if the wave crashed. I focused on the strength only He could give and the joy my mother was experiencing in heaven, and I was no longer anxious or afraid. I didn't have to run to the bathroom to sob. Instead, I silently thanked Him and laughed at my aunt and uncle's banter over Duke's versus Hellmann's.

———◆———

The alarm clock rang at 6:00 A.M., which was the earliest it had chimed since I'd moved to Whitten. I was used to sleeping in, having a cup of coffee on the deck while Patsy sniffed the trails that raccoons had made throughout our yard in the night. I would eventually shower, get dressed, and paint furniture or do chores around the house. Molly slept until at least ten after gabbing with friends on the phone all night, and then she'd eat lunch before going to basketball practice for a couple of hours. That had been our summer routine, but now it was over. We weren't early risers and never had been. Even Patsy enjoyed snoozing until the sun had been up for several hours.

Molly entered the kitchen that morning in a Led Zeppelin T-shirt, tattered blue jeans, and new Converse shoes. Her hair was pulled into a messy, yet precious, bun, and small silver hoops dangled from her ears. She'd applied a hint of blush and frosty pink lip gloss. She looked like a young lady, not a kid. She took my breath away for a moment.

"Do these kids even know Led Zeppelin?" She tugged at her shirt.

"If they were raised right, they do," I answered before nursing my cup of steaming coffee. "You look beautiful, Molly. Are you nervous?"

"No," she said confidently while pulling the waffles from the toaster.

I remembered her first day of kindergarten. She wore a Hello Kitty T-shirt and turquoise shorts. I braided her hair and helped her tie the sparkling tennis shoes that lit up when she walked. An oversize Barbie backpack hung from her small shoulders, and a matching lunch box dangled from her baby hand. Carter and I posed her next to the river birch in the front yard on Sullivan Street and she gave a big, toothless grin. Her father and I walked her into Mrs. Penner's class, and after giving us both a quick hug, she tossed her things into her cubby and immediately mingled with a group of little girls playing with blocks on a choo-choo train rug. One of those little girls was her future best friend, Lauren.

Carter had draped his arm around me as we walked out of Belmont Elementary School and my tears fell. I cried like a baby after dropping my baby off at school for the first time. I worried she would forget to go to the potty. I worried kids would tease her. I worried she would eat lunch alone. I worried she wouldn't nap. I worried about every little detail and counted down the minutes until I picked her up that afternoon. When she finally crawled into my car after school, with the big backpack in her way, she was beaming and told me all about finger paints and the swirly slide on the playground and her new friends. And then I cried because I felt she didn't need me quite as much anymore.

Watching her lean against the kitchen counter and chew the waffle in her hand while looking over the freshman schedule she'd received in the mail a few days before, I wanted to cry again. My baby was going to high school. She was growing up so quickly, and before I knew it, she'd be calling me from some college dorm to tell me about the boy she hoped to marry. It was almost too much to bear.

"Your dad is going to pick you up after basketball practice this afternoon, remember? He's going to take you to dinner and then bring you home."

She nodded and continued to read the schedule.

I quickly dabbed my eyes with the back of my hand before she noticed my tears and said, "Good gracious, Mama, get it together."

When Molly walked through the front door that evening, her backpack comfortably draped across her shoulder, I muted the television, sprang from the couch, and rushed to her. I wrapped my arms around her and gave her a tight squeeze.

"You act like I've been deployed for two years, Mama. It was only my first day of school."

"Your first day of *high school*. Was it great? Did you make friends? Did you eat lunch with someone? Did you remember to go potty?"

She gave me a confused look and tossed her bag to the living room floor. "Everything was fine. I ate lunch with some girls from the basketball team. I went to the potty twice."

"So it was good?" I asked as Carter walked through the front door.

"Yeah, it was good. I have a couple of classes with people I know. They knew who Led Zeppelin was. It was fine."

"Oh, I'm so glad." I smiled and tucked a stray piece of dark hair behind her ear.

"I'm ready to shower though. Practice was brutal today. I sweated off ten pounds." She walked to her father, who was still standing at the front door, and kissed his cheek. "Thanks for dinner, Daddy. I love you."

"Love you, baby. I'll see you Friday night," he said and shoved his hands into the pockets of his khaki pants.

"Oh," I sighed in relief. "I'm so glad she had a good day."

"Sounds like she loves it here. I don't know why I worried. She can make the best of anything. She makes friends easily. Remember the little girl she befriended at the beach? I think they wrote letters to each other for a year or so."

"She's a good kid." I sat back down at my familiar spot on the couch. "You want to sit?"

"Yeah," he said, to my surprise. "I can stay for a few minutes."

He sat at the opposite end of the couch and pulled one of the oversize pin-striped pillows into his lap. Patsy waddled to him and rested her head on the pillow. "Hey, old girl. I've missed you."

"So? How's work? Everything going well?" I attempted to make small talk while *Fixer Upper* played quietly on the television.

"Still watching those two renovate houses?" He tipped his head toward the television while rubbing Patsy's ears. "I came across that show the other night. I ended up watching an entire episode. They made the kitchen and living room one open space and painted the walls gray. It was quite the plot twist," he said sarcastically.

"Oh, hush. It's a good show," I said. "It inspired everything you see here." I waved my hands around the living room like I was Vanna White introducing a prize.

"The house looks great. I meant to tell you that the last time I was here. You're good at this kind of thing."

"Thank you very much," I said.

"Well." He paused. "I, uh, I got a call from my brother the other night."

"How is Jarrett?" I leaned into the sofa cushion and crossed my legs.

"He isn't doing so well. He fell off the wagon again. Melanie kicked him out and won't let him see the kids."

"Oh, Carter, I'm sorry. He was doing so well after his last stint in rehab, wasn't he? He was sober for, what, at least two years?"

"I thought he was." Carter shrugged. "But he's been drinking the whole time he's been out. He called me from a friend's house. He's sleeping on the couch. Lost his job. He owes everybody he knows money. He asked me for a grand. I wouldn't give it to him. Do you think that was wrong?"

"I don't think you need to enable him. You know how I feel about that. How many times did we loan him money? He never did the right thing with it."

After years of battling alcohol and drug addiction, Carter's mother, Jackie, abandoned her devoted husband and two sons when the boys were in high school—Carter a freshman and Jarrett a senior. She ran off to Las Vegas to be with a man she met in an online chat room. He was fifteen years her senior and said he was a real-estate millionaire. Turned out he tended bar, which was probably more appealing to her than being with a tycoon anyway. Jackie rarely called her sons, and the first time Carter had seen her since she left was when she came to our wedding, stoned out of her mind and wearing ripped blue jeans and a leather jacket that reeked of tequila. She was a real sight at the reception when she grabbed my father by the arm to dance and fell into the gift table. Jackie had only seen Molly a couple of times. She really didn't even exist as far as we were concerned.

Carter and Jarrett had a wonderful, hardworking father and loving grandparents who cared for and supported them. Still, Jarrett was so affected by his mother's rejection that he started drinking heavily in college and never stopped. He wanted to be a lawyer but instead flunked out of law school, married three times, and rarely saw his four children. He'd gotten clean a couple of times but always seemed to backslide.

"I thought I'd send some money to his kids. Are you okay with that?"

"Well, Carter," I said, "your money is no longer *our* money. You can do what you want with it."

"I know." He sighed. "I just want your opinion. Do you think that's what I should do?"

"I think that's kind of you," I answered. "You love your brother, and I know you love his children. I'm sure Melanie would put the money to good use for them. She's always been trustworthy."

"Dad is getting on in years. He's getting forgetful and confused. I called him the other night and he thought I was Jarrett the whole time we were on the phone. He kept asking me about lawyering and how many cases I'd won this year. I finally just played along. Before we hung up, he put Aunt Paulette on the phone. She's taking good care of him, but she said he's getting worse. I just wish I had Jarrett to talk to about it. I wish he would get his act together. For Dad."

My heart was saddened. I'd always loved Carter's father. Mr. Henry called me a few days after Carter left me and wept over the phone. He didn't know why Carter had made such a terrible decision, he'd said. He promised to always love and support me and Molly in whatever way he could. He was a fine man.

"I'm so sorry to hear this." I picked at the threads on the couch cushion in my lap. "I know you miss your brother. You need him right now. You need to come together to decide what's best for Mr. Henry. I'm sorry you don't have him to lean on."

"Dad also thought Molly was married with a couple of kids. He said he wished he'd been invited to her wedding. Aunt Paulette said he failed his cognitive testing. It's early dementia, Rae. He's not going to get any better."

I looked down to my lap and shook my head in sorrow.

"Maybe you could go up to Tennessee with me to see him, Rae?" Our eyes caught. "He's always loved you so much. Maybe seeing you would do him good. Maybe we could go by and see Jarrett too. Talk some sense into him. You are the one who convinced him to go to rehab the first time. He listens to you. He respects you. We could go next weekend. You, me, and Molly?"

"Oh, Carter, I don't know. I—" I began.

"Please, Rae?" he pleaded, nearly on the verge of tears. "Please go with me. I need you."

"Okay. Whatever you need me to do, Carter. Yes."

CHAPTER 13

On the third Thursday in August, I walked through the front door of Mrs. Dora's white wooden farmhouse and was greeted with, "Shhhh! Harold is napping in the back room. Don't let that storm door slam behind you. He'll wake early and be in a ripe kind of mood."

As I followed Mrs. Dora and her jeweled wrists, I heard the television blaring loudly from the back of the house. I could clearly make out every word of a commercial about catheters being delivered right to your door. I had no idea how Mr. Harold could sleep over the booming television, much less hear a storm door slam, but I tiptoed behind her to the dining room.

"Raeley Ann," Aunt Maxine called from the shiny red mahogany dining chair as Mrs. Dora shut the French doors behind me. "So glad you could make it."

"I'm only five minutes late, Aunt Maxine." I bent down to kiss her rouge-covered cheek before I sat in the empty chair at the end of the table.

"A Southern woman is always punctual. Five minutes might as well be forty-five," she said. "However, you look lovely today. Rare to see you in a sundress instead of those shorts splattered with paint."

I tapped at the blue-and-white seersucker dress. "Well, you hinted that I should have dressed up a bit at last month's meeting."

"You look beautiful, sweet Rae. How have you been?" Mrs. Fannie asked from the chair next to Aunt Maxine.

"I'm well," I said, eyeing the table beautifully set with a fresh, colorful hibiscus bouquet from the bush at the corner of Mrs. Dora's porch. There was a silver platter topped with some fancy cheese and almond butter and crackers. Perfectly scooped balls of watermelon and cantaloupe filled a crystal bowl, and lemon icebox pie had already been cut and placed on four small floral plates. Matching saucers were filled with dark coffee. "Wow, this all looks delicious, Mrs. Dora. Look at the perfect meringue on that pie. I'm starved."

"Dora splurged on the Sociables crackers this time around. I guess Maxine's spiel about saltines a few months ago got through to her." Mrs. Fannie winked at me.

"Harold loves saltines. I assumed everyone else did too. I'm so glad Maxine set me straight before word got out that I served them to guests and Harold and I were blackballed from the country club," Mrs. Dora replied sarcastically while taking her seat at the table.

"How was Molly Margaret's first day of high school? I sent her a word message on Monday morning on her portable phone, but I don't think it went through. It somehow disappeared on my end and she never replied. Those dadgum buttons are so small I can barely see what I'm typing." Aunt Maxine shrugged.

I chuckled at her confusion regarding technology. "She's had a wonderful week. You know Molly. She makes friends easily."

"Such a precious girl. I miss hearing your mother boast on her all of the time. That child sure was the apple of her eye." Mrs. Fannie reached for a cup of coffee.

"I was so pleased when Janelle Holbrooke told me Molly Margaret signed up to keep the nursery at church next month too," Aunt Maxine said.

"While I was singing last Wednesday night, I was nearly in tears when I looked out at the congregation and saw you sitting there near your mother's spot. You're taking a step in the right direction, Rae. Your mama is proud of you. We are too." Mrs. Fannie smiled.

"I'm thankful for each one of you and for your prayers." I looked around the table. "The Lord and I are working through some things. I'm letting go of anger. I'm giving Him control. I'm studying. I'm learning. My joy is being restored little by little. My first thoughts when I wake up in the morning aren't those of grief or depression. I—I feel good."

"Glory, hallelujah," Mrs. Dora said quietly as she spread cheese on the fancy cracker.

"I wanted to call Margie yesterday. I decided to make some chowchow and couldn't remember how many tablespoons of cloves our mama used—"

"One tablespoon, Maxine." Mrs. Dora shook her head. "It's always one tablespoon."

"I know that now, Dora." Aunt Maxine rolled her eyes. "The point is, I wanted to pick up the phone and call my sister and have her tell me. So many times I just want to pick up the phone and call her. Well, I found myself sitting at the kitchen table crying over a cutting board of peppers and tomatoes. When Wilson walked in, I blamed it on the onions, but I just really missed Margie yesterday. I can't do it alone either, Raeley Ann. I had to pray a good long while for some peace for my broken heart. And, as always, the peace came."

"He's faithful," Mrs. Fannie said.

"I am, um, I'm really enjoying getting to know Kent, Mrs. Fannie. We have fun together. He's a great guy."

"That's so sweet, Rae. He's certainly fond of you. He is a fine gentleman, isn't he? He's like his daddy. Theo was a remarkable young man. Kind, courteous, humorous, handsome. Dora had a thing for him back during our school days, didn't you, Dora?"

"I never!" Mrs. Dora passed the crystal bowl of melon to me. "I've never loved anyone but Harold Kinney."

"I didn't say you loved him, Dora, but I remember a time when Theo received a large box of chocolate-covered almonds from Clooney's with the inscription, 'Your secret admirer.' Well, I would have recognized that chicken scratch anywhere. Don't deny it, Dora. You have the handwriting of a serial killer," Mrs. Fannie teased.

"That is a bald-faced lie," Mrs. Dora huffed. "I've never sent chocolates to a man in my life."

"And Theo was allergic to nuts. Almost killed him, didn't you, Dora?" Aunt Maxine chuckled and wiped cracker crumbs from the corner of her lips.

"You are both becoming more and more delusional in your old age." Mrs. Dora's bangles clinked against her plate as she stuck her fork in a melon ball. "Don't believe a word these old biddies say, Rae."

"As I was saying," Mrs. Fannie continued, "I don't know what will come of you and Kent, but I am certainly glad he has you for companionship. Now, he made it clear that I didn't tell him to ask you out, didn't he? I don't want you to think I was prying in your life, dear. I simply hinted that you were a lovely young lady, recently divorced. He took it upon himself to make the call."

"I know he did, Mrs. Fannie. I'm glad he called. He's filled some lonely nights with laughter and friendship. I'm thankful for him."

"How is Carter handling this new relationship?" Mrs. Dora asked before finishing her cup of coffee.

"He is fine with Kent as long as Molly is, and she is very fond of him. Of course it was awkward for her at first, but she really does like him as both a coach and as the guy who takes her mom out to eat," I said as they all nodded. "But, well, speaking of Carter, he, um, he's been going through a lot with his dad and his brother. He has come to me for some advice. Confided in me."

"His brother? The drunk?" Aunt Maxine asked as Mrs. Fannie passed her a plate of pie.

"Jarrett, Aunt Maxine," I said. "His father isn't doing well either. He's got dementia. He, um, Carter asked me to ride up to Tennessee with him this weekend to see his family."

Aunt Maxine's tiny fork fell to her plate. "He wants you to go with him to Tennessee? And you are going to go?"

"I think so."

"Well, Raeley Ann, why would you—"

Mrs. Dora interrupted. "Maxine, Rae is a grown woman. She is perfectly capable of making decisions without your opinion."

"He wants us to be friends, Aunt Maxine. We'll always be connected. We share a child. I don't want to spend the rest of my life hating Carter. I don't want to sneer at him at Molly's wedding or refuse to speak to him once we share grandchildren. I think it would be good for us to start over—as friends." I took a sip of coffee.

"I have to agree with Rae, Maxine. They must be cordial. For Molly," Mrs. Fannie added. "What does Kent think about this though? Taking a road trip with your ex-husband?"

"I haven't told him, Mrs. Fannie," I said as a look of disappointment crossed her face. "It's not that I'm keeping anything from Kent. I just haven't had an opportunity to explain it all yet. I'm going to tell him everything when we go to dinner this evening. There's nothing for him to worry about. Carter and I are not going to get back together. I'm not going to hurt your nephew. I promise."

Mrs. Fannie situated the large diamond on her thin, pale finger. "I believe that, Rae, and I think it's wonderful that you and Carter are finally reaching a place of restoration. That's the healthiest thing for all of you, especially Molly. Your mama would want that."

"I don't know though," Aunt Maxine chimed in. "I can just see him weaseling his way back into your life. He hurt you once, Raeley Ann. What makes you think he won't—"

"You told him just a few weeks ago to make up for his mistakes. He's really making an effort to be friends, Aunt Maxine. You've got to cut him some slack."

"Maxine cut someone slack? That's a fat laugh." Dora reached over and patted my hand.

"Are you insinuating I'm not a forgiving person, Dora?"

"I'm just saying you'd probably kick poor Wilson out of the bed for eating crackers. Whether they were saltines or Sociables, it wouldn't matter."

Aunt Maxine glared at her. "We've got a lot to cover today. Two deaths, two marriages, and three newborns. Shall we get started?"

"Yes, ma'am." Mrs. Dora and I exchanged grins.

Once sympathy and congratulations cards had been signed by everyone and the ladies had argued over family trees, laughed over a legendary ice cream fight at the diner back in their school days, and prayed a lengthy prayer, we helped Mrs. Dora clear the dining table before we were quietly ushered out the front door of the country home. I guided both Aunt Maxine and Mrs. Fannie down the wobbly wooden steps and onto the gravel walkway where they both complained a rock was going to grab their kitten heels and send them hurtling across the shady lawn.

"Maybe Harold should skip a nap one day and asphalt this walkway," Aunt Maxine muttered as she sat in her old Lincoln with a patina-covered hood. She cranked up the old car and blew the horn at us before backing down the shady drive.

"Lord have mercy, that horn surely woke up Harold." Mrs. Fannie shook her head as I laughed.

"Why do they pester one another so much?"

"Maxine and Dora?" she asked as we approached her shiny Cadillac parked beneath a silver maple. "Oh, they've always been that way. I'm a few years older than them, you know, but we managed to run in the same circle every so often when we were younger. Those two bickered back and forth at the movie theater, the diner, wherever they were. That ice cream fight we laughed about today? Dora dumped two scoops of butter pecan on Maxine's head." She laughed. "Margie was the one who intervened in their squabbling. I've always just sat back and laughed at them. I tell you, though, it takes a good, solid friendship to be able to hurl insults back and forth like that one day and then pray with each other the next. Those two love each other. Don't let them fool you."

I nodded. "Well, it sure was good to see you, Mrs. Fannie."

"Rae, wait just a minute. I've got something for you."
She opened the heavy door of the pearl-colored car, sat in the
driver's seat, and rummaged around in the console for a few
moments. Finally, she handed me a pink envelope.

"Mama's stationery. And that's your name in her handwriting." I brushed my thumb over the letter and looked
down at Mrs. Fannie.

"Sight better than Dora's penmanship, isn't it?" She
smiled. "Your mama gave me that a few weeks before she
passed on. I think you ought to take a look at it."

"I don't want to invade your and Mother's privacy. She
wrote this to you, Mrs. Fannie. You should—"

"Take a look at it," she repeated.

"Yes, ma'am," I agreed. "She left letters for me too. I've
been finding them around the house."

"What a great comfort that must be, my dear. Like she's
still right there with you."

"Yes."

"But you know she is, Raeley Ann." Mrs. Fannie pointed
her finger with the large diamond at the chest of my blue-
and-white seersucker dress. "She's right there in your heart,
darling. Always. Can't nothing separate you from your
mama's love. Not even death."

I reached into Mrs. Fannie's plush Cadillac and wrapped
my arms around her thin body. "I love you, Mrs. Fannie.
Thank you for this."

I knew I couldn't wait to get all the way home to read the
letter. Once I turned out of Mrs. Dora's driveway, I pulled

over on the side of the country road surrounded by green open fields and grazing cattle. The sun beamed down and the air conditioner roared to life as I carefully peeled open the envelope and read my mother's words.

Fannie,

You knew my James and his family long before you ever knew me. (I believe my mother-in-law, Mrs. Bonnie, and you were often in competition for Volunteer of the Year Award, weren't you? She may have sold more raffle tickets, baked more pies, and raised more money for the veterans than you ever did, but I don't doubt for a second you're going to have one of the finest mansions on those streets of gold.) And although my mother-in-law wasn't your favorite person, you welcomed me with open arms the first time I visited First Baptist. You invited me to your Sunday school class, taught me the Word of God, and prayed with me through life's ups and downs. You gladly babysat Jamie and Rae, brought us meals when we were sick, and praised James's barbecue nearly as much as I did.

I will never forget that April when my mother died and I was consumed with depression, hidden away in my dark room, sobbing. James called you late one evening. I overheard him on the phone. He said something like, "Fannie, you've got to come talk to her. Pray over her. She needs you." And you were there within ten minutes. That may have been the first time I ever saw you without a full face of makeup (and wearing that net sleeping cap! Lord, I will never forget that!) and you knelt next to my bed, held me, and prayed peace over me.

Before you left late that night, you made me promise to come to church the following Sunday, whether I felt like it or not. And I did. I remember not even caring that Jamie's hair wasn't properly combed or that Rae wore blue jeans. I didn't care about anything but simply getting through that service and getting back home to my dark bedroom where I could cry over my mother for the rest of the day.

And then you stood before the church and sang, Fannie Culpepper. Our eyes caught as your angelic voice rang out "My Anchor Holds."

"Tho' the angry surges roll on my tempest-driven soul, I am peaceful, for I know, wildly though the winds may blow, I've an anchor safe and sure, that can evermore endure."

As you sang each stanza, I was reminded of something I'd always known but had forgotten in my sadness. I was reminded of the anchor and the loving God who knew my heartache intimately and wept right along with me, yet He was faithful and strong enough to hold me. I remembered I could have peace and joy again because I had Him.

Fannie, Jamie is a mama's boy. He's going to hurt when I'm gone, but I have incredible peace in knowing his faith is strong. Thank the Lord he's also got a loving, wise wife by his side who will remind him where his help comes from when he feels he can't endure the loss. I worry more about Rae, especially now that Carter is gone and her faith is lukewarm. I have asked God to allow the heartache she'll endure when I pass to bring her back to the anchor and remind her of His unwavering love. But if you don't mind, will you remind her of that as well? Remind her the anchor holds.

You've been a good and faithful friend to me for so many years, Fannie, and I thank God He placed you in my life. Iron sharpens iron. And you, my precious friend, have sharpened me more times than I can count. (And I'd rather spend eternity next to your mansion instead of Mrs. Bonnie's. But don't tell her I said that when we all meet again.)

Love,
Margie

That evening Molly and I met Kent at Bea's for supper. As Molly and I approached the dark wooden door of the red cypress building, Mr. Harold walked out with a to-go order.

"Well, Mr. Harold, were you able to get a good nap with all of us yapping at your dining table this afternoon?"

"I could nap through an F5 tornado, but not through the blaring horn of Maxine's Lincoln," he said as the scent of the hushpuppies in the plastic sack he was holding surrounded us. "She does that on purpose, you know. She blows that doggone horn every time she comes over and I'm asleep."

Kent was already seated at a booth near the back of the restaurant and munching on an appetizer of Bea's famous buffalo shrimp dip. He stood when he saw us walking toward him.

"Hey, ladies. I hope you don't mind that I ordered an appetizer while I waited. I know you like the dip, too, Rae. Your drinks are on the way. Sweet tea and Dr Pepper, right?" he asked as we slid into the booth across from him and he sat back down.

"Always." I smiled as I picked up the menu.

"Good practice today, Molly." He topped another cracker with the dip.

"I don't know why my shot was off today." Molly shrugged.

"Keep working on setting your feet to the eleven o'clock position. Elbow down."

"I keep wanting to turn my elbow out. I don't know where in the world that came from. I've never had that problem." Molly reached for a cracker. "Ella was a beast on defense today too. I think she stole the ball from me three times."

"Ella is really improving. Now, the best defense we'll see this year is Ryland. They have a senior who is going to play college ball. Her footwork is great. It's hard to get past her."

I tuned out their basketball rhetoric and scanned the

menu. I squinted my eyes to read because the anchor-shaped chandelier dangling above our table had something absurd like 10-watt bulbs that may as well have not even been on. I pulled my tortoiseshell readers from my purse next to me in the booth.

". . . and I've just been off the last couple of days," Molly finished.

"Don't stress too much. We'll work on defense this weekend," Kent assured her.

I knew it was time to talk about the Tennessee trip with Carter.

"About that, Kent," I said as I put on my glasses. "Carter's dad is sick and he's asked Molly and me to go with him to Tennessee this weekend to visit him. We're leaving Saturday morning and won't be back until late that evening."

"Oh." A slight frown creased his forehead. "Okay. That's fine."

"Mom, I want to see Granddad, really I do, but I've been thinking a lot about this since you told me we were going out of town. I don't want to miss practice this weekend. My shot is struggling. We always do a full scrimmage on Saturday. I need to scrimmage. I need to be there," Molly said as the young waitress with a long blond ponytail placed our drinks on the table. She reminded me of Autumn. I glanced at Kent to make sure she hadn't caught his eye. I guessed I'd always be intimidated and somewhat afraid of young blond waitresses.

"Are y'all ready to order or do you need a few minutes?" she asked in a slow, Southern drawl.

I held up my finger to signal we needed more time as she nodded politely and walked away.

"No, Molly, really, it's okay. You should go with your parents," Kent urged her. I wasn't sure, but I had a feeling his persistence might have been fueled a tad by jealousy and worry that I still had feelings for my ex-husband.

"Can't just you and Dad go?" Molly turned to me in the booth. "Aunt Maxine could take me to practice on Saturday, or I could catch a ride with someone on the team. I really don't want to miss. I shouldn't miss."

I glanced across the table at Kent, who was quickly dipping crackers and pretending not to be paying attention to our conversation.

"I think you need to come with your dad and me, Molly. You haven't seen your grandfather since Christmas. He's not well. Who knows when you may see him again?"

"Dad said he's going back to Tullahoma in a couple of weeks. I could talk him into going on a Friday after practice and be back before Saturday's practice. We start games in a few weeks. I need to be at practice as much as I can. Tell her, Coach Richardson," she pleaded with him.

He quit dipping and said, "Molly, if you miss practice, you won't be penalized. This is considered a family issue. It's not like you're missing to hang out with friends. This would be an excused absence."

"Coach Richardson, I *want* to be there. Mom, please. I'll go with Dad in a few weeks to see Grandad."

"I guess we could both go with him on a Friday afternoon

in a couple of weeks. We don't have to go this weekend," I conceded.

"Thank you," she said, relieved.

Kent looked pleased and stopped shoving crackers in his mouth. He evidently felt more comfortable at the thought of Molly being with us, and he was more than willing to allow her to skip practice for that very reason. Honestly, I was kind of nervous at the idea of taking a road trip with Carter alone too.

We didn't talk about the trip or Carter again for the rest of the evening. Kent and I shared a crab cake platter, and when Molly excused herself to go to the restroom, we both leaned over the table for a quick kiss beneath the dim anchor chandelier that hit me in the head as I slid back into my side of the booth.

Once I was in my comfortable, cool bed that evening, slathered in multiple creams for my eyes, face, and hands, I read my devotional about trusting in God, rolled Patsy off of my hot, smothered feet, and dialed Carter's number.

"Carter, we can't go with you this weekend. I'm sorry. Molly has basketball practice and she says she can't miss it. She keeps dropping her elbow or something."

"She dropped her elbow?" he asked over his television playing softly in the background. I heard the laughter of a live studio audience. I knew he was probably in bed, too, in that familiar tattered Vanderbilt T-shirt and faded plaid pajama pants. "She can't miss practice to see her grandfather? Kent won't let her?"

"No, Kent is fine with it. He urged her to go. She just doesn't want to miss practice. You're planning on going up again in a few weeks, right? Maybe we could both tag along with you then?" I said as Patsy began to pant like an obese lion on top of the white down comforter.

"But, Rae." He sighed. "I already told my dad you are coming this weekend. I'm not sure if he'll remember, but if he does, he'll be heartbroken when you don't show up. He was so excited. Aunt Paulette told me a few days ago any kind of change really discourages and angers him. What if he actually remembers you are coming and then you don't show? He's not himself. I don't know what he would do. This is really important to me. And to him."

I sighed. "I guess I can make Molly come." I cradled the phone against my shoulder and picked my nails.

"Just let Molly stay in Whitten and go to practice." He paused. "I really don't want her to see Jarrett in the shape he's in anyway, and I would like for you and me to visit with him while we're there. Molly can go with me in a couple of weeks to see Dad, but you and I can go on Saturday. We'll leave early in the morning, and I'll have you home that night in time to catch that eleven o'clock rerun of *Fixing Up Houses*."

"*Fixer Upper*." I chuckled.

"Please, Rae?"

I never could tell him no.

CHAPTER 14

On Friday morning I gulped half my coffee and then nervously dialed Kent's number to tell him the trip was back on . . . and only Carter and I would be making the drive. I didn't know why I was so worried about telling him. If there was a future for our relationship, Kent would have to accept that Carter and I would always be in communication, always have some kind of connection because we shared a child. Maybe one day we'd be like Dale and Donna Jameson and their new spouses and share a booth at Bea's. Kent and Carter would rib each other with playful insults like Aunt Maxine and Dora do, and I would jovially chat with Carter's future wife about shiplap and chalk paint and Molly's basketball games and . . . No, the thought of Carter having a future wife made me uneasy. I could not mentally go there.

Kent wasn't thrilled with my decision to take the little voyage with Carter, and he admitted it made him nervous. He was, indeed, worried Carter and I would rekindle some old flame.

"I know our relationship is new, Rae, and it's not even official or anything. It's not like I've even asked you to be my girlfriend. Be my girlfriend? What am I, fifteen?" We both giggled. "I just really care about you. I like the possibility of where this could go. I'm a little nervous about losing you to Carter. Losing what we have."

"Kent, that's sweet and I completely understand. I like the idea of where this relationship could go too. As for Carter and me, you have nothing to worry about," I assured him. Although I wasn't really sure of that last sentence either.

I didn't know how I felt about Carter. I was on board with being friends for Molly's sake. I often prayed to truly forgive him the way the Bible instructed me to do. I wanted us to start over with a clean slate, but I was nervous because I had so easily fallen in love with Carter when we were teenagers. I knew it was possible to develop those feelings again. I didn't know if I could ever be just his friend.

On Saturday morning I got out of my warm, cozy bed before the sun was fully over the magnolia tree on the east side of the house. Patsy didn't even budge as I groaned and rolled out from under the covers and put my feet onto the carpet. I was so jealous of her snoozing soundly.

When Carter rapped on the door an hour later, I still wasn't fully awake even though I'd downed two cups of black coffee. He left me in the quiet kitchen to pour the rest of the pot into a travel mug while he went back to Molly's room to kiss her cheek and tell her to go back to sleep.

"She's got a ride to practice? She'll be okay while we're gone?" he asked when he stepped into the kitchen.

"Her teammate's mom is taking her to practice, and

Aunt Maxine is going to pick her up and take her back to her house to can some vegetables and hang out." I yawned like a grizzly fresh out of hibernation.

"Still not a morning person, I see." He grinned and situated his white ballcap over his thick, dark hair.

"Don't start with me, Carter Sutton. Just because you actually enjoy getting up to sit in a deer stand at five in the morning doesn't mean everyone else likes to roll out of bed at the butt crack of dawn."

As I climbed into Carter's tall truck, the August humidity was already preposterously high, and I knew the baby hairs around my face were going to frizz and leave me looking like Albert Einstein with a ponytail. I'd fidgeted with my hair multiple times before we'd even turned out of my subdivision and onto the highway that would take us to Tullahoma. And then, as I sat still in the passenger seat, I began to feel awkward. All of this felt awkward. I'd known this man since I was eighteen years old, and I didn't know what to say to him. Or what to do with my hands now that I was sure I'd made my hair look worse instead of better. I just knew the silence was deafening. I searched my mind for conversation. I felt the need to speak. To fidget. To bite my nails. To ask him to stop at the Dollar General so I could buy an iron and straighten my hair. To do something.

And then he said, "We can still share comfortable silence, can't we?"

I never realized the silence Carter and I had shared for all those years was comfortable, because I didn't know otherwise. I never knew uncomfortable silence with him—not even on our first date at the Burger King when he chewed like a horse. We immediately clicked. He never made me nervous. But now I was uncomfortable, and I didn't know what that meant.

He pulled a pack of peanut M&M's from the console and handed the yellow bag to me. They'd always been my favorite snack on road trips. I had consumed thousands of the things on our vacations to the Gulf Coast.

"Thanks," I said and tore open the small bag. "Do you still like a plug of that disgusting chaw on the road?"

"Sure do." He tapped on the console. "I've got a can of wintergreen right in there."

"Oh, Carter. I've never understood why you do that." I grimaced.

"You know I always dip when I'm on the road, and never unless I'm in the truck for more than thirty minutes. I've been dipping a lot since you've moved to Whitten, I guess."

"So gross," I said and chewed my chocolate candy. "You do remember the time Molly thought it was actually Coke in that Coke bottle and took a swig of tobacco and spit? The poor child threw up for ten minutes. I was so angry with you."

"Bless her heart." He laughed heartily. "We can laugh about that now, though, can't we?" He glanced at me.

"I'll never laugh when it comes to our eight-year-old ingesting nicotine and vomiting for ten straight minutes." I smirked. "I had the poison hotline on the phone!"

"She was fine, though, wasn't she? What about the time you backed out of the garage while the door was still down? I can laugh about that now. Can't you laugh about the spit bottle?" He reached over and playfully poked me in the arm.

"Never," I said dryly and ate another M&M.

"Rae, I really appreciate you making this trip with me, especially after all I've put you through," he said.

"Maybe I can laugh about that someday." I stared out the window.

The rest of the hour-and-a-half trip didn't seem so awkward, thank the Lord. We discussed Molly's new friends and a potential love interest (a freshman in her American History class) I'd heard her mention a couple of times since she'd started school. I asked him about our old gang back in Huntsville and wasn't surprised to learn Danielle had a breast reduction and Dillon joined a hair club to remedy his own reduction. We reminisced about Danielle and Dillon's wedding and the bird that pooped on the cake at the outdoor venue.

I enjoyed our conversation. I enjoyed hearing his hoarse laugh and watching the way he took off his hat to scratch his head and then put it back on. I enjoyed his music playlist— the same songs we'd been listening to for decades. Everything began to feel familiar. As if I was still his wife sitting in the passenger seat. As if he'd never fallen out of love with me.

"Man, Dad's house is looking rough," Carter said as we turned onto Lake Cove and his childhood home at the end of the cul-de-sac came into full view. "Look at the roof."

"When was the last time you were here?" I eyed the thirty-year-old vinyl and pink brick two-story ranch-style in front of us.

"Too long. April," he said as he slowly pulled in to the crumbling driveway next to Aunt Paulette's Maxima. "All the rain in the spring really did a number on that roof. And look at the mildew on the vinyl. That gutter is shot. Weeds are growing the driveway. I've got to get somebody here to fix this place up. I sure wish Jarrett was capable of doing it. I mean, he doesn't have anything else going on besides drinking all day and then passing out on a couch."

I recognized the anger in his voice. I knew his annoyance came from worry. It always had. He was concerned about his dad, his dad's home, his brother, and he was mad about all of it too.

We stepped onto the brick porch steps with blades of grass growing through the crumbling mortar and Carter's aunt Paulette pushed through the storm door that wasn't completely latched and reached out to hug Carter.

"I'm so glad you're here, son. So glad you're here," she said as she patted his back.

"Me, too, Aunt Paulette," he responded. "There's no excuse for why I haven't been here sooner."

"Never mind that," she said. "Rae, you're still pretty as ever." She reached out and pulled me into her arms, too, and the three of us stood there in a huddle for a few seconds.

Aunt Paulette was Mr. Henry's younger, and only, sister. She was a kind, gentle, soft-spoken woman, but her facial features reminded me of Miss Gulch from *The Wizard of Oz*. She was tall and thin with long dark hair pinned atop her head and always wore lengthy dresses or skirts and minimal makeup due to her Pentecostal faith. But I'd never seen her ride a bicycle while holding a cairn terrier hostage in a picnic basket.

"He's having a good day." She grabbed Carter's hands. "He remembered you are coming. He hasn't had any angry outbursts or forgotten who I am."

"That's a relief," Carter said. "I'm so thankful you're here with him."

Aunt Paulette gave him a small smile. "Now, if he begins to ramble, starts talking nonsense, the best thing to do is just go along with it. You won't change his mind. And if you try, he'll just get frustrated and mad. I spent half the day yesterday pretending I was the Wicked Witch of the West. He swore I had flying monkeys hidden in the kitchen cabinets." She stifled a chuckle.

Carter and I exchanged glances and held back our own laughter. I'd mentioned to him more than once who I thought Aunt Paulette resembled.

Aunt Paulette turned, opened the door wider for us to enter, and merrily called, "Brother, you've got company!"

We stepped onto the maroon rug I'd help Mr. Henry pick

out nearly a decade earlier when he told me the place needed a "woman's touch" and I was happy to oblige. Back then, I was obsessed with a burgundy and dark green color scheme. The room looked exactly the same as it did when I'd finished painting the wine walls and tossed hunter-green accent pillows on the chocolate-brown leather sofa and recliner that I had also picked out at Hammill's Furniture. I now grimaced at the room and how dim and outdated it was. I had the overwhelming desire to paint everything greige and shiplap a wall.

Mr. Henry never stood to his moccasin house shoes but turned completely around in the bulky caramel-colored recliner to see us walking toward him.

"Carter! And Rae! Get over here, you two."

"Dad, it's great to see you." Carter leaned down to hug his father. "It's been too long."

"I'll say. What? Five years?" Mr. Henry asked. His bright white mustache, a tad unkempt, was hanging over his thin upper lip.

Carter had seen his father in the spring, but he played along. "At least."

"And, Rae, come here and squeeze my neck, you sweet thing." I reached down to hold him and felt his weak hands pat my back. "Now, both of you, sit down. Sit down." He motioned to the long brown sofa across from him. "Paulette, bring us some sweet tea, will you?"

She nodded and disappeared through louvered doors to the kitchen that I assumed was still painted maroon with a wallpaper border of French chefs holding trays of red wine and bread loaves.

"How was your flight?" he asked, a pleasant expression on his face.

"Uh." Carter glanced to me beside him on the leather couch. "Uh, it was great, Dad."

I sensed the anxiety in Carter's voice. He was beginning to realize just how significantly his father's cognitive health had declined since April.

"And Jarrett? Did he come with you?" Mr. Henry brushed his mustache with his fingertips.

"No." Carter rubbed his hands together. "No, Dad, Jarrett wasn't able to come."

"Too busy with work, I guess? Big-shot lawyer." He grinned as Aunt Paulette entered the living room and handed him a yellow Tupperware cup of tea from a matching serving tray.

"Yep," Carter said as we both took our cups.

"And Molly?" Aunt Paulette said as she placed the server on top of the Jacobean-stained entertainment center (that I'd also picked out) and then sat next to us on the couch.

"She's doing great," I said. "She's a freshman this year. Just started school last week. She made the basketball team and is really adjusting well to Whitten."

"Oh, that's right. You moved to your mother's home, didn't you, Rae? I was so sorry to hear about her passing. I wish I could have come to the funeral, but"—Aunt Paulette nodded toward Mr. Henry—"you know."

"I received the lovely arrangement and card you sent, Aunt Paulette. Thank you for remembering us."

"I'm sure your aunt Maxine is lost without her sister, isn't she? I've been meaning to send her a note, but I just haven't gotten around to it. I always—"

"Who died?" Mr. Henry interrupted.

"My mother passed away," I answered.

"Was she from here?" he shouted over the cup of tea. "Paulette, was it someone we knew?"

"No, Henry, she wasn't from Tullahoma. Margie lived in Alabama," she answered while reaching over to softly pat my hand resting in my lap.

"Margie? Was her father in the timber business? Did they live close to Murfreesboro?" he asked.

"Maybe so, Henry," Aunt Paulette pacified him. "Maybe so."

Mr. Henry knew both my parents well. He and Daddy went on a hunting trip not long after Carter and I began dating. They went to Louisiana to catch redfish. They shared a cigar outside of the hospital the day Molly was born. And Mr. Henry was fond of my mother too. They talked on the phone about us kids and took turns taking care of Molly every few weeks. Mr. Henry, Daddy, and Mama *all* shared a cigar in relief once Carter's mother left our wedding.

On top of the dark wooden cabinet that housed a rear-projection television with built-in VHS/DVD combo were framed photos—one of Molly's elementary school portraits; one of Jarrett's children; another of my mother, my father,

Mr. Henry, Carter, and I standing on the church steps on our wedding day; and one of Jarrett and his first wife, Krista, with the Appalachian Mountains as a backdrop.

"Rae was saying Molly is doing well, brother. She's a freshman this year," Aunt Paulette said.

"She's all grown up, isn't she? Why didn't she come with you today? I haven't seen my granddaughter in so long. I bet she's grown a foot, hasn't she?" Mr. Henry inquired, sounding clear-minded.

"She had basketball practice today. She's coming back with me to see you in a couple of weeks though," Carter assured him.

"Who is she playing basketball for? Alabama or Tennessee? Don't tell me she's a part of the Crimson Tide." And just like that, we'd lost him again.

Mr. Henry had once been a strong, broad-shouldered man with thick, dark hair and a Tom Selleck-ish mustache. He grew up a poor farm boy but got a job right out of high school working as a teller at First State Bank in Tullahoma. He climbed the banking ladder until he was CEO and retired a wealthy and highly respected man. He was intelligent. He could do long division in his head and rattle off multiplication answers in a matter of seconds. He was an above-average golfer who often boasted that he consistently shot under par. He was a devoted outdoorsman (which was evident by all the mounted deer heads and ducks that hung on the living room wall before I convinced him to convert the sunken den on the back of the house to a lodge and display them there).

Mr. Henry was so much more than the frail man sitting feebly in that recliner and staring into space with an unkempt mustache and trembling cup of tea.

"How are your children and grandchildren, Aunt Paulette?" I changed the subject.

"Oh, dear. Well, let's see. Hayley is a dental hygienist in Nashville and still hasn't gotten married, but that's the Lord's will, I guess. Kimberly and Jack are in Houston, and their four children are doing fine. Their oldest daughter will graduate high school this year. Bradley and Annalee are working real estate in Jacksonville, and their oldest will start medical school next fall."

"Oh, wow. Sounds like they are all doing well. It's been so long since I've seen any of them," I said.

"I know, dear," Aunt Paulette said. "I sure miss the big holidays we used to have right here in this house. Seems everyone is scattered nowadays."

"Who went to medical school?" Mr. Henry asked.

"Bradley's son, Joshua!" Aunt Paulette shouted with a hint of annoyance. I had a feeling she had answered that question more than once.

"What's that got to do with anything?"

"Nothing, brother. Rae was just asking about my children and grandchildren. I was telling her." She sighed.

"Well, speaking of Rae, let me just say something right now." He looked right at me. "My son may love you very much, but you can't compare to his first wife."

"Dad." Carter chuckled. "Rae *is* my first wife."

"I know that," Mr. Henry answered matter-of-factly as he set the cup of tea on the TV tray next to the recliner. "You may think you love this one, son, but Rae was it for you."

"He doesn't remember you now, dear. Just play along," Aunt Paulette whispered to me.

"But, Dad, this is—"

"Carter," Aunt Paulette interrupted him. "I think your father is correct. You won't ever love another like Rae."

Carter nodded to indicate to Paulette that he understood the game.

Mr. Henry reclined the chair and sank his back into it comfortably. "Carter went down to some party in Huntsville with Bradley and some friends from Vanderbilt and when he got back home, he told me he'd met a girl. I knew by the sound of his voice—I knew right then he was head over heels in love. Because, dear"—he looked at me again—"the ladies sure loved my boy. He wasn't a jock like his brother, but he was a smart, good-looking kid. Old William Duffey's daughter was smitten with him in high school, and she was a real looker too."

"Dad, stop." Carter blushed.

"But he never talked about any of those school flames the way he talked about Raeley Ann Reeves. He said he knew he was in love with her the moment he saw her. And I said, 'Well, by golly, son, you've been hit by the thunderbolt!' I was hit by the thunderbolt once—with my Jackie. I fell in love with her real fast. Jackie was a beautiful woman. And her laugh! Her laugh filled up a room. I thought my love would make her quit drinking and drugging and let go of all her hang-ups, but it wasn't enough. Nothing I ever did for her was enough. I don't know where Jackie is now . . ." His voice trailed off.

I glanced over at Carter and his eyes were glassy. Tears hadn't streamed down his cheeks, but they threatened to do so.

"But, you know, you only get hit by that thunderbolt once, son. This girl you've got with you today may be pretty and she may be nice, but Rae was it for you. I hope you aren't offended that I said that, ma'am."

I quickly wiped my eyes and shook my head. "No, sir."

"Well then." Mr. Henry looked at us both and gave a big smile. "I sure am glad you stopped by. I've got a tee time with Judge Duffey soon, though, so you better run along. You don't want to miss your flight."

"So soon?" Carter asked. "I thought we'd stay a while. Catch up."

"No, son, I'm sorry." He stubbornly shook his head. "I would love to chat some more, but I can't be late for my game. Judge Duffey would never speak to me again if I am late."

"Sure, Dad," Carter said as we all stood from the sticky leather.

"I'm glad I got to see you, Mr. Henry." I smiled at him as I passed his chair.

"I'm always glad to see a pretty lady. And don't be angry about what I said, now. You kids be careful getting home." He reached for the cup of tea on the TV tray.

Carter stopped at his dad's chair, tapped him on the shoulder, and said, "I've got to ask you something before I go, Dad."

"Yes, son? What is it?"

"What's 17 times 24?"

"That would be . . . 408."

Carter smiled. "Sounds right to me."

As Carter and I stepped onto the front porch, Aunt Paulette followed us and quietly closed the storm door behind her.

"He still knows his figures," she chortled.

"I don't understand." Carter pulled off his hat and scratched his head. "He knows Rae, and then he doesn't. He knows Molly but thinks she's in college. He remembers every detail of the weekend I met Rae, but he thinks he has a tee time with a friend who's been dead fifteen years. He can still do math in his head. I just—"

"It's a tricky disease, Carter. In a few minutes I will drive him to the golf course and we'll sit in the parking lot for a little while. Then I'll ask if he had a good game, and he'll tell me all about shooting under par and Judge Duffey's foul language, and we'll come home."

Carter put his hands on his hips and stared at the concrete porch while Aunt Paulette continued. "He can still tell me the restaurant our father took us to in Savannah when we were children. He remembers our mother's recipes. He remembers things my Sammy, who has been dead nearly thirty years, said to him one Saturday night on the telephone. But then he can look right at me and ask me who I am and why I'm in his house. It's a tricky disease."

"And it's heartbreaking," I added.

"I will, um, arrange to have someone get this place cleaned up, Aunt Paulette. The roof needs replacing, and I see so many other things that need to be done. I'm sorry I haven't taken care of everything sooner. I'll be in touch, okay? And Molly and I will be back in a couple of weeks."

"Sure, son. I'm so glad you both came. Are you going to see Jarrett while you're in town?" She took Carter's hand.

"Yes, ma'am."

"I know your father would love to see him. He asks about him often. Try to talk some sense into him, okay? You, too, Rae."

"I'll try," I said.

"Thank you for taking care of Dad, Aunt Paulette. I am so grateful for you. If it becomes too much, I can always bring him to Huntsville. There's an excellent Alzheimer's care—"

"We made a pact years ago, Carter. No nursing homes. I'll be right here with him as long the good Lord allows. Don't worry about a thing. He's my big brother." She gave his hand a good squeeze before letting it go and walking back inside the house.

When Carter and I got inside the truck and the air conditioner filled the hot, stagnant cab with warm air, he leaned his head against the steering wheel. I heard him sniffle. I'd only seen Carter cry a handful of times. Large, salty tears streamed down his tan face, onto the steering wheel, and eventually dripped to the knees of his jeans. I reached my hand over and rubbed his back.

"I don't know who that man is, Rae. That confused man isn't my father," he choked out.

"I know" was all I could muster. "I know, Carter. I'm sorry."

"My dad is slipping away."

CHAPTER 15

The short drive to the apartment where Jarrett was staying was silent. I knew Carter's mind was filled with thoughts of his father. He was certainly mourning Mr. Henry's disease and coming to terms with how his mind had deteriorated. I told him maybe we should save the trip to see Jarrett for another time because it had already been an emotional day, but he refused.

The apartment complex was not the finest in Tullahoma. Multiple broken-down cars on three wheels or flat tires sat in the parking lot. Trash was stuck in the holly bushes that lined the property and cigarette butts littered the asphalt. It certainly wasn't the type of place you'd think a brilliant former law student would live.

"He texted me the address. Do you see 21B?" Carter navigated slowly through the parking lot.

"Here's 20," I said. "And there's 21."

Carter pulled in to a space next to a rusted green fishing boat filled with beer cans. "Nice boat," he said. "Fishing for Coors instead of catfish, I see."

We exited the truck and walked up the concrete and

metal steps to the top floor. Carter tapped on the navy-blue door of apartment 21B.

A few moments passed and then Jarrett stood before us. I'd never seen him look so disheveled and thin. His beard was unruly and wiry and peppered with gray strands. His brown hair was long and tucked behind his ears. The beige T-shirt he was wearing was stretched out and his jeans were tattered. I really wouldn't have known it was him until he opened his mouth and revealed his familiar Southern drawl.

When I thought of Jarrett Sutton, I thought of him standing in a courtroom in suspenders and wooing a jury with his thick, Southern, gentlemanly enunciation. Oh, he would have gone places. He would have done great things. He would've been the inspiration for a John Grisham novel.

"Well, I'll be," he slurred. "You brought the beautiful Mrs. Raeley Ann Sutton. Or is it Reeves again? I honestly cannot remember."

"Jarrett, you look . . ." Carter paused. "You look like you just listened to a Jefferson Airplane album."

"Oh, I get it." He laughed slowly. "I look like a hippie. Haight-Ashbury stuff, yeah? You always have been a witty guy, haven't you, little brother? Always got jokes. Well, come in. Come in. Welcome to my lovely abode."

"*Your* abode?" a gruff voice called from the kitchen directly beside the living room.

"You're right, Matt, you're right. I'm merely your guest.

Your mother pays the rent, not mine." Jarrett laughed at his scruffy roommate in a Pink Floyd T-shirt and sweatpants.

"Hey, Carter," Matt called from the kitchen as we entered the messy apartment that reeked of cigarette smoke and beer and old pizza.

"Hey, Matt." Carter waved to him. "Been a long time."

"Yeah," he said as he threw a sandwich on a paper plate and disappeared to the bedroom at the back of the apartment.

"You'd think he would have stuck around to catch up, but you know Matt has always been rude," Jarrett said as he cleaned a pile of clothes off the stained plaid couch and motioned for us to sit down. He fell into the matching loveseat next to us. "So, are you two married again or what?"

"No." I shook my head.

"Carter, you fool. You didn't know what a good thing you had, did you?" He reached over the cluttered coffee table between us to grab his pack of cigarettes. "I still can't believe it, Rae. I thought he was supposed to be the level-headed one."

"We just went to see Dad." Carter changed the subject and leaned into the uncomfortable couch as Jarrett lit a menthol and the small room filled with smoke.

"Oh yeah? How's the old man doing?" Jarrett placed the glass ashtray beside him on the loveseat.

"He's not well, Jarrett. You need to see him. How long has it been?"

"Couple months." He shrugged. "I called and talked to Aunt Paulette not long ago. She said everything was cool."

"Well, it's not," Carter said, frustrated. "It's not cool. He's not himself. He doesn't know where he is or what he's doing half the time. He didn't even recognize Rae the last few minutes we were there. He said he was going to play golf with Judge. He's not well."

"What do you want me to do about it, Carter?" Jarrett huffed and tucked his greasy hair behind his ears.

"I want you to go see him. Go help Aunt Paulette. Clean the place up. Pressure-wash the house, mow the yard, do something! You live ten minutes from him, Jarrett."

"You've always been the good son, haven't you? Smart, responsible Carter Sutton." Jarrett took another drag. "Well, aside from leaving your wife."

"Oh, Jarrett, don't start with that good-son, bad-son crap." Carter threw his hands in the air. "This isn't a competition. He's our dad. You live in the same town as him. Why can't you do something for him? What other pressing engagements do you have? Are you working? Taking care of your kids? Helping Mel?"

Jarrett casually took a long drag from the cigarette and remained silent.

"How much have you had to drink today, Jarrett?" I quietly interjected, infuriated at his nonchalant attitude.

"Oh, Raeley, not you too?" He flicked the cigarette and shook his head.

"You know drinking has always been the problem," I said.

"I do know that, all right? I'm past the denial stage.

I know drinking is the issue. I can't quit. Rehab doesn't help. I know because I've been twice. Counseling doesn't help. Talking through all my abandonment issues because dear Mommy left doesn't help. Not seeing my kids doesn't help. Melanie cussing me out doesn't help. Nothing helps, okay?" he demanded. "I am most content, most carefree, when I wake up to a vodka and orange juice and go to bed with whiskey and Coke. That's just who I am. That's who I always will be."

"Jarrett, you don't have to be that person." I leaned forward. "You have choices—"

"I'm okay being this person, Rae. I know the consequences of my actions, and I no longer feel guilty about it. Is this the only reason you came to see your big brother, Carter? To throw a guilt trip on him? Because it won't work."

"No, Jarrett." Carter took off his hat again and scratched his thick, dark hair. "No one is here to throw a guilt trip on you."

"Well, since Rae brought up drinking, I think I'll have a beer. Anyone else?" Jarrett stood from the loveseat and walked to the refrigerator.

"How are Melanie and the kids?" I asked as he opened the door and retrieved a silver can.

"They're fine. Better without me, actually." He returned to the loveseat. "They are living at her parents' house. They've got a pool and ten acres. The kids feed the chickens. They ride the horses. Melanie has built-in babysitters she can rely on. She doesn't have to worry about coming home from work to Bailey sitting in the floor eating cold SpaghettiOs out of the can because Daddy was too 'dizzy' to work the microwave and passed out on the couch."

"You feel guilty about that, Jarrett? Sounds like it," I said.

"Nah, not anymore. I'm just telling you what Melanie has said to me repeatedly for the last eight years. And besides, what would Matt do without my company? I'm his Xbox partner. We're taking down some kids on *Call of Duty* later tonight. He'd never get past the Hardened level without me."

"You know," I hesitated, "when my mother died—"

"And I sure was sorry to hear that, Rae. Your mom was cool. She was always really nice to me." He nursed the beer.

"When she died, I was a wreck. I mean, I still am. It's only been two, almost three, months. But I've recently discovered how the Lord can mend our hurts and take our burdens—"

"Stop right there, Tammy Faye Bakker. I don't need to be preached to. I've sought a higher power. That's what half those twelve steps are about, aren't they? Step two says a power greater than myself can restore me to sanity. I've been told to turn my life over to a higher power. Tried it, sister. Didn't work." He sipped from the beer can again while the cigarette smoldered in his fingers.

"Higher power," I huffed. "Say God's name. Think of Him personally, Jarret. Not some orb, some higher power, floating in the sky."

"Still won't work." He shook his head.

"There's nothing we can do here, Rae," Carter mumbled.

"That's the most sensible thing you've said, little brother. There really is nothing you can do here unless you want to grab that controller on the floor and try your hand at *Call of Duty*. Rae, you could be helpful and grab one of those Red Barons out of the freezer and pop it in the oven."

"Maybe we should just go, Carter," I suggested.

"Yeah, go ahead. I didn't think you came here to talk about anything other than what a disappointment I am. I didn't think you'd walk in with a six-pack and shoot the breeze with me for an hour. That would be too brotherly, wouldn't it, Carter? Instead, you and your ex-wife made the two-hour drive to tell Jarrett what a disappointment he is and what a bad son he is. You want me to reimburse your gas money? Oh, wait. I don't have any money." He angrily squeezed the can in his hand and smashed the cigarette in the full ashtray.

"You've talked about what a disappointment you are twice in ten minutes, Jarrett. I didn't say it. You did. Sounds like you're wrestling with that a little bit. Sounds like you aren't as content with your life as you say you are," Carter shouted.

Jarrett paused. "Do you remember when we were kids, Carter? We were friends. We never fought like other siblings. We hung out together. Remember all those nights at the arcade? Making grilled cheese sandwiches at two in the morning? We liked each other's company. You were my best friend. What changed?"

Carter took off his hat again and scratched his head. "Mom left and you chose alcohol over me. Over our friendship."

"Yeah," Jarrett said. "I guess I did."

"Well, we'll get out of your way." Carter motioned for me to stand.

"That's it? You really drove two hours to lecture me for ten minutes?"

"There's no reason to stay," Carter said as we both stood and walked toward the front door. "We aren't going to agree on anything. You're not going to quit drinking. You're not going to see Dad. Might as well get back home."

"Well, okay." Jarrett remained on the loveseat. "Hey, Rae. Do me a favor?"

"Yeah?" I turned back to him.

"Pray for me, will you?" He laughed.

Carter and I walked out the front door and into the humidity.

"I just don't understand him. No remorse. No sense of responsibility. I want to punch him in the throat," Carter spat out from the driver's seat and stuffed his lip with a wad of nicotine.

"He's not going to stop drinking until he's ready," I said as he turned onto the highway that would take me home. "There's nothing you can do. Only the Lord can change him, Carter."

"And you think God will?" he asked.

"I know He's capable of doing it. It's not too hard for Him. But Jarrett is going to have to surrender. It's out of your hands. You can't make Jarrett do the right thing. You can't make him visit your father. You're just going to have to trust God to do the work."

"His victim mentality makes me sick. Mom left me, too, and I didn't turn into an alcoholic. I didn't turn into a no-good—" He stopped and looked over to me. "But I did leave you, didn't I? I abandoned you the same way she abandoned me. Oh, Rae, I've never thought of that before. I've never . . ." He remained silent for a moment before awkwardly asking, "Do you want me to stop at a convenience store and get another bag of M&M's?"

"No, thank you," I muttered as he proceeded to spit brown liquid into a water bottle. I looked out the window to a herd of cows grazing in the hot sun.

We rode silently for a few minutes while I checked my phone. My thoughts kept going back to Carter's statement about his mother. He did abandon me, just as she had done him. I'd never realized it either, until he'd said it. I never understood that sort of thing—I never understood how children of alcoholics became alcoholics after what they'd been through. I never understood vicious cycles or family curses. I never understood how people could wound others in the same way they had been wounded—why they didn't learn from their own experiences. Did misery really love company? Why had the man who claimed to love me for so many years hurt me in the same agonizing way his own mother had hurt him?

When he was done dipping and spit the wad of disgusting tobacco into the water bottle, he said, "I really want to thank you for making the trip with me today. Nothing really went as I had planned. I'd hoped to stay at Dad's longer, but he kind of rushed us out of there, didn't he? I guess I hoped we'd have some sort of intervention for Jarrett and take him back to rehab today. I don't know what I thought."

"You got to see your dad. That's what really mattered." I patted the frizzy baby hairs around my temples.

"You sure you don't want me to stop and get you some more M&M's?" he asked again.

"Enough with the M&M's!" I shouted. "What is going on here? What do you want from me, Carter? Why did you invite me today? You could have made this trip alone."

"I miss you, Rae." His eyes never left the road.

I didn't know how to respond. I was feeling so many emotions. Anger that he'd cheated on me. Relief that he missed me. Flattery that he'd asked me to make the trip with him. Elation at the thought of restoring our family. Guilt for considering reconciling with him when I had a good man like Kent. And again, anger that he'd cheated on me.

"Why did you leave?" I interrupted the silence. "What did I do to send you running to Autumn?"

"You didn't do anything wrong. You were good to me. I think I was just scared. Scared of the routine. Thinking maybe there was more to life than—I don't know."

"More to life than what? Me? Being my husband?" I glared at him as he continued to watch the highway.

"I really wish I had an answer that made sense. I just don't, Rae." He quickly glanced at me and then back to the highway. "What's important is I regret it now. I never should have left and torn our family apart. It's the stupidest thing I've ever done. I was wrong, Rae."

"You shattered me. You know that? Since you brought it up, you did to me exactly what your mother did to you. You know how that feels—to be left behind? To be rejected? I've spent the last year and a half of my life not only worrying over my mother having cancer but worrying what I did wrong. Wondering how I could have loved you better. Wondering what I could have done to make you stay. You wrecked me, Carter. You weren't there when I needed you the most. I don't know if I can ever forgive you for that. I don't know if we can ever be Dale and Donna Jameson," I grumbled angrily through clenched teeth and looked back out the window.

"I know," he said softly, remorsefully. "I lie awake at night, alone in the house—*our* house—and hate myself because you and Molly aren't there. I hate the thought of you crying over your mother and I'm not there to hold you. I hate what I've done."

"Too little too late." I sniffled. "I've moved on, Carter. Molly and I both have a new start in Whitten. Molly loves her new school and is making friends. I'm in a relationship."

"Kent," he scoffed.

"What's that mean? Is that why you're suddenly sorry?" I turned in my seat toward him. "You thought I'd pine for you the rest of my life, didn't you? You thought I'd wait for you while you went out and had your fun with some silly little girl named after a season she wasn't even born in?" I shouted. "Now Autumn is gone and you're jealous, aren't you? That's what this is all about. You aren't really sorry you hurt me. You don't want me, but you don't want anyone else to have me either. Is that it?" I wanted to reach across the console and punch him in the jaw that cracked when he chewed.

"Rae, no." He looked over to me. "I don't like the idea of you with another man, but that's not why I'm regretful. I still love you. I've never stopped loving you."

My heart was pounding in my throat. I turned back in my seat and faced the windshield. I wanted to open the truck door and jump out—roll onto the gravel shoulder at seventy-five miles an hour. I didn't care if it killed me. I just didn't want to be in the truck with Carter for one more second.

"I'm not saying it back." I crossed my arms and huffed like a child. "I don't love you anymore. I never will."

As soon as the words escaped my mouth, I knew they were a lie.

"I understand," he said quietly. "I don't blame you."

We rode quietly for the next thirty minutes or so. I stayed busy on my phone, checking social media and emails and texting Molly to make sure she'd gotten to Aunt Maxine's safely. She responded they were boiling Mason jars and making salsa. She was fine and having a good time and told us not to rush home to pick her up. I think she was ecstatic her parents were together—alone—possibly saying kind words to each other and mending their broken marriage.

Instead, I was infuriated at all the ways this man had hurt me. I was infuriated that he picked now to tell me all of this—at the time I was finally moving on with my life, attempting to get over him and develop romantic feelings for a new, great guy. Feelings of excitement at the notion of reconciliation surfaced earlier, but the more I thought of Kent and how blessed I was to have him, the more my feelings for Carter steered toward anger again.

I did not trust Carter. If we reunited, if we restored our family, how did I know he wouldn't cheat on me again? I couldn't go through that pain a second time. I wouldn't. If I couldn't trust him, I couldn't be with him. That was all there was to it.

"Sid's Secret Hideaway." His laughter broke through the silence and my thoughts.

"What?"

"Sid's Secret Hideaway in the Ozarks. You remember?" He looked over to me and laughed again.

"Yeah." I grinned as the memories flooded in and dampened my anger. "Beautiful cabin in the mountains with all the amenities, stunning views—"

"And a stripper pole in the middle of the living room." He was laughing so hard he could barely spit out his words.

"Molly said, 'Mama! They've got a pole like the playground does. A fireman's pole.'" I snickered.

"She dropped her little Minnie Mouse suitcase and ran to climb it and you made me stop her. You looked all over that cabin for disinfecting wipes while she begged to climb the pole. You made sure it was operating-room sterile before you let her touch it."

"She was missing both of her front teeth, remember? Grinning from ear to ear and sliding down the 'fireman's' pole over and over again. After a while, you were worried she enjoyed it too much and made her get off and promise never to get on another pole again."

"Oh." He grabbed his stomach. "It hurts. I've laughed so hard it hurts."

Our laughs tapered to chuckles and then he sighed heartily and said, "That. That's what I miss. I miss laughing with you, Rae. I miss making memories with you . . . I miss *you*."

"Here's another story," I said as the anger resurfaced. "I thought all was right in the world, and then you cheated on me. You told me you didn't want to be married anymore. Remember that story?"

He didn't respond. We remained silent until he dropped me off at my house, thanked me for going with him, and I walked inside.

CHAPTER 16

*B*etween the Burger Basket and Taylor Faye's Boutique on historic Main Street was a dilapidated, yellow-painted brick building with faded newspapers taped to the windows and a For Sale sign on the green wooden door. Several businesses called the small building home during my childhood, but it had sat empty now for a couple of years. When I glanced over at it while sitting at the red light on Main Street, I thought of my mother's suggestion to open a store and *"fill it with junk furniture you find on the side of the road and paint gray and wrap in chicken wire. You can call it vintage and sell each piece for three hundred dollars or more."*

I saw potential in that neglected building. I envisioned painting the chipped yellow brick a bright white and hanging a black-and-white striped awning over shiny teal French doors. Above the awning beautiful black cursive would read Restorations by Rae. The large front window was the perfect place to showcase freshly painted dressers or dinettes or chests or chairs I had brought back to life.

I couldn't rely on alimony and Mama's inheritance forever. I really did enjoy refinishing furniture for friends and neighbors and was giddy at the thought of making a living doing something I loved. I tossed and turned in the bed that night while praying for guidance in the matter. And finally, peace replaced my worried thoughts of the business failing. I took that peace as a sign and thanked God for it.

———— ✦ ————

On a warm September morning after I dropped off Molly at school, I peered inside the building through cracks of the brittle newspaper as Dawn and Aunt Maxine pulled in to a space in front of the store.

"She drives like a bat out of hell!" Aunt Maxine was shouting as she carefully exited the passenger door of Dawn's silver sedan.

"You exaggerate, Aunt Maxine." Dawn climbed out of the driver's side with her keys and a folder in her hand.

"You've lived here your whole life, Dawn Elizabeth. How could you forget there's a stop sign on Periwinkle? Huge red stop sign, Raeley Ann. Just rolled right through it." Aunt Maxine huffed and walked, humped over, toward me.

"She says the same thing about me, Dawn. Don't take offense." I laughed as Dawn shook her head and smirked. "How many more pounds have you lost?"

"Another seven gone, girl." She put her hands on her hips and modeled her beautiful tan, silky pants.

"I'm proud of you, sister," I said and hugged her neck.

"You ready to go inside?" She placed a key into the rusty

lock and pushed the wobbly door open as we were pelted with a cloud of heat and dust.

"Lord have mercy!" Aunt Maxine coughed at the dander and followed us inside. "This was a gin joint when I was a young'un. I think this is the bar where Fannie's daddy used to play billiards and get drunk as a skunk. An old man named Sal ran the place." She coughed again as Dawn and I walked around. "That Sal sure was a no-good. I don't know how he stayed in business for so long. He drank more liquor than he sold. I don't think they even buried him when he died. Probably just left him to ferment somewhere."

"Oh, Aunt Maxine." Dawn sighed. "You're too much."

It certainly was a charming old building. It was a single eight-hundred-square-foot room with a small bathroom and storage area in the back right corner. The walls were made of the original oversized dark red bricks, and the pipes running along the red oak hardwood ceilings were exposed. The floors matched the stunning oak ceilings and seemed to be in great condition.

"Sal's grandson still owns the place. He wanted to do something with it, but he's decided it's time to let it go. It sure would enhance the beauty of historic Main Street, Rae." Dawn kicked at some aged newspapers on the floor.

"I can afford this," I thought aloud while looking up at the spectacular fifteen-foot ceiling. "With the money Mama left me, I can afford this."

Aunt Maxine coughed again. "But do you want this, Raeley Ann? Looks like a lot of hard work to me."

"I would be in heaven fixing this place up, Aunt Maxine." I nearly twirled right through a pile of busted Sheetrock and old water bottles.

"I think it's time you expand your business from the shed in your backyard. You'd have plenty of space here to work and display your pieces. And financially, I think it's a smart move. Interest rates are wonderful right now too," Dawn said.

"I want it, Dawn." I smiled. "I've got peace about this. I want to do this. Restorations by Rae."

Dawn beamed. "Girl, I know how you love alliteration."

"Would he take any less?" I asked.

"I think we could talk him down. He's ready to sell."

"I'm going to do it. I'm going to do this. Aunt Maxine, I'm going to do this!" I skipped around like a giddy schoolgirl.

"If anyone can get this place in shape, it's you, dear." Aunt Maxine swatted at a fly buzzing around her head. "I know your mother would be beaming with pride. But what about Restorations by Raeley Ann? That has a nicer ring to it, don't you think?"

———————◆———————

Things moved quickly once Sal's grandson accepted my offer. The building was inspected, and surprisingly, it was structurally sound with no major issues. A new roof would be a priority soon, but other than that, it just needed cosmetic repairs. Within a week of looking at it for the first time with Dawn and Aunt Maxine, 127 Main Street was officially mine. I couldn't believe it. I was an entrepreneur. God had been so good to me.

With the key in my pocket, I left the bank and drove straight to my new place with a Shop-Vac and cleaning supplies and cans of paint I'd bought earlier that morning in tow. I worked all day—vacuuming, scraping, scrubbing, sanding, dusting, and vacuuming some more.

When basketball practice was over, Kent walked through the squeaky front door with a beautiful bouquet of mixed wildflowers and a takeout box of chicken, rice, and cheese from Rubio's.

"I'm proud of you." He kissed me and handed over the lovely flowers and delicious food.

"You're sweet, Kent. Thank you." I set the flowers and food on my mother's black-and-white houndstooth card table I'd brought from home. "Did Carter get Molly from practice?"

"Yeah, he did. You've made a lot of progress today." He looked around the room illuminated by several lamps on the floor. "I don't see a single cobweb or dust bunny."

"I vacuumed this whole place at least ten times." I sat at the table to eat. "I bet I tossed a hundred and fifty pounds of dirt into the dumpster out back. Does it smell better? The air purifier has been running all day."

"Smells clean." He tucked his hands into the pockets of his basketball shorts. "What's next?"

"Well." I took a bite. "I'm going to finish restoring the

floors and hang up some cool chandeliers in here. I think I'm going to use the dresser I just refurbished as the counter for the cash register. Then I'll move outside. Paint the exterior, get a new door, and order some signage and the awning. I think I'll be in business in a few weeks. Kelly Simpson stopped by earlier and said she's going to run a piece in next week's paper to get some buzz going."

"You know I'll do whatever you need to get this place up and running," he offered.

"I know. Thank you."

"Listen, we haven't really talked about your trip with Carter a few weeks ago." He walked over to the table where I was eating. "I was wrong to say anything. He's the father of your child. I know you need to reconcile for Molly's sake. I spoke to him for a few minutes after practice today. He's a good guy. He's a good dad to Molly. I was wrong to feel jealous."

"You spoke to him? About what?" I asked.

"Nothing, really. We talked about Molly and basketball. I asked about his dad and he told me about the dementia. I told him about my father having Alzheimer's and everything we went through with him. We had a good talk about it. And he thanked me for being cool about you going to see his family with him."

Having a father with Alzheimer's would be the thing Carter and Kent had in common. That's what they would talk about when we achieved Dale and Donna Jameson status—when we celebrated Molly's birthdays together.

They'd talk over a glass of wine about Alzheimer's and I'd talk to Carter's future wife about . . . No, I still couldn't go there.

Stupid Carter. Since our trip a couple of weeks earlier, he'd consumed my thoughts. We hadn't spoken about our little getaway. But I thought of him and our conversation on the way home from Tennessee nearly every waking second. I thought about his remorse and our laughter and still being loved by him and it prompted a desire to run back into his arms. It prompted me to fully forgive him of the infidelity.

But then I'd think of Kent and how much I really do care for him too. I felt good about our relationship. He was such a kind, thoughtful, good-looking man who gave me butter-flies when he smiled at me and offered to do nice things for me. He was good to Molly. I felt safe and at ease with Kent Richardson. I knew I could trust him, and I wasn't sure I'd ever trust Carter again.

At that moment, while watching this tall, handsome man inspect the gorgeous, ornate molding in the room, I was ready to declare my love for him. To take the next step in our new and exciting relationship. To throw the plastic fork topped with rice and cheese to the clean floor and run to him. To drape my arms around his neck and hold him close. To tell him those three words I hadn't said to a man in so long.

What wasn't to love about Kent? He'd been a blessing in my life. He'd prayed with me. He'd comforted me over my mother's death. He'd brought me joy and companionship.

He'd encouraged Molly in the game she loved. Kent Richardson was a good, decent man and maybe he was the very reason I moved to Whitten. Maybe our entire relationship was ordained by the good Lord.

I could imagine marrying him one day. I could visualize him and Molly at our kitchen table discussing basketball plays over a breakfast of bacon and eggs. She'd call him "Kent" at home and "Coach" at school. He'd prepare her for college ball and accompany me to all of her games at some Southern university. I could imagine sharing inside jokes and bouts of laughter with him—growing old with him. Raeley Reeves Richardson. I loved alliteration.

"Rae, I've got to tell you something that happened yesterday." He ran his hand along the brick wall.

"What?"

"I've been offered a job . . . in Tuscaloosa."

"Tuscaloosa?" I asked, confused. "What's the job?"

"Well." He walked to me as the sun set outside the large storefront window. "There's a position available for an assistant coach at the University of Alabama. An old college buddy is the athletic director. He gave me a call last night and offered it to me. I couldn't believe it. My alma mater. Assistant coach." I could hear the enthusiasm in his voice but noticed he was trying to dial it down.

"Kent." I gulped and put the plastic fork in the take-out box. "That's amazing. You simply must take the job. You can't pass up an opportunity like this. You can't." I attempted to exaggerate what little enthusiasm I had.

"I don't know what to do," he said as he sat in the folding chair next to me. "I'm happy taking girls and boys to state. I love those kids. I love getting the chance to mold them into good people, good athletes. I love the idea of maybe watching them play for Alabama one day. This is what I'm supposed to do." He smiled. "And you. I'm happy right here with you, Rae."

"Kent, b-but y-you—" I stuttered. "We're talking about the SEC. We're talking about coaching college kids—molding *them*. Maybe watching *them* play in the NBA one day. And you certainly can't stay here for me. We hardly know each other. We—"

"I know everything I need to know about you." He took my dirty, calloused hands into his and gave them a squeeze.

"No." I persistently shook my head. "No. You're going to resent me for this. You can't pass up this opportunity. I can't let you. I won't wonder every day if I've kept you from your destiny." I pulled my hands from his and anxiously got up and walked around the room. "And what if you change your mind later, Kent? What if you decide to go? I can't put Molly through another change. I can't move her to Tuscaloosa."

"Hey, just being asked to coach was enough. I promise. I'm content right here. As for the future, I wouldn't ask you and Molly to pick up and move to—"

"You'd go without us. I'd be alone again. Carter already left me for another woman. I sure can't compete with the University of Alabama," I frantically thought aloud.

I watched the streetlamps on Main Street flicker to life in the evening sky and folded my arms. I sighed in relief that I'd kept my premature declaration of love for him to myself. Kent remained in the folding chair, silent.

CHAPTER 17

September in Alabama. The breeze was cool, and the leaves on the trees had begun to fade from bright green to hues of orange and yellow. The humidity was no longer unbearable, and my hair required less effort from the straightening iron.

The third Thursday happened to be my thirty-seventh birthday. It was the first year I didn't wake up to my mother calling to sing to me and tell me the story of the crisp morning I was born. "It was the easiest birth imaginable," she would say. "I pushed once and there you were. I've had ingrown toenails that were more painful."

If my birthday hadn't landed on the same day as the meeting with Aunt Maxine, Mrs. Fannie, and Mrs. Dora, I would have stayed in bed and eaten a gallon of mint chocolate chip ice cream. I would have dug out the old VHS tapes of my childhood birthday parties and longed for those days until I fell asleep curled up next to Patsy. But I had things to do. Aunt Maxine had asked me to bring croissants for the chicken salad and I couldn't let her down.

"Happy birthday to you!" they sang when I walked into Aunt Maxine's airy kitchen. The windows were open and the autumn breeze blew the blue-and-white striped tier curtains over Aunt Maxine's sink.

"Thank you!" I grinned at the precious, well-dressed ladies standing around the strawberry cake in the center of the table.

"I didn't have thirty-seven candles, so one will have to do." Aunt Maxine leaned over the back of the kitchen chair. "Make a wish, Raeley Ann!"

I bent over and blew out the lone white candle. I wished my mother was there, but somehow, I think she was.

"Okay!" Aunt Maxine moved the round pink cake to the counter. "Dessert comes after lunch. Raeley Ann, did you bring the croissants for the chicken salad?"

I handed the bag of fresh bread to her and took my place at the table between Mrs. Dora and Mrs. Fannie.

"Oh, thirty-seven!" Mrs. Dora clapped her jeweled wrists together. "Let's see. When I was thirty-seven, I had a ten-year-old and a five-year-old. I worked part-time at Dr. Dinwiddie's as a receptionist and Harold—"

"Slept every day at noon. We know, Dora." Aunt Maxine placed a glass bowl of homemade cranberry chicken salad and a plate of croissants before us.

"I can't remember when I was thirty-seven. Or sixty-seven, for that matter." Mrs. Fannie chuckled. "I can't even remember what I did yesterday."

Aunt Maxine put a jar of homemade pickles and a crystal pitcher of sweet iced tea on the white tablecloth before sitting down to lead us in prayer.

"Lord, we just thank You today for our sweet Raeley Ann. Thank You for the work You've done in her and the blessings You've bestowed upon her. Let her next year on this earth be one of beauty for ashes. Amen."

"So, Raeley Ann. Big plans today?" my aunt asked as we all fixed our plates.

"No, ma'am." I placed a pickle on the pink-and-gray china. "I bought some old nightstands Mrs. Turner was selling on Facebook. I'm going to start working on them this afternoon. After Molly gets home from basketball, we are all going to Jamie and Dawn's for a birthday dinner."

"Tell us all about the new business, Rae," Mrs. Fannie inquired. "I saw the wonderful write-up in the paper. Kent says the place is coming along beautifully. You two just painted the storefront?"

"Yes, ma'am," I said. "Kent has been such a great help. That beautiful white paint really updated the place. Grand opening is next weekend. I've already got some pieces of furniture moved in and priced to sell. It's funny. After the article ran in the paper, several people dumped old furniture outside the door for me to refinish. I didn't pay a dime for a foyer table, a set of kitchen chairs, and a dresser I'm going to restore as a buffet."

"You need to look through Fannie's attic, Rae. She's got a treasure trove up there." Mrs. Dora wiped chicken salad from the corner of her lip.

"Oh, yes, there are certainly some pieces you can have. There's a trunk up there that is nearly falling apart, but you're welcome to take a crack at it," Mrs. Fannie offered.

"I would love to. Thank you."

"I'm proud of you, Raeley Ann," Aunt Maxine said. "Thirty-seven years old. I can't believe it. I remember the cool morning you were born. Wilson and James sat in the waiting room smoking cigarettes and reading the newspaper, not even caring that Mama and I were coughing up a lung. Margie pushed one time and you were here. I'll never forget looking through the maternity ward window and seeing you for the first time—a precious little thing bundled in a pink blanket. Margie always said giving birth to you was less painful than an ingrown toenail."

We all laughed.

We had a slice of the delicious strawberry cake while chatting and making notes for the meeting. There was another funeral for the ladies to attend, flowers to be sent, encouraging cards to be written, and wedding gifts to be bought. The hospital gift shop had Mrs. Fannie's credit card on file for when one of us ordered our "usual"—a balloon bouquet tied to a vase of fresh flowers. When word got out that a baby in the community had been born, Mrs. Annie at Clooney's Pharmacy put back a chenille baby blanket for the new mother before one of us even stopped by to pick it up.

I'd come to appreciate the circle of life more since being a part of the "ministry." Every month we recognized births, celebrations, sickness, death. For every sad occasion we discussed, there seemed to be two joyous ones. Because of that, I always left those meetings better than when I arrived.

I'd come to value the importance of their friendship as well. I rarely talked to my former friends in Huntsville or even the old schoolmates who lived in the same small town as me. We'd text now or again or chat when we passed one another in the grocery store aisle, but these ladies were the only women I regularly saw or talked to. Iron sharpens iron, and they had certainly sharpened me. Aunt Maxine, Mrs. Fannie, and Mrs. Dora were truly some of the dearest friends I'd ever had.

Each one of them called me several times a week. Sometimes Mrs. Dora would talk in a low hum because Mr. Harold was napping, and she never failed to rib Aunt Maxine at least once while we were on the phone. Mrs. Fannie checked in with me before driving down to Beck's Beauty Spot to have her hair washed and styled. And Aunt Maxine, well, if she wasn't calling me on the phone, she was walking through my door with a Tupperware dish of food. Each lady was concerned for me and my daughter. Each one prayed for me. Each one contributed something positive to my life. Each one reinforced a connection to my mother.

Mama was gone, and I'd never see her again this side of heaven, but I had three mother figures step up to the plate in her absence. They counseled me and poured their wisdom into me, the same way my own mother had done. They taught me how to correctly can pepper relish and the importance of sending notes of encouragement to those who were struggling. They'd each had a hand in restoring me—sanding off the old mess to reveal the joy within. My best friends—my reminder that the anchor holds—were elderly women who smelled of muscle rub and were covered in liver spots and were in the bed by eight thirty. And I loved them dearly.

When half the cake was gone and the kitchen counter was cluttered with glasses of watered-down tea and messy plates of croissant crumbs, we were ready to adjourn.

Mrs. Fannie said, "Before we go, I have to tell you, Rae. Kent stopped by yesterday and told me about the college coaching position."

"What's that now?" Aunt Maxine's ears perked up.

"He was offered an assistant coaching job in Tuscaloosa," Mrs. Fannie answered. "He's not taking the job."

"Well, why on earth not?" Aunt Maxine exclaimed.

"He loves those high school kids. And dare I say he loves your niece too." She grinned at me.

"Ohhhhhh," Aunt Maxine purred with glee.

"Do you think he's making the right decision, Mrs. Fannie?" I crossed my arms on the kitchen table.

"I believe love is always the right choice. Jobs come and go. Love is lasting." Mrs. Fannie patted my hand with assurance.

Mrs. Dora picked at the charms on her bracelet and added, "Harold had an opportunity to ride bulls on the Amarillo, Texas, circuit. He could have gone professional."

"But what, Dora? He was worried he might fall asleep on the bull if the rodeo was at noon?" Aunt Maxine blurted while standing up to put a pile of dishes into the sink behind her. Mrs. Fannie stifled a laugh.

"You old nag," Dora said before looking to me. "He turned down that cowboy life for me, Rae. He turned down the honky-tonk scene and the big belt buckles and the dust and the mud."

"And the bulls and the blood and the roar of a Sunday crowd?" I teased, knowing Mrs. Dora didn't know the Garth Brooks lyrics.

"Well, yes, that too." She looked at me, confused. "I worried he would resent me, but he still says it's the best decision he ever made. He chose me. He's never regretted it."

"I don't know about that," Aunt Maxine muttered.

"I think our story is romantic. Maxine, maybe you're just mad Wilson never turned down anything for you—never chose you over something else he loved."

"Wilson turned down naps for me. He chooses to stay awake and watch *Jeopardy!* with me even when he wants to doze off."

"Ladies, that's enough," Mrs. Fannie interjected. "Rae, I'll tell you the ultimate sacrifice. My Pratt nearly lost his entire family because he fell in love with a poor girl from the wrong side of the tracks. His family threatened to disown him, cut him out of the lumber fortune. He didn't care. He chose me. He chose me over and over again. And eventually, his family chose me too. Kent is a smart man. He knows what's important. He knows love requires sacrifice. He is able to make his own decisions. Instead of feeling any kind of guilt because he's choosing you, thank God you have a man smart enough to see what truly matters."

I was still concerned about Kent's decision to turn down the job and stay in one-horse Whitten. I felt I would always worry about resentment and even future rejection. I had prayed fervently about our relationship, but I didn't have any peace about Kent's choice. The anxiety and worry refused to subside.

When Mrs. Fannie and Mrs. Dora had gone, Aunt Maxine asked me to stick around and help her with the dishes. We washed, dried, and put the dessert plates into the cupboard as Uncle Wilson came inside from mowing the yard, fixed a glass of tap water, and said, "I'm going to rest awhile."

"Don't you tell Dora that Wilson takes naps too." She wiped her hands with her terry-cloth apron printed with fall leaves and acorns and said, "I've got something for you. Margie wanted me to give it to you on your birthday."

"A letter?" I perked up. "She left a letter?"

"She did."

I sat at the table. "She's left several letters for me. The one we found that day going through the mail, another in her music room, and one in the shed in a table drawer. When I find one, it's like she's still right here, Aunt Maxine."

"She left a couple for your brother too. You know he's not one to be emotional about things, but I was riding with him down to the farmer's market when he discovered one in the console of his truck. I haven't seen your brother tear up with joy like that since he got that dirt bike when he was just a boy. But that was our Margie, wasn't it? Making sure everyone is taken care of—even after she's gone." She opened a cigar box on her kitchen counter and retrieved the pink envelope. "She gave this to me a couple of weeks before she passed. I was looking around the kitchen for that candle for your cake and found it in the cigar box. As if the Lord reminded me to give it to you. Go ahead and sit down and read it. I'll leave you alone and go check on Wilson."

The autumn air continued to whip through the kitchen as I peeled open the envelope and a photo that I had not seen in years fell to the table.

Rae,

If Maxine remembers to give this to you on time, then the date is September 17. You are thirty-seven years old today. Giving birth to you was less painful than an ingrown toenail. You know the details of that day, so I won't bore you with them again.

I was looking through photographs this afternoon and came across one of you blowing out the candles on your third birthday cake that Mrs. Daisy Evans made. You loved *Sesame Street*, so the cake was decorated with Big Bird and Cookie Monster. Your curly pigtails were tied up in pink ribbon, and you wore a little sundress my mother made for you in a Bert and Ernie pattern. (You always confused Bert with Ernie.) I remember that day well. You sang the *Sesame Street* theme song for everyone and told Maxine a long story about how you felt sorry for Snuffy because he always seemed sad. Then you laughed when Maxine kept trying to pronounce Snuffleupagus.

I found another photo of you on your sweet sixteen. I made the cake that year. Strawberry—your favorite. We had a small party on the back deck with a couple of your friends. Paige was there, and Kerry and the Wheeler girl who wore braces for a hundred years but still had crooked teeth even when they came off. (Bless her heart, Rae. She got her father's teeth, didn't she? Mr. Wheeler could open a beer bottle with his.) Your fingernails were painted black and you were wearing one of your many rock band T-shirts. I have another picture of you opening up those ugly combat boots you begged me to buy for you.

My favorite photo I found today, though, was this one of your twenty-third birthday. You are sitting at our kitchen table, holding Molly Margaret in your lap while you blow out the candles on the familiar strawberry cake. She was a chunky little thing in that polka-dot dress with unruly curls pinned back in a bow and a pacifier in her mouth, and she is looking up at you. She wasn't concerned with the cake or the bright flames flickering on it just a few inches away. Do you see how she was gazing at her mama with affection and adoration?

You, too, radiate joy in this photo—even more so than grinning next to your Cookie Monster cake or posing with your friends and those ugly boots. You were a new person, a woman—a mother. You knew the precious love for a child and the love of a child and your life had changed for the better. My life changed for the better on the day you were born thirty-seven years ago too. I was already a mother to Jamie, and you know how much I adore him (Mama's boy, you always teased), but it has been one of the greatest joys of my life to be the mother of a daughter—your mother.

This picture of you and Molly Margaret perfectly sums up the love between mothers and daughters. I hope you'll frame it and remember no matter what's going on around you, Molly Margaret is looking to you. It is the ultimate bond. Unwavering. Undeniable. Unbreakable.

And although I'm not physically there with you on your birthday, our bond will never be broken. Happy birthday, my beautiful little girl.

I love you with my heart.

Until we meet again,

Mama

It had turned quite chilly that evening as Kent, Molly, and I walked out Jamie and Dawn's back door to see a table near the deep end of their pool with a spread of barbecue and all the fixings. Lit tiki torches shimmered from the flower beds that surrounded the completed concrete, and rose-gold balloons were tied to the back of the patio chairs. Their backyard was met by acres of thick woods, and although there was a nip in the air, bullfrogs and cicadas were singing a farewell song to summer.

My nephews both greeted me with hugs, followed by Dawn, who looked to have lost another ten pounds since I'd seen her only a few days before. Not only was she eating healthy and drinking gallons of water, she'd taken up running and said she felt better than she had in her whole life. I loved seeing the progress she'd made and how her self-esteem had soared. Her face had a youthful, healthy glow, and she was rocking her skinny jeans.

Aunt Maxine, Uncle Wilson, and Mrs. Fannie were all sitting at the table, wrapped in sweaters and cardigans and waiting on Jamie to start a fire in the new outdoor stone fireplace.

"We're all on blood thinners, son. Let's get some heat going!" Uncle Wilson gruffed from beneath his heavy coat before blowing me a birthday kiss.

"I'm trying, Uncle Wilson!" Jamie shouted from the fireplace next to the table as he poked at some smoldering embers. "It won't catch. The wood is wet."

"Throw some newspaper in there. Lighter fluid. Something!" Uncle Wilson huffed back. "I'm going to catch my death of cold."

Aunt Maxine sighed loudly at their bickering and then said, "I brought what was left of the strawberry cake, Raeley

Ann. Fannie brought the coleslaw and baked beans. I know how you love Fannie's coleslaw."

"It all looks so good. Thank you all for being here to help me celebrate," I said as Kent pulled one of the rattan and bamboo chairs out from the table for me.

"Chivalry isn't dead," Aunt Maxine whispered loudly to Mrs. Fannie.

"My brother sure raised you well."

"Fine man, that Theo." Aunt Maxine nodded in agreement.

The fire soon caught and we were immediately blanketed by warmth. Uncle Wilson shrugged off his heavy coat and said contentedly, "That's more like it."

We finished our plates of barbecue, and Dawn placed a candle on what was left of the cake from earlier that afternoon. I thought of Mama's letter and glanced over at Molly sitting beside me. She had a smile on her face, gazing at me, but what she was thinking, I didn't know. I thought back to the times I stared at my own mother in an effort to memorize every line, every wrinkle, every lipstick shade, every outfit she wore.

She was older than my friends' mothers, and her passing away was always on my mind, even when I was young. I'd had Molly when I was just a kid myself, so I didn't know if she thought of me as older or of the day when I would no longer be here. Maybe she did, now that Mama was gone and I talked so often about missing her. Maybe she wasn't trying to memorize my crow's-feet or lipstick shade at all— maybe she was simply thinking about basketball plays or the cute boy in her class or homework while she was contently watching me. Nevertheless, once the candle flickered out, she stood from her seat next to mine, draped her arms around me, and said, "Happy birthday, Mama." My heart was full.

The first gift I opened was from my aunt and daughter. Aunt Maxine had taken Molly to the hardware store to pick out a new set of paint brushes and packages of sandpaper for me. They knew I loved practical gifts and how much I needed those very things. Then Jamie and Dawn presented me with a framed black-and-white photo of my building when it was Sal's.

"I thought it would be neat to hang in the store," Dawn said. "Look at those wooden windows and the detail on the original door, girl. It really is a cool building."

"My father was probably in there, stone-cold drunk, the very moment that photo was taken," Mrs. Fannie said as she used the dancing light from the fireplace to peer at the picture from behind her glasses. "What a place that was. My mother threatened to burn it down many a time before my daddy came to know Jesus. I'm glad I can pass it on Main Street now and associate something good with it."

Kent quietly pulled out a small box wrapped in silver paper with a black bow and slid it across the patio table to me.

"My Lord, it's a ring, isn't it?" Aunt Maxine blurted loudly.

"Maxine, for heaven's sake!" Uncle Wilson glared at her. "Stifle thy tongue, woman!"

I blushed immediately and Kent did, too, before saying, "It's not a ring, Mrs. Maxine."

"Maxine, good heavens." Mrs. Fannie chuckled and playfully swatted at my aunt's arm.

"Well, no matter what's in there, Kent, it won't live up to Aunt Maxine's expectations." Jamie laughed and patted Kent on the back before walking over to stoke the fire again.

"I'm sorry." Aunt Maxine shook her head at herself. "I can't control my tongue sometimes."

"Sometimes? That's an understatement," Uncle Wilson said.

I peeled open the small box and saw a beautiful set of earrings. Studs, like I always wore, in shiny silver and white.

"Oh, Kent," I said. "I love them!"

"I saw them and thought of you. They're nothing fancy, but I thought you would like them."

"And I do." I leaned over to kiss his cheek.

"Gross!" Molly joked dramatically before standing up and tugging on Liam's arm. "Let's go inside so I can beat you at Ping-Pong."

The kids went inside, I put on the lovely earrings, and Kent and Mrs. Fannie began discussing their family tree as Aunt Maxine and Uncle Wilson interjected their own memories of the Richardsons. My telephone rang and I saw

Carter's name scroll across the screen. My first reaction was to decline the call, but I stood from the table and walked away from the warmth of the fire with the phone to my ear.

"Happy birthday, Rae."

"Thanks."

"Have you had a good day?" he asked.

"Yeah," I answered. "And it's not over. We're still at Jamie's. I've got cake left on my plate. What do you need?"

"Nothing. I just wanted to wish you a happy birthday. I'm sorry I didn't call sooner. I just got out of work."

"I didn't expect you to call at all. And I would have been okay if you hadn't."

My words and my tone were harsh. I was annoyed with him since our trip to Tennessee. I was annoyed at myself because I knew if I could trust Carter, I wouldn't hesitate to take him back. Somewhere, beneath all of the heartache and pain, there was still some adoration. But I didn't trust him. Anger still festered. I still seethed at the memory of seeing him with Autumn for the first time when I made an unannounced visit to our home on Sullivan Street to pick up some things I'd forgotten to move to the apartment. He gave a humbling confession about their affair while Autumn stood, embarrassed and terrified of my reaction, in the corner of my living room. I silently stared at them, offering no response, and walked out that front door in shambles with the overwhelming desire to run to my mother, but she was incredibly sick from chemotherapy and staying at Jamie and Dawn's house. I would never forget those things. I would never forget the betrayal and the agony. I would work on forgiving him and salvaging some sort of friendship for the sake of our daughter, but I could not erase the gut-wrenching memories.

"Why are you so mad at me?" he asked.

"I'm not, Carter," I lied. "I'm just in the middle of celebrating my birthday with my family. It's really not a good time to talk."

"I was thinking," he continued anyway. "You remember the year we went down to Gulf Shores for your birthday? We left Molly with Mrs. Margie and took off for the weekend."

I was drawn into the memory. "Hurricane season," I added.

"Ivan dumped water on us the entire time we were there, but you were determined to put your feet in the ocean. The beach was closed and the winds were unbearable, but we managed to run from the hotel down to the water. The lifeguards rolled up in their truck with sirens blaring and demanded we get off the beach. You told them, 'I'm not going to swim. I just want to stick my toes in the water once before I go home. It's my birthday.' They threatened to call the police and ushered us to their truck, and right before we got in to ride back to the hotel, you took off running back to the ocean and managed to stick your foot in for half a second before one of the lifeguards picked you up by the waist and carried you away."

"I didn't even feel the water on my toes because my feet were already soaking wet from the rain."

"I loved that you did that. You were on a mission and not even a hurricane could keep you from it."

"It was stupid." I chewed on my nails and watched sweet Kent laughing with his aunt.

"I've always been proud of your determination. The way you remodeled our entire house, the way you pulled yourself together after I left, how you coped with the deaths of your parents, starting your own business. You've always been resolute, Rae. When you make up your mind to do something, you're hell-bent on accomplishing it. I love that about you."

There he went again—making my heart skip a beat, making my knees weak, making me want to forget every hurt he'd caused and tell him I love him, making me want to throw away the wonderful thing I had with Kent Richardson.

"Well, I need to get off the phone now and rejoin my family and Kent."

"Then there's nothing else I can say. Happy birthday." He hung up.

CHAPTER 18

I stood outside the renovated alabaster-white building with my name above the striped awning. Mayor Haywood handed me an oversize pair of scissors and I cut the red ribbon taped across the matte black French door as my family, friends, a newspaper reporter, and members of the Whitten Chamber of Commerce cheered. Kent immediately wrapped his arm around my waist and Molly let out a loud "Woo-hoo!"

Restorations by Rae had plenty of inventory. Nestled in the corner was a headboard I'd brought back to life with plush beige upholstery. I also had a dining table, several chests of drawers, three trunks, two end tables, two buffets, multiple chairs, a bookcase, a sewing table, a foyer table, and a porch swing in the shop. I'd repurposed pallet wood into multiple picture frames that were showcased on the bookcase and buffets. A couple of old doors, lamps, and a collection of vintage Coca-Cola trays were also on display. My favorite piece in the shop, though, was a washstand Mrs. Fannie had given me that I'd turned into a bathroom vanity with a fireclay farmhouse sink.

I sold a couple of chairs, a chest of drawers, and one of

the buffets in the first hour I was open. I'd made quite the profit since the chairs were found in an old barn I had permission to rummage through, the chest was a ragged piece of junk that I'd scored at a yard sale for next to nothing, and the buffet was the dresser I had restored. I didn't know if business would always be this good, but I relished in the revenue of the day.

When the shop officially closed at five that evening, I locked the front door and took a seat, alone, in an antique captain's chair stained in weathered oak. I sighed in delight as I looked around the charming store at the mended furniture and the white candle-style chandeliers hanging from the fabulous wood ceilings.

"Mama, I sure wish you were here," I said aloud. "I wish you were here to see this. To share in this moment with me. Thank you for the money to make this possible. Thank you for always believing in me. Thank you for being the best mama a girl could have. I love you with my heart. Always."

A few days passed and more pieces sold. A couple of clients even brought in their own furniture for me to restore. I gladly accepted the challenge of refinishing a rolltop desk and reupholstering a plaid glider chair from the '70s.

I had repurposed some old shutters as a room divider and set up a space at the back of the shop to work on furniture in my downtime. A box fan roared while I applied a coat of de-glosser to the deacon's bench I was working on, but I faintly heard the jingle of the bell on the front door. I wiped my hands on my rag and walked around the divider to see Carter standing inside.

"Rae!" he exclaimed when he saw me. "This is great. Look at this stuff!"

"Thanks." I wiped my hands again on the legs of my jeans stained with paint and polyurethane.

He examined the headboard I'd leaned against the brick wall after finishing it that morning.

"What is this headboard made of?" He ran his hand across the ornate detailing.

"It's made from the frame of an old mirror," I said.

"That's amazing. Look at the patina on that. You came up with that idea? An old mirror frame?" He smiled.

"I did."

"You've got a gift." He continued to look around the shop. "Business is good?"

"It's good," I answered and then paused. "Carter, what are you doing here?"

"I got done with work this morning and wanted to see the place. Thought I'd pick up Molly from practice today and take her to dinner tonight. She's always talking about the seafood at Bea's." He shoved his hands into the pockets of his khaki pants and shuffled his tan tassel loafers across the hardwood. His sunglasses were tucked into the pocket of his white, heavily starched dress shirt. His skin was still tan from his summer weekends on the lake. His hair was a bit longer than usual and curled up at his neck.

"What are you really doing?" I asked him and leaned against the pub table that served as my counter.

"I just told you, I wanted—" he began.

"I know what you told me, but what do you want from *me*, Carter?"

He hesitated. "You want to grab a late lunch? Is the Burger Basket next door pretty good?"

"I've already eaten. I brought food from home," I answered.

"Then go next door with me and have a sweet tea."

"Why?" I asked. "What do you—"

"Rae," he asked in a serious tone, "will you please have a glass of tea with me? I just want ten minutes of your time."

I locked the store and we silently walked a few steps in the autumn sun to the fire-red brick building next door. When we entered, we were pelted with the wonderful smell of grilled beef and greasy fries that often wafted into my shop and tempted me. If I'd caved to my taste buds, I would have a double bacon cheeseburger, curly fries, and a chocolate milkshake from the Burger Basket for lunch every day of the week.

Carter ordered two sweet teas from Mr. Thomas, wearing his cow-print apron behind the counter. I sat at one of the tall red tables in the corner and looked around the restaurant. Like my shop, the ceilings were beautiful wood, the walls were antique brick, and the pipes were exposed. The flooring was black-and-white checkerboard to give it a '50s diner feel.

Carter sat on the red barstool across from me and placed our drinks on the table. We quietly looked out the window to cars coasting down sleepy Main Street. I noticed the parking lot of Harper's Funeral Home packed with cars and remembered Aunt Maxine, Mrs. Dora, and Mrs. Fannie were at Dennis Johnson's funeral. I made a mental note to send a card of encouragement to Mrs. Johnson at our next third-Thursday meeting.

"So?" I asked over the sizzle of grease frying in the kitchen.

He slurped from the straw and then fidgeted with it. "Do you remember the day I came inside when I dropped Molly off at your house? You gave me fried green tomatoes?"

I nodded.

"I didn't come over that day to tell you I want us to be like Dale and Donna Jameson. I kind of exaggerated their story a little bit. They did go to some football games and have a few double-date dinners together, but that ended when Mrs. Donna slapped Mr. Dale's new wife over a surf and turf dinner at Catfish Cabin."

"What?" I couldn't help but laugh.

He showed me his familiar smile. His teeth were one of the first things that attracted me to him. Straight. Pearly white. And he'd never worn braces a day in his life. "Rae, I came over that day to . . . to ask you to come back to me."

"Milkshakes up! Jalapeño poppers up!" Mr. Thomas

interrupted the awkward silence as a couple across from us went to the counter to get their food.

"What stopped you?"

"I lost my nerve. You happily talked about your new relationship with Kent. And then Aunt Maxine showed up." He continued to tug at the straw in the red textured plastic cup. "Autumn didn't leave me for a younger man. I made that up so you could gloat a little bit. So you could tell me, 'I told you so.' But you didn't do that. The truth is, I ended things because nothing felt right with her. I pretended it did and stuck it out, hoping that something would click between us, that it would justify our divorce, but I quickly realized she wasn't you. And I knew no one else would be you."

"Onion rings up! Fries up!" Mr. Thomas shouted.

"How much food did they order?" Carter asked, frustrated.

"Carter, I don't know what you want me to say."

"Tell me, Rae. Do you love Kent? Do I even have a chance after what I've done to our family? I need to know," he pleaded.

"I think—I think I could love Kent. I mean, I-I do," I stuttered as Carter's eyes disappointedly shifted down to his hands. "I love him for being there for me. I love him for caring about me and caring about Molly. I trust him."

"I know you don't trust me anymore. You have no reason to trust me. But, Rae, think on all the good years we had together. Before Autumn, I was faithful for thirteen years. I never even looked at another woman. I've always loved you.

I just made a stupid mistake. I made one stupid mistake! Are you going to hold it against me forever?"

"Burgers up!"

"Dude! Are you done yet?" Carter shouted at poor Mr. Thomas.

I put my head in my hands and sighed. "Stupid mistake is an understatement."

"Look at me, Raeley. Look at me." He grabbed my hand as I lifted my head. "Do you still love me?"

Lord, yes, I still loved him. I'd loved Carter Sutton since I was eighteen years old. He was the father of my child, my husband of thirteen years. He knew me better than anyone else on this earth. He knew my secrets, my ugly side, my temper, my weaknesses, my strengths. He'd seen me at my worst and had loved me anyway. He was still the most handsome man I'd ever seen. He was still the love of my life.

"I don't know," I fibbed.

"The night I left, I sat in that hotel room knowing I'd made the biggest blunder of my life. I knew I'd regret it. That first night, I knew. And I don't know what stopped me from begging you to take me back immediately. I don't know, Rae. I was confused. My pride got in the way. I was tempted, I guess, by a young girl and the unknown. What I wouldn't give to go back to that night."

I pulled my hand out of his and quickly rubbed my eyes with my palm before he saw my tears fall.

"I've hurt you and our daughter. I'll never forgive myself for it, Raeley, but if you ever give me the chance, I'll make it up to both of you. I'll love you well for the rest of my life. I'll earn your trust again. I promise."

"I can't do this, Carter." I shook my head and took a big gulp of the sweet lemony tea. "I can't talk about this anymore."

"Please don't go, Rae." He grabbed for my hand again.

"I have to," I said. "Leave me alone for a few days, okay? Don't get Molly from practice or take her to dinner tonight. Just leave me alone."

I quickly stood from the red vinyl chair and walked back to my shop.

———◆———

After the conversation with Carter, I couldn't concentrate on the rolltop desk. I sanded one corner too much and dug into the wood and yelled out in frustration. For the first time since the store had opened, I was thrilled when five o'clock came. I had to get out of there. I needed fresh air. I needed to talk to Dawn.

I picked up Molly from basketball practice, briefly chatted with Kent through my car window, and then Molly and I headed straight to Jamie and Dawn's house. I didn't mention that Carter had come into town that afternoon. I just said I wanted to stop by my brother's house and she could hang out with Logan and Liam while I talked with her aunt about some things.

Dawn was pleasantly surprised to see Molly and me on

her porch decorated with hay bales, corn stalks, and pumpkins. She invited us in for homemade pizza and was quick to point out hers was made with a low-carb cauliflower crust. Molly made herself at home and plopped down with a plate of pizza at the kitchen bar in her sweaty basketball clothes. Jamie immediately began playfully teasing her about her need for extra deodorant.

Dawn and I walked out the back door with plates of steaming homemade pizza and sat on the wicker outdoor sofa. The autumn air was chilly, so I pulled the orange throw draped across the back of the couch around my sweatshirt.

I proceeded to tell my sister-in-law everything Carter had said to me that day. She listened intently while chewing her low-carb crust and interrupting me every few sentences with her trademark, "Girl!"

"Girl, I'm not even going to ask if you still love Carter because I know the answer. How could you not? There's so much history there."

"Good history and bad," I added. "Just tell me what to do, Dawn," I said as I set the empty plate on the table beside the couch. The October wind picked up and blew the crumbs from the plate onto the concrete patio.

"I can't tell you what to do. Only you know the answer to that."

"I don't know the answer. That's why I'm asking you."

"Well." She tucked her knees up to her chin to get warm. "I know, from a biblical perspective, you have to forgive Carter. Fully. Now, whether or not you remarry him, that's your decision. Restoring your family would be ideal for Molly, though, wouldn't it?"

"Yes." I picked at my dark nail polish that had chipped from sanding furniture earlier. "Am I capable of forgiving him? Of forgiving Carter?"

"Colossians 3:13, girl."

"You know I don't know what that says, Dawn. I'm still on baby Christian milk over here."

"'Bear with each other and forgive one another if any of you has a grievance against someone. Forgive as the Lord forgave you,'" she answered. "You have to forgive him. You are capable of it with God's help."

"Okay, so I forgive Carter, but what about Kent? I really do care about him, Dawn. I have thought so many times God must have sent him into my life. He's been such a blessing to me. I can't just throw him away."

"You're going to have to pray, girl. Get on your knees in your closet. Open your Bible. Look for the answer. That's the only advice I can give you. Pray. And you'll know."

I sighed and wrapped the blanket tighter around my shoulders. The breeze was blowing the leaves on the pool cover into a little tornado. "I can't hurt Kent. I can't do it. I care too much for him," I thought aloud.

"Then stay with Kent."

"But I don't have peace about his decision to turn down the coaching job. Maybe that's my sign to let him go."

"Then let Kent go."

"Big help, Dawn."

She tugged the blanket away from me and put it over her jeans. "You're not going to know what to do tonight. Or even tomorrow. My suggestion? Go home and keep praying about it. Right now you don't have any peace, but when you do—whether you have peace about being with Carter or peace about being with Kent, then there's your answer. That's how God speaks to me, at least. I have peace in the decision. Pray until you get peace."

"I don't have peace, but I can pray until I get it. I can do that."

"It's kind of exciting, though, isn't it? Two men pining for you at the same time?" She playfully punched me in the arm.

"I feel popular. Kind of like Elise England."

"No, not like Elise England. She's popular because she's a whore."

"Dawn! What a cruel thing to say." I shook my finger at my sister-in-law. "One minute you're telling me to pray, and the next you're calling someone a whore."

"Like the Bible doesn't mention whores. Girl, didn't you hear about Rahab?"

CHAPTER 19

*I*t was my first time to host the third-Thursday meeting. I dropped Molly off at school, ran by the shop to put up a sign that I would open at 1:30 P.M. (which I planned to do every third Thursday of the month), and then spent the rest of the morning cleaning the house. I certainly didn't want the ladies to see a speck of dust or fingerprints on the storm door's glass. I showered and dressed in a nice sweater and my "good" jeans before ironing Mama's orange eyelet table-cloth. I draped it over the round kitchen table and placed a fall centerpiece of small gourds, pine cones, beautiful yellow leaves, and candles in the middle.

I was proud, and relieved, the pumpkin caramel poke cake had turned out perfectly. I cut it into slices and carefully placed them on Mama's gold-rimmed fine china. The coffee was piping hot and poured into the matching saucers just before I heard Aunt Maxine, Mrs. Fannie, and Mrs. Dora walk through the front door, arguing.

"That's the most ridiculous thing I've ever heard you say, Dora." Aunt Maxine huffed as she held on to the door frame and walked over the threshold and into the living room.

"Maxine! When you prune a butterfly bush, you always

cut the old wood away within a few inches of the ground." Mrs. Dora's wrists jingled as she talked with her hands.

"Rae!" Mrs. Fannie changed the subject as the storm door shut behind them. "It smells divine in here. Pumpkin spice?"

"Yes, ma'am. I made Mama's pumpkin caramel poke cake," I said as I ushered Patsy away from sniffing their shoes.

"Margie's favorite fall dish. Oh, I've missed that cake."

Aunt Maxine and the other ladies draped their coats and placed their purses on the couch before entering the kitchen that smelled of cinnamon and nutmeg. Patsy stayed behind to thoroughly smell their coats. She sneezed twice at the combined scent of muscle rub and perfumed powder.

"What a beautiful centerpiece, too, dear." Mrs. Dora leaned in to kiss my cheek. "You've done a fine job here."

"Thank you. Y'all make yourselves at home."

They all put their pens and notebooks on the orange tablecloth and situated themselves into the brown bistro chairs. Aunt Maxine muttered "butterfly bush" under her breath while dumping a spoonful of sugar into the steaming saucer of coffee.

"Rae, we were talking on the way over. Would you mind hosting us next month too? It's my month to host, but Lee and that no-good son-in-law of mine will be arriving that morning for Thanksgiving." Mrs. Fannie sighed.

"Bless your heart, Fannie. A whole week with him in your house?" Dora shook her head.

"He's a burr in my saddle." She took a sip of her coffee.

"Yes, ma'am, I can host next month. I hope to have the carpet and this old linoleum pulled up by then. I would love for you all to see it."

"I remember the original flooring in here. Pine, I think," Aunt Maxine said.

"So Kent tells me you are going to accompany him and help chaperone at the high school Halloween dance tomorrow night. Make sure no one pours liquor into the punch." Mrs. Fannie stirred her coffee.

"Harold used to make a liquor punch," Mrs. Dora began as we all looked to her. "Well, that was before we knew Jesus."

"Molly is old enough for a school dance? Where has the time gone?" Aunt Maxine asked as I placed the dessert plates of cake before them and they all oohed and aahed.

"Yes, I'm going with Kent to help chaperone. I've got to figure out what costume to wear."

"My sister, Ruthie, showed me a picture of her granddaughter last Halloween. Sixteen years old and looked like a woman of the night. Barely enough cloth to make a baby blanket. I tried to be nice, but all I could muster was 'bless her heart.' Well, Ruthie didn't like that one bit." Mrs. Dora sliced into the cake as I joined them at the table.

"Sounds like the apple didn't fall far from the tree. Ruthie went around the block a few times," Aunt Maxine said.

"Maxine! Don't you dare—"

"And, Dora, don't act so holier than thou, what with

those tawdry romance novels you read. At least your sister's granddaughter had clothes on, unlike those heroines in your books," Aunt Maxine muttered.

Mrs. Dora turned red. "Maxine, you're about one comment away from—"

"I like the pun costumes," Mrs. Fannie interrupted. "My granddaughter went as a deviled egg one year. She drew a big yellow circle on a white T-shirt for the yolk and wore some red horns. I didn't particularly like seeing her in anything representing Satan, but it was a cute idea."

"That is a cute idea," I said. "I will come up with something."

"This cake is delicious, Raeley Ann. Tastes just like your mama's." Aunt Maxine wiped her lips and smudged her lipstick with the linen napkin. Mrs. Dora and Mrs. Fannie nodded in agreement.

"Before we get started, let's not forget to send Dennis Johnson's wife a card. Bless her heart. She's struggling with his death. She's been his nurse for the last five years while he was sick. She told me a burden has been lifted, but she just doesn't know what to do with her time anymore," Mrs. Dora said.

"I was that way when Pratt died. I'd just sit in the living room and listen to the grandfather clock tick. I didn't know what to do with myself," Mrs. Fannie added.

"I was the same after the divorce. I didn't have a grandfather clock, but I remember the refrigerator humming. It wouldn't quit. *Hum. Hum. Hum*," I said. "One day Mama came over and forced me to leave the house. She said that refrigerator was going to drive me crazy. We went to lunch at a little deli in Huntsville. No one was in the place, and we could hear the big subzero refrigerator in the kitchen humming. That was the first time I really laughed after Carter left."

They chuckled.

"He wants me back," I blurted out, and the sound of their forks hitting their plates echoed in the kitchen.

"Carter wants you back?" Aunt Maxine asked.

"I don't know what to do." I shook my head and looked to Mrs. Fannie. "I love being with Kent, Mrs. Fannie. I don't want to hurt him. Or you. But do I need to take Carter back to restore my family? Is that's what's best for me? And for Molly? I'm praying about it. I'm listening for the Lord. I'm waiting to have peace about it. I'm just still so confused."

"Well, Raeley Ann—" Aunt Maxine situated her stooped back against the chair.

"Hush it, Maxine!" Mrs. Dora exclaimed. "She's talking to Fannie."

Aunt Maxine pursed her lips and went back to eating her cake.

"Oh, sweet Rae." Mrs. Fannie smiled lovingly at me. "You're doing the right thing by praying. If God has softened Carter's heart and he's repented for his mistakes, then you must forgive him."

"I have forgiven him. I really have. I just don't know if

that means we should get back together." I shrugged and poked at the cake with my fork.

"Kent would be hurt. I would be a little disappointed, too, because I love the two of you together, but it's not up to me. Or Kent. You have to obey God's plan for *your* life."

"This reminds me of a story," Mrs. Dora began.

"No, Dora, I'm telling a story," Aunt Maxine interjected and Mrs. Dora waved, annoyed, as if the floor was all hers. "Raeley Ann, did your mother ever tell you about Cecil?"

"No." I shook my head.

"Oh, Lord, not Cecil," Mrs. Dora mumbled before finishing her coffee.

"Growing up, Cecil Gray lived next door to us. He was in love with your mother from the time he was ten or so. He was relentless in pursuing her. He left flowers for her on our porch. If he saw her outside doing chores, he ran over to help her. He was kind and quick to help our parents with whatever they needed. He was a good boy." She paused to take the last bite of cake. "Margie didn't care much for Cecil at first, but as time went on, he wooed her. She fell in love with him, and by the time she was eighteen, she was dead set on marrying Cecil Gray. They were just waiting to save up some money before they said I do."

"I've never heard this," I said, amazed, because I thought my mother had told me everything about her life.

"And then one day she went to the hardware store to buy some sandpaper for Daddy. That's where she met James. I'll never forget when she came home that afternoon. I was married to Wilson by then and had been out of the house for a couple of years, but I was helping Mama bake that day. Don't ask me what we were baking. And Margie called me to come outside on the porch with her. She said, 'Maxine, how did you know Wilson was the one?'"

"Because he was the only one who would put up with you." Dora smiled and Mrs. Fannie muffled a chuckle.

Aunt Maxine rolled her eyes. "I told her I just knew. And she said, 'Well, I think I know who the one is for me. And it isn't Cecil.'"

"Margie always told me she knew the moment she saw James that he was the love of her life," Mrs. Fannie added.

"Well, this was scandalous. Margie had been with Cecil Gray for years. We had all gotten used to the idea that they were going to be married. And now she was willing to throw all that away and break Cecil's heart for some new kid who had just moved to town and worked in the hardware store." Aunt Maxine shook her head. "But, like Song of Solomon says, she had found the one whom her soul loved."

"What about Cecil? What did he do when she told him?" I asked.

"Cecil went crazy," Mrs. Dora remarked. "Stark raving mad."

"He did no such thing, Dora. Just because he was heartbroken for a while doesn't mean he went crazy."

"Who climbed the water tower, Maxine? And had to be coaxed down by the fire department? I believe it was Cecil Gray? Hmmm?" Mrs. Dora smirked.

"Yes," Mrs. Fannie spoke, "Cecil went through a rough patch, Rae. He was heartbroken when Margie left him, but he recovered. He went on to marry a lovely girl from Ryland and have half a dozen children and own his own business. He passed away a couple of years ago, but he led a good life. Margie did what she had to do. And if she hadn't, you and Jamie wouldn't be here, would you?"

"So, she just knew? She knew she had to throw caution to the wind for Daddy?"

"She knew. She stewed over it for the longest time, but eventually she had the peace that you're praying for. Keep praying. You'll know." Aunt Maxine reached over and patted my hand.

"And just hope Carter or Kent don't end up climbing the water tower," Mrs. Dora added with a wink.

———— ◆ ————

I lost my love for Halloween when I was eight years old. I went trick-or-treating as Wonder Woman that year. As Paige and I ran from house to house in our neighborhood, the flimsy plastic mask covered my eyes, blinding me, and I fell right into a drainage ditch. I sprained my ankle, not to mention my bucket of candy flew everywhere and my plastic cape was splattered with mud. As Mama wrapped my ankle in an Ace bandage, I realized it was easier and less dangerous to ask her to buy me Skittles at the grocery store.

Molly had never fallen into a drainage ditch, so Halloween still excited her. She loved searching for the perfect costume and watching scary movies. This year half of the girls' basketball team decided to dress in their uniforms and the other half of the team dressed as donuts, complete with colorful sprinkles drawn on their shirts and paint on their faces. They were the Dunkin' Donuts.

Kent was wearing a furry wolf suit beneath a basketball jersey and shorts when he picked Molly and me up that Friday evening. He was Teen Wolf from the '80s classic movie. He laughed uproariously when I walked out of the house in a costume Molly had told me was lame no less than forty-five times. I wore a simple black T-shirt and draped a couple of Molly's middle school academic medals around my neck. I clutched two loaves of bread.

"I'm a breadwinner," I said matter-of-factly when I greeted him on my front porch.

"I can see that." Kent laughed.

"Aren't you going to get tired of holding two packages of bread all night? Tell her, Coach. You'll put the bread down and then you'll just be walking around with your teenaged daughter's medals around your neck. Looks like you're going as someone living vicariously through their kid," Molly joked as she walked out the front door.

"I happen to agree with Mrs. Fannie. I like puns. It was either this one or the bull in a china shop. Did you want me to walk into your school with bull horns on my head while holding your nana's teacup? Besides, if you aren't standing by Ella all night, people will think you're just going as a basketball player. That's lame," I argued.

Kent continued to laugh from beneath his wolf mask at our banter and opened his truck door for both of us to climb in.

———◆———

We walked into the purple and white Whitten High School gym eerily decorated with cobwebs, plastic spiders, skeletons, and jack-o'-lanterns. We never had a Halloween dance when I attended the school, but I thought of my senior prom held in that very gym. I didn't have a date. Paige and Emma Wheeler didn't either, and Kerry's boyfriend had just broken his leg in a dirt bike accident, so we all dressed to the nines and went together. I remembered leaning against the purple-and-white striped wall with Kerry, watching my classmates dance with their dates to LeAnn Rimes's hit "How Do I Live" and thinking, *Will I ever be in love?* And less than a year later, Carter Sutton danced into my life and changed everything.

Kent and I were asked by Assistant Principal Abney to man the dessert table. We stood guard over jack-o'-lantern cupcakes, peanut butter and chocolate eyeballs, strawberries dipped in white chocolate to look like ghosts, and witch finger cookies. Every kid who stopped by for a treat gave Kent a fist bump. They all seemed to love Coach Richardson, even those who didn't play basketball for him. I watched his eyes light up inside that wolf mask as he joked with those kids. He really did enjoy being a part of their lives.

A DJ dressed in a Michael Myers mask and coveralls was set up beneath the basketball goal and danced goofily while Michael Jackson's "Thriller" echoed throughout the school. Kids in costumes twirled across the hardwood of the dark gym, illuminated only by the orange, green, and purple strobe lights swirling. Kent and I sat on the bottom bleacher behind the dessert table. We watched the hundred or so kids dance and he held my hand.

"Is Freddy Krueger groping the disco princess?" he shouted over the loud music as he leaned into me.

"No, I see his razor hand." I eyed the kids.

"What about his other hand?"

"I don't think so. I think Freddy is on good behavior."

"Got to keep a close eye on these youngsters. A dark gym. Costumed faces. Hyped up on cupcakes. No telling what could happen." He smiled and gave my hand a tight squeeze.

I laughed. "Thanks for asking me to come tonight. This is fun." I nodded at Molly and her friends dancing to the *Ghostbusters* theme. "Molly looks like she's having a good time, but who is that kid in the T-Rex suit that keeps hanging around?"

"Oh, that's Macon Bennett. Freshman. He's on my JV team. You don't have to worry about him. He's a good kid."

"Is she really old enough to be dancing with a boy in a high school gym?"

He gave my hand another squeeze. "I think she is." He paused. "Have you ever thought of having another one?"

"Another kid?" I asked, surprised. "Well, Kent, no. Not really. I just figured it was God's will for me to only have one. What about you? You want kids?"

"I do," he answered. "I'm only forty. Forty isn't too old, is it?"

"Mama had me at forty," I said. "I don't think you're too old at all."

He smiled and I began to digest what he'd just said. He was implying that he wanted more children . . . with me. It seemed like too much, too soon. We were still getting to know one another. We hadn't even verbally professed our love for one another. Maybe I could envision spending the rest of my days with him and maybe even having children, if my eggs hadn't shriveled up yet. I glanced over at him as he watched costumed kids bob around the dance floor and I asked myself, *Do you really love him, Rae?* I couldn't answer my own question with certainty.

The DJ took a break and the bright lights came on, leaving us all squinting our eyes. Kids rushed off to the bathrooms and swamped all the food and drink tables set up around the perimeter of the gymnasium. Molly hovered by the orange punch table with some friends while T-Rex playfully slapped at her back with his short dinosaur arms. Molly didn't seem to mind one bit. In fact, she flirted back with him by smiling and grabbing at his costume. I didn't know how I felt about this—about my little girl no longer being so little. Kent was serving the kids sugar, and on a whim, I whipped out my phone and took a picture of Molly and Macon standing side by side and laughing. I sent the photo to Carter with the caption, "Do you approve of this?" Within thirty seconds, Carter responded.

NO! Who is the T-Rex?

> He keeps flirting with her. I
> don't think she minds.

I'm on my way.

> You are not.

Wasn't she just trick-or-treating in a Dora the Explorer costume?

> Seems like it.

What costume did you pick? You aren't Naughty Nurse Nookie or Red-Light-District Riding Hood, are you?

> You know better. I'm wearing
> some of Molly's medals and
> there are two loaves of bread
> sitting on the bleachers
> beside me, but I'm supposed
> to be holding them.

????

> Breadwinner, dummy.

Well, that's genius.

I thought so. Especially since
I'm divorced and support
myself now.

Good point. Having a good
time?

Yes.

Danced with Kent yet?

Not yet.

Don't dance to "Fade into
You." It will kill me.

They aren't going to play a
Mazzy Star song at a 2018
Halloween dance.

True. No "Black Magic
Woman," then.

I don't think they are going to
play a Santana song at a 2018
dance either.

True. Well, just don't dance
with Kent at all.

Got to go.

I ended the chat.

When the lights went dark again for the last half of the dance, "I Put a Spell on You" began to play. Michael Myers swayed behind his turntable, but half the kids remained standing to the side of the gym because there wasn't anything more awkward in life than slow dancing with your teenaged, acne-riddled peers. Thankfully, T-Rex didn't take Molly into his short arms either.

"Dance with me?" Kent asked. "Is that appropriate?"

"I think so." I smiled.

"I think so too. Principal Abney has a pirate in her arms. I hope it's Mr. Abney beneath that beard and eye patch. Although, rumor is it might be Mr. Cole, the Algebra 1 teacher."

He led me onto the dance floor, and I saw Molly immediately cover her face with her hands in utter embarrassment. Ella and some other girls dressed as donuts gathered around her in support. One donut put her hand over her heart and pretended to cry as if she wished she were the one dancing with the handsome Teen Wolf.

We knew students were watching our every move, so we didn't press close to one another. We gracefully, and tactfully, swayed across the floor with a handful of kids and chaperones. I secretly wished Molly would snap our photo and text her daddy, "Do you approve of this?"

I really liked Molly's new friend Ella. She was a tall, pretty kid with long blond hair, freckles, and impeccable manners. I had talked to her mom, Melissa (also a single mother), a couple of times while waiting on the girls to get out of practice. She was a few years older than me, but I vaguely remembered her name from school. Aunt Maxine and the ladies had given me enough good reports on her family that I felt comfortable with Molly having sleepovers at Ella's house. So after the Halloween dance, when Molly begged to go home with her for the night, I complied.

"I smell like a bakery," I said as I tossed the somewhat squished loaves of bread to the kitchen counter. "Wine?"

"Yes, please!" Kent called on his way to the bathroom to take off the scratchy wolf suit and change into jeans and a T-shirt.

I turned up the heat in the cool house and made my way to the sofa with the wine glasses while Kent entered the living room. We gave each other a quick kiss as I handed him the glass. We sat close together in the bend of the L-shaped couch and took a sip. The wind whipped through the trees surrounding the house and undoubtedly sent their orange and yellow leaves to the ground. Rain splattered on the roof while Patsy crawled next to us and nuzzled her head on Kent's leg.

"I had a good time tonight," I said.

"I did too." Kent draped his arm around my shoulder and pulled me in closer.

"You sure T-Rex is a good kid?"

He chuckled. "I'm sure. I'll watch him like a hawk though."

"Good."

"I got another call from Sketch today," he said before putting the glass to his mouth.

"Who?" I asked.

"Trent Taylor at Alabama. We always called him Sketch because he drew out every play in elaborate detail."

"Oh yeah?" I rested my head on Kent's shoulder as Patsy began to snore. "They still want you for the job then?"

"I've told him no twice, but he's dead set on me coming down to talk to them about it. Sketch has never taken no for an answer."

"Kent." I leaned up to look him in the eye. "Why don't you? Don't you see what an amazing opportunity this is?"

"No," he said. "You're an amazing opportunity. Us. This. What we talked about earlier."

"What did we talk about?"

"Children? Maybe?" he asked sheepishly.

I looked to my socked feet on the floor as my heart pounded between my shirt. I didn't have any peace when he brought up the subject of more children. I didn't have any peace when he talked about turning down Tuscaloosa.

"Then why even tell me? If you're not going to take the job, then why tell me he called you again?" I became angry. "Are you trying to put some kind of guilt trip on me? Do you resent me already? Is this your subtle way of letting me know you resent me? Are you going to casually mention to me for the next twenty years that *Sketch* called?"

"Hey, calm down," Kent said kindly and placed his wine glass on the coffee table. "I was just telling you that he called. There's no ulterior motive here, Rae. I'm telling you about my day. I had oatmeal for breakfast. Sketch called while I was having a grilled cheese at lunch. One of my players jammed his finger at practice today. His calling was simply part of my day. I don't want the job. I'm just making conversation with you."

I felt silly. My temper had reared its ugly head.

"I'm sorry, Kent," I said. "You didn't deserve any of that."

"Listen." He took my hands into his. "I'm going to tell you one last time. I really love my life here in Whitten. I didn't think I'd stay here more than a couple of months after my dad died, but I'm glad I did. I love my job. I love coaching those kids. I love being with you. I don't need the salary Tuscaloosa has offered me. I do fine with what I have. I don't need the stress. I don't want to travel all over the country. I'm content right here. With my job. With you. Believe me, okay?"

"Okay. I believe you," I said as we leaned back on the couch together.

Still, the peace didn't come.

CHAPTER 20

It was spitting snow on the frigid November morning Molly Margaret Sutton was born. She came into the world at 9:32 A.M., weighing eight pounds and four ounces. Her eyes were the color of coffee, just like her daddy's, and she had a head full of dark hair that Mama said explained why I had terrible heartburn most of the pregnancy. She was a beautiful baby with a flawless complexion. When the nurse placed her on my chest, all I could do was cry tears of joy.

The snowy day she was born seemed like just yesterday, but fifteen years had flown by. I lovingly watched her sitting at the kitchen table eating her traditional birthday breakfast (a Fudge Round and a tall glass of Dr Pepper over ice) on the colorful "It's My Birthday!" plate Mama had given her when she was about five. She resembled her father—her eyes the same dreamy brown hue and her hair long and dark. She had his tan complexion, his mannerisms, even his laugh. No matter the anger I'd harbored toward him in the past, he'd given me my greatest blessing.

"Breakfast of champions." I sat beside her with my cup of coffee.

"You know it." She took the last bite of the Little Debbie cake. "I miss Nana."

My heart fluttered and my eyes threatened to leak. I grabbed her hand resting on the kitchen table and gave it a squeeze.

"I know you do, sweetheart. I do too."

"She always made me feel so special, you know?" She looked to me. "She would have already called this morning to sing to me. I miss her."

"I know, my love."

"So," she said, changing the subject, "Dad is going to pick me up from basketball practice and we're going straight back to Huntsville."

"You've got everything packed for the weekend?"

She nodded as Patsy slowly walked to her and placed her head on Molly's lap for an ear scratching. "I'm so glad my birthday landed on a Saturday. I'm really excited to see Lauren and everyone."

"I know you've missed them," I said. "So tell me the plan. Pizza, IMAX, and then what?"

She shrugged. "I don't know. Lauren said we should go to Game On, but I really don't care about riding go-karts and bumper cars when it's this cold outside. We may just hang around the arcade."

"And then all the girls are staying the night with you at your dad's house?"

"Right," she said.

"Bless Carter's heart for having five girls in the house.

Y'all don't keep him up all night with your whooping and hollering."

"Oh, we will." She patted Patsy's head before standing to put her birthday plate and empty glass in the sink. "Thanks for breakfast, Mama. And for the clothes. I really needed those jeans."

"You're welcome, sweetheart. Happy birthday."

———— ◆ ————

After I dropped off Molly at basketball practice that Saturday morning, I raced over to the shop to open up by ten thirty. I really enjoyed owning my own business and setting flexible hours to accommodate Molly's practices and my ministry meetings with the ladies.

It was a slow morning, but I sold a set of nightstands and some picture frames. One of the buyers, a sweet old lady with awfully dyed orange hair, spent at least forty-five minutes chatting with me about a trip she took with Mama and Aunt Maxine to Chattanooga one summer. I loved getting stopped in the grocery store or at church to hear a story about my mother. This was her town. This was my town. And I felt as if she was with me every day.

When the lady with the orange hair was finally gone, I spent the remainder of my free time putting the finishing touches on an antique changing table a client brought in last week to have repaired and refinished.

When I got home around four thirty that afternoon,

I stood in the living room with my hands on my hips. I wanted to keep myself occupied instead of thinking about Molly's birthday party and how part of me wished I'd gone to Huntsville with her. I decided tonight was as good a night as any to start ripping up carpet in the house.

I knew I wouldn't be able to move some of the bigger pieces of furniture on my own, so I called Kent and asked him to come over and help. I did miss him. I hadn't seen him in a couple of days because he and his teams were putting in a lot of work in preparation for the upcoming first games of the season. I'd also been really busy at the shop. We'd only seen each other in passing when I picked up Molly from practice. He said he'd gladly help me with whatever I needed and offered to make spaghetti for us when he arrived. He needed to do a couple of loads of laundry first and take a shower. I told him to hurry because I really couldn't wait to see him. And then I thought of his talk about kids and Tuscaloosa and that uneasy feeling resurfaced. I pushed it away.

It was such a chilly night that I put on a pot of coffee before moving some smaller pieces of furniture off of the carpet and into the kitchen and carport. Once those were out of the room, I couldn't wait any longer. I tugged on the carpeting near the front door. Without much effort at all, the seams ripped and it pulled loose from the floor. Another tug or two and the beautiful hardwood floor that had been hidden for decades was revealed. I could not believe my parents had covered such magnificent flooring with that beige,

shaggy mess. Mama always defended their decision by saying, "The house always seemed so cold with the hardwood.
I was old and pregnant and insisted your father put down
the plushest carpet we could afford."

I ran my hand across the pine, smiled widely, and told
Patsy, "Now, that's a gorgeous floor, isn't it, girl?" She
couldn't care less and rolled over on the couch.

I continued yanking until I reached the heavy entertainment center and had to quit. I walked to the spot where
the carpeting met the linoleum of the kitchen and began
to tug. The carpet there was quite loose already from so
many years of being a high-traffic area, and it easily peeled
like a banana. The hardwood was revealed and so was my
mother's pale pink stationery. She had slipped a letter for me
under the loose spot of the carpet. I immediately grabbed it
and took a seat in the middle of my kitchen floor crowded
with end tables, lamps, and an ottoman.

Rae,

If you're reading this, then odds are you are living in
our home and have ripped up the carpeting. However,
someone else could have bought the house and decided
to remove the carpet and found this note. If the latter is
the case: Hello, my name is Margie Reeves. This letter
is intended for my daughter, Raeley Reeves Sutton. Her
address at the time of my death was 1500 Harvest Ridge,
Apt. 309, Huntsville, Alabama. Would you please see that
she receives this?

Lord have mercy—now that we've gotten that out of the way.

Rae, I hope you are the one to find this letter. I know it's bringing you a lot of joy to see these old wooden floors. I grew up poor. The last thing I want to see was another scarred floor, rusted doors, and anything with patina (including your aunt Maxine's car hood). But I know you love those things. You love finding the treasure in trash. One thing I've never understood though. Why do you paint old things to look new and then sand and scuff them to look old again?

This is the last letter I plan to write to you. I'm getting sicker. I know my time on this earth is coming to an end. I am not scared, Rae. I am looking forward to being healthy and whole again. I tell you, though, I may have taken seventy-five trips around the sun, but my life has flown by.

You hear "cherish the moment" so often that it has become cliché. Well, listen to this old dying woman—cherish the moment. Every moment. Every time Molly Margaret steps onto a basketball court or sits on the couch drinking Dr Pepper, look at her as long as time allows. Relish in your youth, and hers. Appreciate the good and even the bad, Rae. Cherish the valley, because that is where you find the strength to reach the mountaintop.

I want you to appreciate moments with Carter as well. I know his leaving hurt you terribly. One of my saddest experiences in this life was holding you at the foot of your bed while you cried so hard you could barely speak. My heart broke right along with yours. I was so angry with Carter for tearing your family apart. I could have kicked that boy's behind from here to kingdom come. You didn't deserve that pain, and Molly Margaret didn't either.

I want you to know I forgive Carter for what he did to your family, Rae, and I pray you will forgive him too. He asked me never to tell you this, but I'm going to because what's he going to do about it after I'm dead?

He called me one afternoon last week. He said he needed to see me and showed up at my front door later that evening. As soon as his feet hit the carpet you're now ripping up, he completely broke down. It reminded me of the same sobbing you did on your bed that afternoon. I reached up and took him into my arms, and all he kept saying was, "Mrs. Margie, I'm just so sorry."

I fixed him a glass of tea and offered him some choco-late chip cookies. They were store-bought, but he gobbled them all up anyway. He was still crying while he ate. He looked like an emotional toddler sitting at my kitchen table with chocolate chip crumbs on his mouth and tears in his eyes.

Once he'd pulled himself together, I reached across the table and took his hands into mine and asked him to talk to me. He told me the real reason he left, Rae. He told me all about the young girl from the restaurant. And he was riddled with guilt over it. He insisted he didn't care one iota for the poor girl, but he was sticking it out with her to see if it was possible to love someone besides you.

But it wasn't.

I asked him why in the world he did something so asinine as to betray his loving wife and devastate Molly the way he did. I'll never forget his answer.

"Because I'm a fool, Mrs. Margie."

We had a good therapy session right here in my kitchen, and I quickly pegged the issue. He'd simply undergone some kind of premature midlife crisis. He felt tied down and trapped. He was bored with being married. He was intrigued at the thought of a new and exciting romantic relationship. The impulses that overtook him were destructive and irrational. However, it didn't take long for him to realize his grievous mistake. After a few months into his "new and exciting romantic relationship," he understood being married to you was far better than being in a relationship with someone else.

Old Roy Cox went through a midlife crisis. He was quite a bit older than Carter, but he lost his ever-loving mind. He left his wife of over thirty years and traded in his diesel truck for a stupid little car with a spoiler on the back. Maxine and I were eating at Bea's one night and he came strutting in with some young brunette on his arm. His white hair had been dyed black as night, yet his eyebrows were their original color. He was about five shades tanner than usual and was wearing a Hawaiian shirt, a

gold chain, and ill-fitting jeans with some kind of rhinestones on the pockets. Lord have mercy, Rae, you should
have heard Maxine. I nearly choked on my hushpuppies
as she (loudly) commented on his appearance.

Roy's wife passed away not long after he left her.
Maxine and I went to the funeral, and Roy's hair was
its familiar white, his skin was winter pale, and there
weren't any rhinestones on his suit. He was sobbing over
her casket, and I overheard him tell Marcus Cooper that
he'd broken her heart. He was convinced that's what
killed her. "I never should have left her, Marcus. She was
the love of my life."

Maybe I should have called to tell you about my
conversation with Carter the moment he left my house.
Maybe it would have eased some of your pain to know
Carter still loves you, Raeley, and he regrets what he did
to your family. But he asked me not to tell you, so I honored his wish. I don't know if he'll ever toss his pride aside
and tell you everything he told me, but I hope he does.
Even so, you may find another man who is crazy about
you and Molly. There may be someone besides Carter
Sutton out there who loves you well and dances with you
in the kitchen until you burn the fried green tomatoes.
You may find someone new to cherish.

If so, at least be cordial with Carter. Forgive him.
He's a broken man who made a mistake. But we're all
broken in some way, aren't we? Befriend him for Molly's
sake. I know you can do it because you have such a gift of

restoring things and making them new. Bury the hatchet
the same way I buried the hardwood under the carpet.

    I love you with my heart.

                    Until we meet again,

                    Mama

As I put the letter to the side and wiped my damp cheeks, the peace I had been praying for came. Then Kent knocked on the front door.

CHAPTER 21

Sunday after church, I buffered the hardwood and applied a fresh coat of finish. I stood to the side of the living room to admire the floor. I was so pleased with the way it had turned out and couldn't wait for Kent to get back from Huntsville with the rug I had ordered last week. Mama may have preferred the carpet, but no doubt she would have been pleased with the way the floor gleamed and added charming character to the house.

Kent and I placed the large Persian rug with hints of blue and gray in the center of the living room. We worked together to move all of the furniture back in and then we sat on the couch to revel in the renovation.

"So, what's next?" he asked as I settled into the crook of his arm.

"She's probably going to tear down a wall. It's what she does," Molly said from the opposite end of the couch.

"Kitchen cabinets," I answered. "They are so outdated and must be painted. Then the linoleum has to go. I don't think I'll find hardwood to match this well, so I'm thinking gray-and-white ornamental tile. I saw some online last night that would be so pretty with a subway tile backsplash. Black cabinet pulls. New faucet."

"I don't know what half that means," Kent confessed. "What's a subway tile?"

"Don't ask questions, Coach. Just smile and nod." Molly stood from the couch and walked into the kitchen with Patsy following behind her.

"Let's make vegetable soup." I slapped my knees and stood.

"I'll do the cornbread." He held up his hand for me to pull him off the couch.

I loved cooking with Kent. Carter never stepped foot in our kitchen unless it was to rummage through the refrigerator. But I enjoyed sharing the space with Kent. He even washed, dried, and put dishes away as we went. I thought of dancing with him while fried green tomatoes burned in the skillet. And then he'd be the one to flip them. And I had peace, even joy, with the thought. I really needed God to come down on a cloud and tell me what to do—who to love—because my mind wrestled with my options every single day.

The three of us sat at the kitchen table while steam rose from the piping hot soup in our bowls.

"I've got a trick." Kent walked to the fridge and got three cubes of ice from the freezer. He dropped one into each bowl of soup. "It'll cool quicker this way."

"Well, aren't you smart? To think we've been burning our lips on soup our entire lives. No more!" I joked as I stirred the melting cube into the broth.

"So we play Ryland next week. Give me the scoop, Coach." Molly nibbled on her cornbread.

"You've got to watch number five. She's not afraid to shoot the three. Don't even give her the chance to take the shot. We're going to be working on defense all day tomorrow," he said.

"Which plays are you going to run?" she asked.

I loved when Molly and Kent talked basketball, but still, I tuned them out and stared through the doorway to the beautiful floor. I was so proud of it and was eager to start the kitchen renovation. I continued to scan the living room while I slurped the soup and realized I needed something to go on the wall above the couch. I had a large tobacco basket at the shop that would be perfect.

". . . and full-court press will work," Kent finished.

"I wonder if I can get this kitchen done in time for Thanksgiving?" I thought out loud.

"Uncle Jamie or Aunt Maxine aren't going to host this year?" Molly asked.

"We've always had Thanksgiving in this house. The turkey and dressing have always been made in this kitchen. I don't want that to change just because Mama isn't here. Besides, I would love a reason for everyone to see the floor."

"Enough with the floor. You're obsessed." Molly's eyes grew wide as she teased me. "It's just a floor, woman."

"A stunning fifty-year-old floor," I retorted and stuck my tongue out at her.

"She loves flooring the way we love basketball, Molly. Cut her some slack." Kent laughed.

"Coach, are you going to come to Thanksgiving dinner?"

I'd wrestled with this decision too. I didn't like the thought of Carter being alone on Thanksgiving. I had contemplated inviting him and maybe even driving up to Tullahoma to visit with his dad and Aunt Paulette after dinner. Where that left Kent, I didn't know.

"You and Mrs. Fannie should both come. We'll put the folding tables in the living room and have plenty of room for everyone," I said.

"I would love to," he answered before his eyes turned downcast to his soup on the table. I knew something wasn't right as he remained quiet for a few moments.

"Girls," he finally said. "I've been putting this off, but now is good a time as any since I've got you both together."

He placed the spoon in the bowl and looked back and forth between us.

"Sketch called again," he said, almost ashamed, as his eyes caught mine. "Remember I told you he never takes no for an answer, Rae?"

"You're going to take the job, aren't you?"

"Well, I've been thinking this through, and I know how to make this work," he said with confidence before looking to Molly. "Northbrook High School is one of the best schools in Alabama. Their basketball team is amazing. That's who we lost the state tournament to last year. Coach Vance is in the business of getting girls seen by colleges. You'd have an amazing opportunity playing ball there, Molly."

"C-coach, I—" Molly stuttered.

"Wait, Kent," I interrupted her. "You're suggesting we move to Tuscaloosa with you?"

He paused. "That's what I'm asking, Rae. Yes. I want you and Molly to come with me."

I placed my folded hands on the table. "Kent, we can't do that. I told you we can't do that." I looked to Molly, who held an expression of surprise. "I just moved back to Whitten. I plan to live in my mother's house for a long time. I have plans to renovate the rest of the house. I just opened a business. I'm not subjecting Molly to more change. We're happy here. Stable."

"Coach, I've made friends here. Huntsville, my old friends, my dad are all right down the road. Tuscaloosa is, what, three hours away?"

"I know." Kent pushed his soup bowl away and placed his folded hands on the table too. "I don't know what I'm supposed to do."

We all sat silently for a moment before I asked, "What changed your mind about the job? About the traveling? About leaving the kids here?"

"Sketch changed my mind. He keeps pointing out what a great opportunity this is. I could be promoted to the head coach of Alabama basketball one day. I've been praying on it and had a nudge that this is what I should do. I have peace about it. But I don't want to do it without you, Rae. Without both of you."

Molly looked to me and raised her eyebrows.

"You've got to take the job, Kent." I finally broke the

silence. "You can't let us hold you back. You have peace about it. You have to be obedient to what God is calling you to do."

He looked to me with desperation. "I don't want to leave you."

"And I don't want you to spend the rest of our relationship wondering what could have been. Every time you watch an Alabama basketball game on television, you'll resent me. I can't live with that. I don't want you to live with it either."

"What about this season, Coach? When would you leave? Who will coach us?" Molly asked.

"I wouldn't go until our season is done. I told Sketch I've made a commitment to you girls and boys, and I'm going to see it through. I want us to make it to state again this year. I know we're capable of it. And then I'd sign on with them when school is out."

"Well, I agree with Mama," Molly said. "You have to go."

His sad eyes shifted around the kitchen. I knew this decision was weighing heavy on his mind. I wanted to cry into my bowl of soup because I really did care about this man.

"Hey," I said, "we have the rest of this season. Once you move, you will still come see us when you visit Mrs. Fannie. Molly and I will come to some home games. You'll get us courtside seats, right?" I smiled as he grinned and nodded.

"You are the best thing to ever happen to me, Rae," he muttered and reached for my hand.

"Okay, I'm going to leave you two alone now." Molly

stood from the table. "It's starting to sound like a soap opera in here."

She took her bowl of soup to her room and Patsy followed the scent. She knew Molly would let her lick the bowl when she was done.

"I love you, Rae."

"I love you," I replied as tears welled in my eyes. "I love you enough to let you go."

"You think this is the right thing to do?" He searched my face for confirmation and gave my hand a squeeze.

"I do, sweetheart. I really do," I said with confidence. With peace. And I silently thanked the Lord.

———— ◆ ————

Kent stayed at the house pretty late that night. Molly went on to bed while we continued to talk about the job offer, and I buried my head into his chest and cried. He'd been just what I needed when Mother died. He helped to mend me, to restore my joy. He was placed in my life by God. But only for a season.

Our hug at the front door that night lasted longer than usual. We shared one last kiss before he disappeared inside his truck and reversed down the driveway covered in dead leaves.

Even though we had promised to remain friends, I knew it wouldn't happen. I knew what would happen though: He would coach Molly for the rest of the season, and we'd make small talk after the games. Maybe we'd meet at Bea's or Rubio's to catch up. But in six months, he'd be living in Tuscaloosa and we'd rarely communicate, if at all. The friendship would cease. I would miss him, and his companionship, but I'd remember who holds the anchor and move on.

I tossed and turned for hours while the winter wind whipped through the trees outside my bedroom window. My brain wouldn't shut off. One thing was certain: Kent's leaving didn't mean I was going tell Carter to rent a U-Haul and move all of his belongings into our house on Hazel Tree. It didn't mean I was going to fall into his arms and pick up where we'd left off nearly two years ago either. Kent's leaving meant I was going to take the time to continue healing emotionally from my divorce, Mama's passing, and now Kent's absence. I made the adamant decision to pursue forgiveness and friendship with Carter, but nothing more, then I finally fell asleep.

CHAPTER 22

The third Thursday in November was the coldest day of the month. The windchill was a bitter eleven degrees and sleet covered the roads. I called Aunt Maxine early that morning and suggested postponing our meeting, but she scolded me through the phone. "We've traveled through snow, sleet, and even braved a tornado for our ministry. We're like postal workers. Nothing can keep us from our duty." So I hung up and got to work preparing for their arrival.

I had refinished my kitchen in ten days. I worked from the time I came home from the shop until late at night, sometimes till two or three in the morning. Molly had opened her bedroom door and shouted at me from the hallway, "Mama! I'm trying to sleep. What are you doing in there?" more than once as I painted the oak cabinets white, changed the hardware to sleek black square knobs, yanked out linoleum, and installed the gray-and-white decorative tile. I installed a matte black kitchen faucet and chandelier in the same finish where the old flush globe had resided. Mama insisted the globe looked like a woman's breast and called it a "boob light."

On Thursday morning I finished vacuuming dust from

the renovation and made a pot of butternut squash soup with pumpkin cheesecake for dessert. I placed the orange eyelet cloth on the table not long before the ladies walked through the front door.

"Why in the world is that child out there shooting basketball in this cold, Raeley Ann?" Aunt Maxine shouted at me before hanging her heavy wool coat and scarf on one of the newly installed hooks by the front door.

"She didn't have school today because of teacher meetings. If she's not at school, she's shooting basketball," I answered.

"These floors! Oh mercy!" Mrs. Dora said while removing her coat, the orange-and-yellow leaf bangled bracelet on her wrist clinking.

"The house is gorgeous, Rae," Mrs. Fannie added. "And it smells delectable too. We're going to ask you to host every single month if you keep this up."

I ushered them to my refurbished kitchen as they remarked at the transformation. They were sure to let me know how proud they were of me for doing everything on my own. I hated to toot my own horn, but I was proud of myself too.

I ladled the steamy soup into the autumn-themed bowls I recently purchased. They were cream with the cutest little acorns adorning them. I bought coffee cups and dessert plates to match. I had gotten them especially for this occasion—and for the same reason I repurposed old crystal doorknobs and hung them as coat hooks by the front door. I wanted to keep hosting these ladies for years to come, and they needed somewhere to hang their coats in the winter, their umbrellas in the spring, and they certainly deserved acorn-covered dinnerware for autumn desserts.

I placed the soup on the table before them and dropped an ice cube into each bowl.

"Well, I'll be. My brother, Theo, always did that, Rae. It works like a charm, doesn't it?" Mrs. Fannie remarked.

I had to admit, the house seemed colder with the hardwood flooring exposed throughout. Instead of regretting my decision and ordering a new batch of beige carpet, though, I simply put an oscillating heater in the middle of the living room and a nice draft of warm air made its way to us in the kitchen. The soup also warmed us from the inside out.

"I don't remember it being this frigid before Christmas," Aunt Maxine said. "January is usually our coldest month."

"Well, I don't like it one bit," Mrs. Dora added before taking another slurp of soup. "The cold makes my knees hurt. And poor Harold, bless his heart, nearly froze to death feeding the chickens this morning. Spring can't get here soon enough."

"I don't mind the cold. I enjoy sitting under my electric blanket with a good book."

"Well, Fannie, you keep your house at 110 degrees all summer, so you've never known what cold is," Mrs. Dora responded.

Mrs. Fannie laughed and then continued, "Pratt gave me my first electric blanket one Christmas. They weren't very safe many years ago. The thing caught on fire, and Pratt was jumping on it and beating it with his fist and doing all he could to keep it from setting the settee on fire. Well, it wasn't funny then, but I can look back on it and laugh now."

"Didn't you lose an entire roll of yarn in that little blaze?" Mrs. Dora asked.

"Yes, you are right, Dora," Mrs. Fannie said. "I forgot about that yarn. We had just started meeting on Thursdays and I was knitting a blanket for one of those Tatum babies from church. I sure forgot all about that."

"Jill Tatum's boy," Aunt Maxine added.

"Jenny Tatum's boy," Mrs. Dora corrected her.

"Y'all have been doing this for a long time." I rested my spoon in the empty bowl and leaned back in my chair.

"Fannie, Maryanne Haltom, and I were the first to meet. It was just a random Thursday and we got together for coffee, and before we knew it, we were discussing how we could be an encouragement to others in the community. Maryanne died about two years after that. So we asked Dora to fill in for her, and Margie joined us not long after," Aunt Maxine explained.

"I was the rebound." Mrs. Dora winked at me.

"Sure were," Aunt Maxine agreed. "What I wouldn't give to have Maryanne back."

"Maxine, be nice," Mrs. Fannie said quietly.

"Oh, poo. Dora knows I'm kidding with her. Don't you, Dora?" Aunt Maxine grinned at her.

"Sometimes I wonder," Mrs. Dora answered.

Once our bowls were empty, I served the cheesecake on the acorn-adorned plates and we began our meeting. One baby had been born, one of Mrs. Fannie's classmates had died, and two elders from First Baptist were in the hospital recovering from surgeries. Mrs. Dora also requested special prayers for Mr. Harold, who didn't nap yesterday afternoon. With worry in her voice, she explained he was unable to fall asleep at precisely noon like he has every single day for the last fifteen years. She was convinced he must have been sick or anxious.

I wrote out a couple of cards while the ladies argued over family trees. I had learned Aunt Maxine was the worst in the group at remembering names. I secretly rooted for Mrs. Dora when she put Aunt Maxine in her place. It was something I'd wanted to do many times throughout my life, but I loved and respected her too much to do so. I couldn't help but look to Mrs. Fannie and giggle when Aunt Maxine retreated in defeat and puckered her lips while Mrs. Dora sat a little taller in her chair and mentally noted she'd won another battle.

When I hung up with Mrs. Annie at Clooney's after giving her the new mother's address for delivery and paying for the blanket over the phone, Mrs. Fannie asked, "Rae, have you spoken with Kent?"

"I talked to him for a minute after basketball practice yesterday. He said they've already reserved him a really nice apartment near the campus. He's planning to move in May." My tone was dejected.

"You miss him, don't you, dear?" Aunt Maxine asked.

"I do." I sighed. "It's hard to see him at basketball games. I'm constantly wondering if we made the right choice. But I have to remember he's at peace with this decision. He's prayed about it and feels it is what the Lord wants for his life. I can't argue with that. I have to let him go. His fate isn't up to me. And I felt uneasy about him turning down the job for me. I knew that wasn't the right choice. I do miss him. But this is for the best. Isn't it, Mrs. Fannie?" I searched her face for confirmation.

"Yes, dear. Although, I won't lie, I rooted for the two of you," Mrs. Fannie said. "But my plans and the Lord's plans aren't always the same. I learned that when Lee married that no-good, gold-digging son-in-law of mine."

Aunt Maxine chuckled and then added, "Raeley Ann, your mother had to choose James over Cecil. Kent has to choose Tuscaloosa. Fannie has to choose not to hit her son-in-law with a cast-iron skillet. The best decisions aren't always the easiest ones. Remember what Romans 8:28 says?"

" 'In all things God works for the good of those who love him.' "

"Rae, I don't think you need to worry about love and relationships right now anyway. You need some time to focus on yourself and your work. Speaking of, how is the business?" Mrs. Dora's bangle clinked against the coffee cup.

"Business is good. I'm paying my bills and have money left over. I can't believe some of the treasures people have in their outbuildings and buried in the basement. Allison

Campbell brought in the most gorgeous church pew she found in her grandmother's shed. It's got this amazing ornamental woodwork like it came out of the Vatican. There's no telling what it's worth. I'm just cleaning it up really well and putting some fresh stain on it."

"Now, Allison Campbell is Harriet Mathurin's granddaughter." Aunt Maxine looked to Dora.

"Nope. Wrong again." Mrs. Dora closed her pale blue eyes and shook her head. "Allison Pritchard is Harriet Mathurin's granddaughter. Allison Campbell's grandmother is Mildred Purcell."

"Well, that can't be right. Mildred Purcell was—" Aunt Maxine waved her hands in the air.

"Not this again. Ladies! Harriet, Mildred, what does it matter? They've both been dead and buried for a decade. The point is, someone took a church pew to Rae. It's beautiful. It's worth a lot of money. That's it," Mrs. Fannie declared, fed up.

Mrs. Dora and Aunt Maxine both gasped at Mrs. Fannie's outburst. I'd witnessed her remain soft-spoken and listen to their banter for years without a coarse word. She might as well have told them to shut up. I could not help but hold the linen napkin over my mouth and laugh.

"Well, someone woke up on the wrong side of the bed this morning, didn't she, Dora?" Aunt Maxine muttered quietly.

"Sure did, Maxine," she responded and folded her arms

while glaring at Mrs. Fannie. "I think I'll put Fannie on the prayer list too."

Mrs. Fannie ignored them and asked, "Have you talked to Carter much since you and Kent broke things off?"

"Yes, ma'am. Carter and I are friends. We're cordial. We have to be for Molly's sake."

"Is he still professing his love for you, dear?" Aunt Maxine asked.

"Well, yes. But like you said, Mrs. Dora, this is my time. I'm not running back to him just because we're both single."

They all nodded in agreement and took their last sips of coffee.

"Well, that no-good son-in-law of mine ought to be rolling in within an hour or two. I need to get home in time to hide all the silver." Mrs. Fannie sighed.

"Fannie, you don't really think he'd steal your silver."

"I most certainly do, Dora. I see the way he snoops around my house, mentally putting a price tag on my belongings. He can't wait to put me in the ground so he can get his grubby hands on all my things. They'll be at auction before the dirt has even settled on my grave. And my sweet Lee—my sweet, naive Lee can't see through his antics. She says, 'Oh, Mama, he'd never do anything like that. He loves you. Why are you so paranoid?' Well, because he's got the eyes of a cheetah scoping out an antelope. I see it clearly."

"Fannie, you're terrible." Aunt Maxine laughed.

"He's terrible. I tell you what."

They slowly stood from their chairs and let out little groans while straightening their aching backs and knees before walking into the living room to retrieve their bulky winter coats from the hooks by the door. I cherished that moment—watching them fuss over whose scarf was whose and the weather outside. Oh, how I loved them. I loved our time together. I loved how they managed to keep my mama alive. They were just what I needed at this stage in my life, and I prayed they would be around for many years to come. I would never grow tired of their prayers, their wisdom, their banter.

"Now, Raeley Ann," Aunt Maxine said as Dora helped her pull her coat over her thick brown sweater. "I will be glad to come over and help you cook for Thanksgiving on Wednesday. Just let me know, otherwise I'll bring the corn casserole and sweet potatoes on Thursday. You did ask Dawn to bring the green beans and her yeast rolls, right? Lord, I hope she doesn't show up with some kind of low-carb hippie bread made with coconut flour."

I laughed. "She promised nothing would have coconut flour or flaxseed, Aunt Maxine."

"Well, that's a relief." Aunt Maxine exhaled. "Dora, you should have gone out and warmed your car up for us. Go do that while Fannie and I wait."

"No, Mrs. Dora. Molly can do that for you while she's out there. Where are your keys?"

While Mrs. Dora searched through her navy patent leather bag for her large gold keychain, I opened the wooden front door to call Molly to come get them. I saw Carter in his black heavyweight coat jump up to block his daughter's shot. Molly laughed while Carter did a victory dance and she threw the basketball at his back.

"Is that Carter out there?" Mrs. Fannie squinted through the glass storm door while Mrs. Dora sat on the couch to continue searching for her keys and Aunt Maxine hovered over her, fussing.

"He must've just gotten here," I said. "I wasn't expecting him."

I watched Carter and Molly converse while he dribbled the ball. He went in for the layup but missed terribly. Molly teased him and imitated his victory dance. I smiled widely while watching my daughter and her father. I cherished this moment, just as Mama had suggested I do.

Mrs. Fannie stood close to my side, and I could sense she was staring up at me. She put her thin arm around my waist while Mrs. Dora continued rustling through her bag and Aunt Maxine demanded she check the inside pocket again. Mrs. Fannie knew what I was thinking. It was written all over my face—in my broad smile and the gleam in my eye. Mrs. Fannie knew Carter was still the love of my life. She knew her nephew and I were meant to part ways. She knew I was going to give my ex-husband the chance to earn my trust and restore our family. She knew I would welcome him inside after the driveway basketball game with a hug and a warm cup of coffee. She saw the supernatural peace that covered me.

She lovingly rubbed my back with her ring-covered fingers and said softly, "Bless your heart, Rae Sutton."

ACKNOWLEDGMENTS

*W*hen I was a child, my mother made up tales about fairies and farmers as I drifted off to sleep in my canopy bed. Her fabulous stories inspired me to write my own. And so, since I was eight years old, I've dreamed of becoming a published fiction author. My favorite Christmas gift was the Brother typewriter I received from "Santa" when I was nine. When my friends came over, they wondered why I had a typewriter in my room—that was something only adults owned. But I spent countless hours on that typewriter, clicking and clacking, well past my 8 o'clock bedtime.

My mother and I also often watched classic black-and-white movies together. As the ceiling fan in her bedroom swirled above us, we were captivated by handsome, broad-shouldered gentlemen in fedoras and elegant ladies in A-line dresses. Rock Hudson. Grace Kelly. Kim Novak. Jimmy Stewart. We were drawn to those stories and those characters on the screen. And many of those scripts inspired me to retreat to my room and write my own mystery about a sophisticated lady and her affair with a private detective.

And still, stories come to me when I'm driving, walking my dogs, shaving my legs. I recently watched an elderly man help his wife out of the car in a restaurant's parking lot and envisioned them as characters in a book. How long had they been married? What were their happiest moments? What nearly tore them apart? Before the little old lady had even made it out of the Buick with her husband's help, I wanted to write what I imagined to be their story.

Thank you, Mama, for telling me all about Farmer Brown and his rogue chickens, for introducing me to the fascinating characters and scripts on the movie screen, and for instilling a love of writing in me. Thank you for always encouraging me in my storytelling—unless I made up a long one about my whereabouts when coming in after curfew. Carrie Anne didn't even have an apartment in Jackson.

I also want to thank my incredible agent, Dave Schroeder, for his wisdom and encouragement to pursue the fiction I love to write and for his part in getting Rae Sutton's story off my computer and into bookstores.

Huge thanks to everyone on the Thomas Nelson/HarperCollins team who had a hand in this book. From the cover to the edits to the back cover copy, you have made this such an easy and fun process. Kimberly Carlton, I'm looking at you.

Aunt Eula, thank you for inviting me to your book club several years ago. That is where this story was born. Watching you ladies laugh and playfully argue and discuss all the latest Brownsville news stayed with me. Mama had just died, and it was just what my weary soul needed.

I also want to thank my grandmother, Rebecca Joyner, for allowing me to tag along with her to play Rook on Friday nights when I was a kid. That is where I met Maxine Joyner and Dora Parks, two precious and hilarious ladies who, along with my Granny, inspired the characters in this book.

Thanks to my husband, Jason, and my children, for their support and encouragement. To my mother-in-law, Kristi, you are such a blessing. So much of this book was written while you were caring for the kids and allowing me uninterrupted time to work.

Thank you to my dogs, goats, and cats for allowing me to use your names in this story—Pepper, T. J., Tucker, Zeppelin, Floyd, Ella, Daisy, Cookie, Dolly, Roy, Dennis, Alex, and Sketch. I will give each of you a belly rub and chicken nugget as compensation.

Thank you to all my fans and followers on social media who have stuck with me through the years, believed in me, and enjoyed what I have to say (most of the time).

Most importantly, thank you, Lord, for giving me the desire to write. You are the ultimate Author—the Author of our lives, of our stories. And You have written my story much better than I deserve.

DISCUSSION QUESTIONS

1. Aunt Maxine, Mrs. Dora, and Mrs. Fannie were a blessing to Rae's life. Have you had any similar mentors?

2. Is there a particular character you identified with?

3. Were you rooting for Rae to choose Kent or Carter? Why?

4. Has the Lord ever served as your anchor in the way He was to Rae?

5. Did the setting and language in the story convey "Southerness" as you know it?

6. How do you feel the story ends? Will Carter keep Rae's trust?

7. Who was your favorite "old lady" and why?

8. What inspired you about the third Thursday meetings? Are you a part of a similar "ministry"?

Please enjoy
an excerpt from

Can't Make This Stuff Up!

In her highly-anticipated nonfiction debut, humorist, popular blogger, and *USA TODAY* bestselling author, Susannah B. Lewis (Whoa! Susannah) uses dry wit and an eye for the absurd to find laughter in even the most challenging circumstances.

NELSON BOOKS
An Imprint of Thomas Nelson

Available in print, e-book, and audio

CHAPTER 1

Write, Rinse, Repeat

My mother was quite the storyteller. Whether humorous fiction or factual accounts of her youth, her stories captivated me, molded me, and planted a seed within me that would one day grow into a calling.

Mama began filling my head with tales when I was just a little girl. She sat on the edge of my canopy bed, stroked my long hair, and wove a humorous plot about Farmer Brown's wife and the chickens that flew through her kitchen window. What a mess they made in poor Mrs. Brown's farmhouse. Those foul fowl wreaked havoc. Silly chickens were the last thought I had before drifting off to sleep.

I also heard numerous anecdotes while I rode in the passenger seat of my mother's Oldsmobile. She'd point to places in our hometown and tell stories about them. I still know the exact spot where she fell off her bicycle on College Street and will never forget the harrowing tale of the drifter who jumped off the train on Boyd Avenue, banged on her aunt Ottie's back door, and paced the porch whistling an eerie tune. I'll forever picture the older couple who lived on Washington Avenue and were terrified their new color television was going to damage their eyes, so they wore sunglasses. I would laugh so hard that I snorted when Mama regaled us with the tale of visiting them and being forced to put on dark glasses to watch *Gunsmoke*.

I especially loved to hear my mother talk about the summers she spent with her refined and elegant Aunt Nancy on Fairfax Avenue in Nashville. Aunt Nancy was a beautiful woman who wore diamonds and sapphires and loathed dirt. She went so far as to wrap newspaper around the gas and brake pedals in her car to keep them spotless. Aunt Nancy was also often embarrassed by her husband James's lack of filter. Mama loved to recount the time Uncle James told a chatty dinner guest to "quit talking and start chewing" while Aunt Nancy turned twenty-four shades of crimson and my young mother covered her face with her napkin to stifle her laughter.

And Lord have mercy, I'll never forget the story about Betsy.

Betsy went to school with my mother and lived in a beautiful house on the hill near the high school. On her way home from school, Mama passed right by Betsy's house where Betsy's mother kept her 1959 Impala parked on the street out front. Betsy was not quite old enough to drive, but she would sit inside that car, and each time someone passed her house she'd pump the brakes so it seemed that she'd just parked the massive Chevrolet. She spent many afternoons doing this just so her classmates would think her parents allowed her to drive. Mama said sometimes Betsy would honk the horn and wave too. That visual of young Betsy trying her best to fit in with the older kids will forever live in my mind.

I'd always loved hearing my mother's stories, but it never occurred to me to write my own until I was eight years old. I had checked out a book at my elementary school library called *The Trouble with Tuck*. I vividly remember the picture on the cover: a dog and a girl sitting under a tree. The girl's shirt was tucked into terribly short shorts, and it looked awful uncomfortable, so I thought maybe the trouble she was having was with that shirt *tucked* into those tiny shorts, but after reading the back cover, I realized that Tuck was the dog. And as a dog lover, I was sold. I took the book home, not knowing it would change my life.

I was lying on my bedroom floor, a chubby kid with a Little Debbie in one hand and the book in the other, when I reached the part where Tuck went blind. Tears poured from my eyes and dampened the pages. I was terrified I was going to get in trouble for soaking (and getting Fudge Round on) those pages by our strict librarian who kept a wooden paddle with holes drilled in it on her desk. But once the fear subsided, I realized something beautiful had happened. That book made me feel something. It brought me joy and laughter as I read about the little girl and her best friend going on adventures, and then the book made me cry my eyes out. Right then I decided that's what I wanted to do. I wanted to write books. Not books about blind dogs per se, but books that made people feel something.

So I started a little series of stories about two friends named Laura and Sarah. On notebook paper, I penned the tale of their friendship and elementary school escapades. I illustrated the covers with stick people, my only illustrative talent, and stapled the pages together. Then I wrote rave reviews on the back and drew *New York Times* bestseller stamps on them. Hey, go big or go home, right?

I loved writing so much I decided to give novels a try. I penned *twenty whole pages* about a girl and her mother who were chased by a truck driver. I cranked out a tale about a haunted garage and another about a kid with the superpower to make things smell like strawberries. I got so lost in those stories every day after school that I forgot to do my homework, but I had found my calling. Math homework did not matter. (Until I got my report card.)

When I was eleven and my father died, I discovered writing was cathartic and therapeutic. I could feel my burdens being lifted when I wrote about the pain and the void that accompanied my daddy's sudden passing. As I banged out words on my Brother typewriter, I recognized writing was so much more than a hobby.

I stuck with it. I was late for high school many mornings because I'd stayed up late writing a book about some zit-faced boy who'd thrown me over for a girl with prettier bangs. I lost interest in other hobbies (I knew basketball wasn't for me when I kept trying to make shots in the wrong goal), but I remained passionate about the written word. And, after graduation, I went to college and took creative writing courses to hone my craft. I was delighted when my writing professors left words of affirmation on my essays. (My math professors did the opposite—in red ink.) I was confident writing really was what I was meant to do.

A few years ago, I wrote a short story that took place in the South in the 1950s. It was about forbidden love between a poor girl and the rich boy across town. Sweet Caroline, in her hand-me-down dresses, wanted only to be accepted by John Williams's prominent family. I read that story to my mama, and when I looked over at her, her cheeks were damp with tears.

"Mama, what is it? Are you all right?"

"You're a fabulous storyteller, Susannah," she said. "You have a gift. What you've written there—that's art."

What my mother had done—what my grandmothers and great aunts had done when they were sitting in rocking chairs recounting memories and embellishing them along the way—was art. It was a gift.

James 1:17 says, "Every good and perfect gift is from above." I thanked God for it.

While staying at home with two children under the age of four, I started a blog called *Write, Rinse, Repeat.* I thought that was a really clever name because I wrote, and I rinsed recycled Similac from bibs and couches and the dog, and I did it all over again. Every. Single. Day.

As my children napped, I logged on to my blog and wrote about daily life as a stay-at-home mother. I wrote about the mundane. I penned humorous tales about trips to the grocery store, the piles of laundry, and the song "Elmo's Potty Time" relentlessly running through my mind when I rested my head on my pillow at the end of a long day. I'm pretty sure Mama and my sister, Carmen, were the only two souls who read my blog posts, but I wasn't writing to gain popularity. I was writing because it was freeing to craft words about the fun of parenting and even the frustration of not having adult conversation.

I self-published several novels and short stories. I won some writing contests and was assigned a column for the local newspaper. And I loved every moment of it. I loved being stopped in Target to talk about the characters in my books as if they were real people. I still wasn't writing for popularity, but it was incredibly surreal that I finally had a platform and my words had an impact on strangers. I was grateful I'd made people feel something, just as I'd set out to do after I read *The Trouble with Tuck* so many years ago.

As I went through my mother's belongings in the weeks after she passed away, I found a copy of a novel she'd been working on for nearly a decade. She never finished it, but I read the words in her beautiful penmanship and thought, *This will live on forever.* That's the beautiful thing about stories. Long after we're gone, the stories last. They are passed down from generation to generation. They are spoken around campfires and on front porches and as a mother strokes her daughter's hair. They are imperishable.

Then my precious mama died. I was so consumed by grief I couldn't bear to write anything humorous. And that's what I was known for—I had been called the "modern-day Erma Bombeck." People visited my blog for a daily laugh. I did not want to disappoint my followers, but I had to write what I was feeling.

So I wrote about my mama's death. The words were real and raw, and I had no idea how many people they would resonate with, but I didn't care. I had to release the pain, so I wrote nearly every day. I wrote as the movers hauled my mother's baby grand piano out of her living room, and as I soaked in the silence of what was once a loud, lively home. I wrote about the denial, the regret, the longing, the void. My fingers rapidly pounded on my keyboard, and tears streamed from my eyes. I left my torn heart on that computer screen.

As the comments and emails poured in, I learned grief is a universal language. Because we live in a fallen world, everyone has experienced pain, longing, and despair. God comforted my broken heart, and then it was as if He put His hand on mine and we wrote words of encouragement and hope together. I understood what Peter said in 1 Peter 4:10, "Each of you should use whatever gift you have received to serve others, as faithful stewards of God's grace in its various forms."

And this was God's perfect plan from the beginning. Isaiah 25:1 says, "LORD, you are my God; I will exalt you and praise your name, for in perfect faithfulness you have done wonderful things, things planned long ago."

Things planned long ago.

When my mother told me the stories about fairies and farmers and sweet Betsy, as I read a book about a blind dog, as my platform grew, God knew all along one day my words would have purpose and comfort others. He had it all planned out.

I look back on the events in my life—the happiness and sadness and loss and redemption and restoration—and it's like a book. God is writing the story of my life. He's writing the story of *your* life. And just like any great read, there has to be plot development. There has to be a test for the testimony. Things have to happen or it would be a snooze fest, wouldn't it? Sometimes the story leaves us crying. Or on the edge of our seats. Or laughing. Or pee-ing our pants. Or wondering what is going to happen next. But the characters always have purpose.

When I write fiction, I am in control of the story. I never fear for my characters. I never think, *Well, I'm going to allow her to go through some things, and I sure hope she perseveres!* No, I already know how the story ends. I'm bigger than the protagonist's problems. I can squash the antagonist with one word. I'm the author. I'm in control.

Just as God is the Author of our stories—of our lives.

Embrace that. Embrace your purpose and trust the Author.

And you know what else I've discovered? God not only writes our story, He rinses us of our sins. He writes. He rinses us white. He writes. He rinses. And repeats.

ABOUT THE AUTHOR

*S*usannah B. Lewis is a humorist, blogger for *Whoa! Susannah*, and freelance writer whose work has appeared in numerous publications. The author of *Can't Make This Stuff Up!*, Lewis studied creative writing at Jackson State Community College and earned her bachelor's degree in business management from Bethel College. She lives in Tennessee with her husband, Jason, their three children, and seven dogs.

Visit her online at whoasusannah.com
Facebook: @whoasusannah
Instagram: @whoasusannahblog
TikTok: @whoasusannah